WARNING

In opening this book, you begin
more than a story.

The beings on the other side are always
watching, always waiting, for any way
through.

Do you have the courage to unleash
what will be lurking?

And, when you are done, do you have
the strength to return it
whence it came?

Also by John Connolly

Every Dead Thing
Dark Hollow
The Killing Kind
The White Road
Bad Men
Nocturnes
The Black Angel
The Book of Lost Things
The Unquiet
The Reapers
The Lovers
The Gates
The Whisperers

Samuel Johnson
vs. the
Devil
round II

HELL'S BELLS
JOHN CONNOLLY

HODDER &
STOUGHTON

Ask Not For Whom The Bells Toll. Just Start Running

First published in Great Britain in 2011 by Hodder & Stoughton
An Hachette UK company

I

Copyright © John Connolly 2011

The right of John Connolly to be identified as the Author of the Work
has been asserted by him in accordance with the Copyright,
Designs and Patents Act 1988.

A CIP catalogue record for this title is available from the British Library

Hardback ISBN 978 1 444 72494 3
Trade Paperback ISBN 978 1 444 72495 0

Typeset in Stempel Garamond by Palimpsest Book Production Limited,
Falkirk, Stirlingshire

Printed and bound by Clays Ltd, St Ives plc

Ceci n'est pas une pipe, 1929, by René Magritte (1898–1967) page 59,
Los Angeles County Museum of Art, USA. © ADAGP, Paris and DACS,
London 2011. Photo: Giraudon/The Bridgeman Art Library.

Hodder & Stoughton policy is to use papers that are natural, renewable
and recyclable products and made from wood grown in sustainable forests.
The logging and manufacturing processes are expected to conform to the
environmental regulations of the country of origin.

Hodder & Stoughton Ltd
338 Euston Road
London NW1 3BH

www.hodder.co.uk

Whenever science makes a discovery, the devil grabs it while the angels are debating the best way to use it.

Alan Valentine (1901–80)

For Cameron and Alistair

CHAPTER I

In Which We Find Ourselves in Hell, But Only Temporarily, So It's Not All Bad News

The place generally referred to as Hell but also known variously as Hades, the Kingdom of Fire, Old Nick's Place[1], and assorted other names designed to indicate that this is not somewhere in which you might want to spend eternity, let alone a short holiday, was in a state of turmoil. Its ruler was unwell.

The source of all Evil, the ancient thing that hid itself in the darkest part of Hell, also had many names, but his followers called him the Great Malevolence. He wished for many things: he wished for every star in every universe to be snuffed out like candle flames between his fingers; he wished for all beauty to cease to be; he wished for cold, and blackness, and a great silence that would last for ever.

Most of all, he wished for the end of mankind. He had grown weary of trying to corrupt every human being, one by one, because it was time-consuming, and frustrating, and a lot of human beings continued to defy

---

💀 [1] Not to be confused with St Nick's Place, which is the North Pole. You don't want to make that mistake, and end up selling your soul to Santa.

him by being decent and kind. While he hadn't exactly decided to give up on his efforts entirely, it just seemed easier to destroy the Earth and have done with it, and so he came up with a plan.

Now for those of you who may not be entirely familiar with our story so far, here is a chance for you to catch up.[2] When last we met, the Great Malevolence, aided by the demon known as Ba'al, was trying to harness the power of the Large Hadron Collider, the massive particle accelerator in Switzerland that was trying to recreate the moments after the Big Bang, in order to open the gates of Hell and force his way into our world. Ba'al passed through a portal connecting Hell to the town of Biddlecombe in England, and disguised itself as a woman named Mrs Abernathy, having first killed the original Mrs Abernathy. At the last minute, just as the Great Malevolence and his army were about to pass through the portal and take over the Earth, Mrs Abernathy's plans were foiled by a small boy named Samuel Johnson, his dachshund Boswell, and an inept, although well meaning, demon named Nurd, the Scourge of Five Deities. The Great Malevolence blamed Mrs Abernathy for this, and as a result was now refusing to meet with her, causing her much hurt and humiliation.

💀 [2] And by the way, what kind of person are you, reading the second part of a series before the first? Now the rest of the readers have to hang around, whistling and examining their fingernails in a bored manner, while I give you special treatment. I bet you're the sort who arrives halfway through the movie, spilling your popcorn and standing on toes, then taps the bloke next to you on the shoulder and says, 'Have I missed anything?' It's people like you who cause unrest . . .

All clear? Good.

The Great Malevolence still wasn't quite sure how his plan had failed, and he didn't care. For a moment, he had glimpsed a hole between dimensions, a possibility of escape from Hell, and then that portal had been closed just as he was about to leave his dreary kingdom behind. All of his bloodied hopes, his shadowy dreams, had come to nothing, and the closeness of his triumph had driven him insane.

This is not to say that he wasn't mad already: the Great Malevolence had always been madder than a bag of badgers, madder even than a colony of bats trapped in a biscuit tin. Now, though, he had passed into another realm of craziness entirely, and significant portions of Hell had been filled with the sounds of his wailing ever since the portal had blinked out of existence. It was a terrible sound, that cry of rage and sorrow, ceaseless and unvarying. Even by the standards of Hell it was very annoying indeed, echoing from the Great Malevolence's lair deep inside the Mountain of Despair, through tunnels and labyrinths, through dungeons and the bowels of the odd dragon, until at last it reached the doorway that led from its hiding place into the dreadful landscape beyond.

The doorway was most impressive, intricately carved with terrifying faces whose expressions were everchanging, and horrific forms whose bodies intertwined, so that the very entrance itself seemed to be alive. At this precise moment the doorway was being guarded by two demons. In the classic manner of double acts everywhere, they were exact opposites. One guard was tall and thin, with features that suggested an irritating, and somewhat overweight, child had spent a lot of time hanging from the guard's chin, thereby stretching the guard's face into a very mournful expression. His colleague was shorter and fatter. In fact he looked like he might have eaten the irritating, overweight child as a favour to his fellow guard.

Brompton, the thinner of the two, had been guarding the doorway for so long that he had forgotten what he was supposed to be guarding it against, given that the most awful being it was possible to imagine was already in residence inside the mountain. During the centuries that he had spent leaning on his spear, occasionally dozing or scratching himself where polite demons didn't usually scratch themselves in public, he could not, until recently, recall a great many instances of individuals trying to get in who weren't already entitled to pass freely. Oh, a couple of demons had tried to escape from inside the mountain, largely to avoid being torn apart as a punishment for something or other, or occasionally just for a bet, but otherwise things had been very quiet around there, in a Hellish way, for a long time.

His colleague, Edgefast, was a new arrival. Brompton regarded him suspiciously from beneath his helmet. Edgefast wasn't leaning sufficiently on his spear for Brompton's liking, and he had not yet proposed skiving off for a cup of tea, or a nap. Instead, Edgefast seemed to be standing up very straight, and he had a disconcerting gleam in his eye, the kind of gleam associated with someone who actually likes his job and, even worse, plans to do it as well as possible. Brompton, by contrast, had not yet found a job that he might be inclined to like or do well, and was of the opinion that such an occupation did not exist, which suited him just fine. A job, as far as Brompton was concerned, was something that somebody made you do when you'd rather be doing nothing at all.

Edgefast glanced nervously at Brompton.

'Why do you keep staring at me like that?' he asked.

'You're not slouching,' said Brompton.

'What?'

'I said, "You're not slouching." Making me look bad, you are. Making me look untidy. Making me look like I don't care.'

'But, er, you *don't* care,' said Edgefast, who understood, from the moment he had set eyes on Brompton, that here was a demon with 'waste of space' written all over him.

'That's as maybe,' said Brompton, 'but I don't want everyone to know that I don't care. You'll get me fired, looking all enthusiastic like that. I might not like this job, but there are worse ones out there.'

'Don't I know it,' said Edgefast, in the manner of a demon who has seen the worst that Hell has to offer, and for whom anything else is pure gravy.

'Yeah?' said Brompton, interested now despite himself. 'What were you doing before this, then?'

Edgefast sighed. 'You remember that time Duke Kobal lost his favourite ring?'

Brompton did. As demonic lords went, Kobal[3] wasn't

[3] Duke Kobal was officially the demon of comedians, although only the really unfunny ones, with additional responsibility for the jokes in Christmas crackers. You know, like: What's the longest word in the English language? Smiles, because there's a 'mile' between the first and last letters. A mile. No,

the worst, which meant that, when he was sticking sharp needles into your flesh, or finding out just how many spiders you could hold in your mouth at once, he would always provide tea and biscuits for everyone who was watching, and tell you how sorry he was that it had to come to this, even as he tried to fit one last spider between your lips. Kobal had lost his best skull ring down one of Hell's sewers, and it had never been found. Following this incident a law had been passed requiring that all of Hell's rotten vegetables, old food, unidentified limbs, and assorted demonic bodily waste products should be searched by hand before being swept into the Sea of Unpleasantness, just in case anything valuable might have been mislaid.

'Well,' continued Edgefast. 'You know all that searching business?'

'You mean, going down on your claws and knees and raking through poo 'n' stuff?'

'Yep.'

'With your nose right in it, so you could be certain that nothing slipped by?'

'Yep.'

'And with nowhere to wash, so you had to try and eat your sandwich at break by holding it right at the

---

a *mile*. Yes, as in distance. Yes, I know there's not really a mile, but – OK, stop talking. I'm serious, you're starting to annoy me. No, I don't want to wear a paper hat. I don't care if it's Christmas, those hats make my head itchy. And I don't want to see what you've won. No, I really don't. Fine, then. Oh great, a compass. If I take it away, will you get lost? See, that's funny. Well, I thought it was.

Christmas: Duke Kobal loves it.

edges with your claws while hoping that you didn't drop it?'

'Yep.'

'But your hands smelled bad so your sandwich smelled bad too?'

'Yep.'

''Orrible. Just 'orrible.' Brompton shuddered. 'Doesn't bear thinking about. Worst job in Hell. Anyway, go on.'

'Well, that was me.'

'No!'

'Yes. Years and years of it. I still can't look at a toilet without feeling the urge to stick my hand down it.'

'I thought you smelled a bit funny, even for a demon.'

'It's not my fault. I've tried everything: water, soap, acid. It won't go away.'

'Very unfortunate for you, and anyone who happens to be downwind of you, I must say. Well, this must be quite the promotion for you, then.'

'Oh, it is, it is!' said Edgefast fervently.

'Somebody likes you.'

Brompton nudged him. Edgefast giggled.

'Suppose so.'

'Oh yes, you're quite the special one. Satan's little pet!'

'Don't know I'm born,' said Edgefast. 'Happiest day of my existence, getting away from all that.'

Edgefast beamed. Brompton beamed back. Just then, a large slot opened above their heads, and the hourly emptying of Hell's drains began, dousing the two guards in the foulest waste imaginable before coming to rest in a series of large, stinking pits at the base of the mountain. When the last drop had fallen, and the slot had closed, a small demon dressed in wellington boots and wearing a peg on its nose entered the pits and began searching through the latest delivery.

'That was me once, that was,' said Edgefast, carefully removing a piece of rotting vegetation from his ear.

'You lucky, lucky sod,' said Brompton.

They watched the demon quietly for a time.

'Good of them to give us helmets, though,' said Edgefast.

'One of the perks of the job,' said Brompton. 'Wouldn't be half as nice without the helmets.'

'I meant to ask,' said Edgefast. 'What happened to the bloke who had this job before me?'

Brompton didn't get the chance to answer. A long, dismal road led through the pits and on to the dreary plain beyond. That road had been empty ever since Edgefast had arrived for this, his first day on the job, but it was empty no longer. A figure was approaching and as it drew nearer Edgefast saw that it was a woman, or something that was doing a pretty good impression of one. She was wearing a white dress decorated with a pattern of red flowers, and a straw hat with a white ribbon around its crown. The heels of her white shoes made a steady *click-click-click* sound on the stones of the road, and over her left arm hung a white bag fastened by gold clasps. The woman had a very determined expression on her face, one that might have given pause to a more intelligent demon than Edgefast. But, as

Brompton had correctly surmised, Edgefast was an enthusiast, and there's no talking to enthusiasts.

The woman was now close enough for Edgefast to see that the dress was more tattered than it had first appeared. It looked home-made, with uneven seams, and the shoes were crude black boots that had been painted white and then carved so that the heels ended in points. The bag had a frame of bone over which skin had been draped, complete with freckles and hair, and the clasps were, on closer inspection, gold teeth.

None of these elements, peculiar in themselves, represented the strangest aspect of the woman's appearance. That honour went to the fact that the only thing more poorly stitched together than her dress was the woman herself. Her skin, visible at her face and arms and legs, seemed to have been ripped apart at some point, the various pieces then sewn back together again in a rough approximation of what a woman might look like. One eye socket was smaller than the other, the left side of the mouth was higher than the right, and the skin on the lower part of the left leg sagged like a pair of old tights. The woman's blond hair sat untidily on her head like a mess of straw dropped there by a passing bird. What he was looking at, Edgefast realized, was not so much a woman as a woman costume, which made him wonder what might lie beneath it.

Still, Edgefast had a job to do. He stepped forward before Brompton had a chance to stop him and stuck his spear out in a vaguely threatening manner.

'You know, I wouldn't do—' Brompton began to say, but by then it was too late.

'Halt,' said Edgefast. 'Where do you think you're going?'

Unfortunately Edgefast didn't get an answer to that question, but he did receive an answer to his earlier one, which was what had happened to the chap who had previously held the guard's job before him, for Edgefast was about to become intimately acquainted with his predecessor's fate.

The woman stopped and stared at Edgefast.

'Oh dear.' Brompton pulled his helmet low over his eyes, and tried to make himself as small as possible. 'Oh dear, oh dear, oh . . .'

Fearsome tentacles, dripping viscous fluid, erupted from the woman's back, ripping through the fabric of her dress. Her mouth opened wide, revealing row upon row of sharp, jagged teeth. Long nails shot from the tips of her pale fingers, curling in upon themselves like hooks. The tentacles gripped Edgefast, lifted him from the ground, and then pulled him very, very hard in a number of different directions at once. There was a squeal of pain, and assorted pieces of what was once Edgefast were thrown in the air; one of them landed on Brompton's helmet. He peered down to see Edgefast's head on the dirt before him, a puzzled look in his eyes.

'You might have warned me,' said the head.

Brompton put his foot over Edgefast's mouth to keep him quiet as the woman adjusted her now even more dishevelled appearance, patted her hair, and then proceeded to pass through the doorway to the Mountain of Despair, untroubled by any further enquiries as to where she might be going.

Brompton tipped his helmet to her as she passed. 'Morning . . .'

He paused, trying to find the appropriate word. The woman's dark eyes flicked towards him, and he felt a coldness enter his belly, the kind of coldness that comes just before someone rips *you* into little pieces and tosses *your* head at the nearest wall.

'. . . Miss,' he finished, and the woman smiled at him in a 'Yes-I-am-so-pretty-thank-you-for-noticing' way before disappearing into the mountain.

Brompton breathed a sigh of relief, and lifted his foot from Edgefast's mouth.

'That really hurt,' said Edgefast, as Brompton began picking up his limbs and placing them in a large pile in the hope that Edgefast could be put back together in a way that might vaguely resemble what he had once been.

'It's your own fault,' said Brompton. He began to fold his arms, then realized that he was still holding one of Edgefast's arms in each of his hands and it all threatened to get very confusing, so he contented himself with shaking one of Edgefast's severed fingers at Edgefast's head in a disapproving manner. 'You shouldn't be asking personal questions of a lady.'

'But I'm a guard. And I'm not sure that *was* a lady.'

'Shhhhh!' Brompton looked anxiously over his shoulder, as though expecting the woman to pop up again and tear both of them into pieces so small that only ants could find them. 'You know, I don't think you're cut out to be a guard,' he said. 'You're too keen on the whole *guarding* business.'

'But isn't that what we're supposed to be doing?' said Edgefast. 'Our job is to guard the entrance. I was just trying to be good at it.'

'Were you now?' said Brompton. He looked doubtful. 'You know what I'm good at guarding?'

'No. What?'

'My health.'

He popped Edgefast's helmet back on Edgefast's head, and went back to leaning on his spear as he waited for someone to come and take the bits away.

'Who was ... um, "she", anyway?' asked Edgefast.

'That,' said Brompton, with some feeling, 'is Mrs Abernathy, and she's in a very bad mood.'

CHAPTER II

In Which We Learn a Little About
How Hard It Is To Be In Love

Time is a funny thing. Take time travel: ask a random assortment of people whether they'd prefer to go backwards or forwards in time, and you'll probably get a pretty even split between those who like the idea of seeing the Great Pyramid being built, or of playing tag with a dinosaur, and those who'd rather see if all of those jet packs and laser guns we were promised in comic books have finally made it into shops.[4]

Unfortunately, there is bad news for those who would like to go back in time. Assuming that I, when not writing books or annoying the neighbours by practising the bassoon at odd hours, build a time machine in my

---

[4] Actually, the decision on whether to go backwards or forwards in time might well tell you something important about the person in question. The English writer Arnold Bennett (1867–1931) was reputed to have said that 'The people who live in the past must yield to the people who live in the future. Otherwise, the world would begin to turn the other way around.' What Bennett was saying is that it's better to look forward than to look back, because that's how progress is made. On the other hand, George Santayana (1863–1952), an American writer, said that 'Those who cannot remember the past are condemned to repeat it.' In other words, it's a question of balance: the past is a nice country to visit, but you wouldn't want to live there.

basement, and offer free trips in it to anyone who fancies a jaunt, those who want to visit Queen Elizabeth I to see if she really had wooden teeth (she didn't: they were just rotten and black, and the lead in her make-up was also slowly poisoning her, so she was probably in a very bad mood most of the time), or to find out if King Ethelred the Unready really was unready (he wasn't: his nickname is a mistranslation of an Old English word meaning 'bad advice') are going to be sorely disappointed.

And why is that? Because you can't go back to a time before there was a time machine. You just can't. The earliest time to which you can return is the moment at which the time machine came into existence. Sorry, those are the rules. I don't make them, I just enforce them in books. So the reason why there are no visitors from the future is that nobody has yet managed to build a time machine *in our own time*. Either that or someone has invented one and is keeping very quiet about it so that people don't keep knocking on his door asking him if they can have a go on his time machine, which would be very annoying.[5]

If Mrs Abernathy had been able to go back in time,

---

[5] There is also the small matter of what is known as the 'Grandfather Paradox': what would happen if you went back in time and killed your grandfather before your mum or dad was born? Would you then cease to exist? But the argument is that you're already in existence, as you were around to travel back in time, so if you do try to kill your grandfather then you'll obviously fail. Hang on, though: is it possible that you might just 'pop' out of existence if you did manage to kill your grandfather? No, because that would imply two different realities, one in which you exist and the other in which you don't exist, which won't do at all. This has led the eminent physicist,

there are a number of things she might have done differently in the course of the attempted invasion of Earth, but principal among them would have been not to underestimate the boy named Samuel Johnson, or his little dog, Boswell. Then again, how could she have imagined that a small boy and his dachshund would prove her undoing? She might have been a demon, but she was also an adult, and most adults have a hard time imagining that small boys, or dachshunds, could possibly be superior to them in any way.

It might have been of some consolation to Mrs Abernathy to learn that while she was struggling with her feelings of rejection and humiliation, the person responsible for most of her problems was experiencing some rejection and humiliation of his own, for Samuel Johnson had just tried to ask Lucy Highmore on a date.

Samuel had been in love with Lucy from the moment he set eyes on her, which was his first day at Montague Rhodes James secondary school in Biddlecombe. In Samuel's eyes, little bluebirds flew ceaselessly around Lucy's head, serenading her with odes to her beauty and depositing petals in her hair, while angels made her school bag a little lighter by helping her with the

---

Professor Stephen Hawking, to come up with the Chronology Protection Conjecture, a kind of virtual ban on time travel. Professor Hawking believes that there must be a rule of physics to prevent time travel, because otherwise we'd have tourists from the future visiting us, and people popping up willy-nilly trying to shoot grandfathers in order to prove a point. In the end, though, if you're the kind of person who, at the first mention of time travel, brings up the possibility of shooting your grandfather, then you're probably not someone who should be allowed near time machines or, for that matter, grandfathers.

burden of it, and whispered the answers to maths questions into her ear when she was stuck. Come to think of it, that wasn't angels: it was every other boy in the class, for Lucy Highmore was the kind of girl who made boys dream of marriage and baby carriages, and made other girls dream of Lucy Highmore falling down a steep flight of stairs and landing on a pile of porcupine quills and rusty farm equipment.

It had taken Samuel over a year to work up the courage to ask Lucy out: month upon month of finding the right words, of practising them in front of a mirror so that he wouldn't stumble on them when he began to speak, of calling himself an idiot for ever thinking that she might agree to have a pie with him at Pete's Pies, followed by a squaring of his newly teenage shoulders, a stiffening of his upper lip, and a reminder to himself that faint heart never won fair lady, although faint heart never suffered crushing rejection either.

Samuel Johnson was brave: he had faced down the wrath of Hell itself, so there could be no doubting his courage, but the prospect of baring his young heart to Lucy Highmore and risking having it skewered by the blunt sword of indifference made his stomach lurch and his eyes swim. He was not sure what might be worse: to ask Lucy Highmore out and be rejected, or not to ask and thus never to know how she might feel about him; to be turned down, and learn that there was no possibility of finding a place in her affections, or to live in hope without ever having that hope realized. After much thought, he had decided that it was better to know.

Samuel wore glasses: quite thick glasses, as it happened, and without them the world tended to look a little blurry to him. He decided that he looked better without his glasses, even though he couldn't be sure of this as, when he took them off and looked in the mirror, he resembled a drawing of himself that had fallen in a puddle. Still, he was pretty certain that Lucy Highmore would like him more without his glasses, so on the fateful day – the First Fateful Day, as he later came to think of it – he carefully removed his glasses as he approached her, tucking them safely into his pocket, while repeating these words in his head: 'Hi, I was wondering if you'd allow me the pleasure of buying you a pie, and perhaps a glass of orange juice, at Pete's emporium of pies on the main street? Hi, I was wondering if—'

Somebody bumped into Samuel, or he bumped into somebody. He wasn't sure which, but he apologized and continued on his way before tripping over someone's bag and almost losing his footing.

'Oi, watch where you're going,' said the bag's owner.

'Sorry,' said Samuel. Again.

He squinted. Ahead of him he could see Lucy Highmore. She was wearing a red coat. It was a lovely coat. Everything about Lucy Highmore was lovely. She couldn't have been lovelier if her name was Lucy Lovely and she lived on Lovely Road in the town of Loveliness.

Samuel stood before her, cleared his throat, and, without stumbling once, said, 'Hi, I was wondering if you'd allow me the pleasure of buying you a pie, and perhaps a glass of orange juice, at Pete's emporium of pies on the main street?'

He waited for a reply, but none came. He squinted harder, trying to bring Lucy into focus. Was she overcome with emotion? Was she gaping in awe at him? Even now, was a single tear of happiness dropping from her eye like a diamond as the little tweety birds—

'Did you just ask that letter box on a date?' said someone close by. Samuel recognized the voice as that of Thomas Hobbes, his best friend.

'What?' Samuel fumbled for his glasses, put them on and found that he had somehow wandered in the wrong direction. He'd stepped out of the school gates and on to the street where he had, it seemed, just offered to buy a pie for the red letter box and, by extension, the postman who was about to empty it. The postman was now regarding Samuel with the kind of wariness associated with one who suspects that the person standing before him may well be something of a nutter, and could turn dangerous at any time.

'It doesn't eat pies,' said the postman slowly. 'Only letters.'

'Right,' said Samuel. 'I knew that.'

'Good,' said the postman, still speaking very slowly.

'Why are you speaking so slowly?' said Samuel, who found that he had now started speaking slowly as well.

'Because you're mad,' said the postman, even more slowly.

'Oh,' said Samuel.

'And the letter box can't come with you to the pie shop. It has to stay where it is. Because it's a letter box.'

He patted the letter box gently, and smiled at Samuel

as if to say, 'See, it's not a person, it's a box, so go away, mad bloke.'

'I'll look after him,' said Tom. He began to guide Samuel back to the school. 'Let's get you inside, shall we? You can have a nice lie-down.'

The students near the gates were watching Samuel. Some were sniggering.

See, it's that Johnson kid. I told you he was strange.

At least Lucy wasn't among them, thought Samuel. She had apparently moved off to spread her fragrant loveliness elsewhere.

'If it's not a rude question, why were you offering to buy a pie for a letter box?' said Tom, as they made their way into the depths of the playground.

'I thought it was Lucy Highmore,' said Samuel.

'Lucy Highmore doesn't look like a letter box, and I don't think she'd be very happy if she heard that you thought she did.'

'It was the red coat. I got confused.'

'She's a bit out of your league, isn't she?' said Tom.

Samuel sighed sadly. 'She's so far out of my league that we're not even playing the same sport. But she's lovely.'

'You're an idiot,' said Tom.

'Who's an idiot?'

Maria Mayer, Samuel's other closest friend at school, joined them.

'Samuel is,' said Tom. 'He just asked out a letter box, thinking it was Lucy Highmore.'

'Really?' said Maria. 'Lucy Highmore. That's ... nice.'

Her tone was not so much icy as arctic. The word 'nice' took on the aspect of an iceberg towards which the good ship Lucy Highmore was unwittingly steaming, but Tom, too caught up in his mirth, and Samuel, smarting with embarrassment, failed to notice.

Just then, he discovered that Lucy Highmore was not elsewhere. She appeared from behind a crowd of her friends, all still whispering, and Samuel blushed furiously as he realized that she had witnessed what had occurred. He walked on, feeling about the size of a bug, and as he passed Lucy's group he heard her friends begin to giggle, and then he heard Lucy begin to giggle too.

I want to go back in time, he thought. Back to a time before I ever asked Lucy Highmore for a date. I want to change the past, all of it.

I don't want to be that strange Johnson kid any more.

It's odd, but people are capable of forgetting quite extraordinary occurrences very quickly if it makes them happier to do so, even events as incredible as the gates of Hell opening and spewing out demons of the most unpleasant kind, which is what had happened in the little town of Biddlecombe just over fifteen months earlier. You'd think that after such an experience, people would have woken up every morning, yawned, and scratched their heads before opening their eyes wide in terror and shrieking, 'The Gates! Demons! They were here! They'll be back!'

But people are not like that. It's probably a good thing, as otherwise life would be very hard to live. It's not true that time heals all wounds, but it does dull the memory of pain, or people would only go to the dentist once and then never return, or not without some significant guarantees regarding their personal comfort and safety.[6]

So, as the weeks and months had passed, the memory of what had happened in Biddlecombe began to fade until after a while people began to wonder if it had really happened at all, or if it had all been some kind of strange dream. More to the point, they figured that it had happened once, and consequently wasn't ever likely to happen again, so they could just stop worrying about it and get on with more important things, like football, and reality television, and gossiping about their neighbours. At least that was what they told themselves, but sometimes, in the deepest, darkest part of the night, they would wake from strange dreams of creatures with nasty teeth and poisonous claws, and when their children said that they couldn't sleep because there was something under the bed, they didn't just tell them that they were being silly. No, they very, very carefully peered under the bed, and they did so with a cricket bat, or a brush handle, or a kitchen knife in hand.

Because you never knew ...

☠ 6 'What do you mean, you're giving me a small anaesthetic? I want a *big* anaesthetic. I want the kind that they give to elephants before they operate on them. I want my chin to feel like it's been carved from rock, like my face is part of a statue on the side of a large building. I don't want to feel ANY pain at all, otherwise there'll be trouble, you hear? Why did you become a dentist anyway? Do you like hurting people? Well, do you? You're a monster, that's what you are, a monster!'

Sorry about that, but you know what I mean ...

In a peculiar way, though, Samuel Johnson felt that they blamed *him* for what had happened. He wasn't the one who had conjured up demons in his basement because he was bored, and he wasn't the one who had built a big machine that inadvertently opened a portal between this world and Hell. It wasn't his fault that the Devil, the Great Malevolence, hated the Earth and wanted to destroy it. But because he'd been so involved in what had happened, people were reminded of it when they saw him, and they didn't want to be. They wanted to forget it all, and they had convinced themselves that they had forgotten it, even if they hadn't, not really. They just didn't want to think about it, which isn't the same thing at all.

But Samuel couldn't forget it because, occasionally, he would catch a glimpse of a woman in a mirror, or reflected in a shop window, or in the glass of a bus shelter. It was Mrs Abernathy, her eyes luminous with a strange blue glow, and Samuel would feel her hatred of him. No other person ever saw her, though. He had tried to tell the scientists about her, but they hadn't believed him. They thought he was just a small boy – a clever and brave one, but a small boy nonetheless – who was still troubled by the dreadful things that he had seen.

Samuel knew better. Mrs Abernathy wanted revenge: on Samuel, on the Earth, and on every living creature that walked, or swam, or flew, or crawled.

Which brings us to the other reason why Samuel couldn't forget. He hadn't defeated Mrs Abernathy and the Devil and all of the hordes of Hell alone. He'd been helped by an unlucky but generally decent demon named Nurd, and Nurd and Samuel had become friends. But now Nurd was somewhere in Hell, hiding from Mrs Abernathy, and Samuel was here on Earth, and neither could help the other.

Samuel could only hope that, wherever he was, Nurd was safe.[7]

💀 [7] Just one more thing about time travel, while we're on the subject. Quantum theory suggests that there is a probability that all possible events, however strange, might occur, and every possible outcome of every event exists in its own world. In other words, all possible pasts and futures, like the one where you didn't pick up this book but read something else instead, are potentially real, and they all co-exist alongside one another. Now, let's suppose that we invent a time machine that allows us to move on to those alternative time lines. Why, then you could set about killing assorted grandfathers to your heart's content, as they're not part of your world but part of someone else's, someone who is not you but is a slightly different version of you, except possibly not with a murderous, inexplicable grudge against his or her grandfather.

And if you think all of these notions of parallel worlds and other dimensions are nonsense, please note that Jonathon Keats, a San Francisco-based experimental philosopher, has already begun selling land in those extra dimensions of space and time. In fact, he sold 172 lots of extra-dimensional land in the San Francisco Bay Area in one day. I'm not sure what that proves, exactly, other than the fact that there are people in San Francisco who will pay someone for things that may not exist, which perhaps says more about San Franciscans than about scientific theory. Also, I'd like to see those people try to enforce their property rights when faced with a ray-gun wielding monster from another dimension. 'Now look here, I paid good money for this piece of land and—' *Zap!*

CHAPTER III

In Which We Delve Deeper Into the Bowels of Hell, Which Is One of Those Chapter Headings that Make Parents Worry About the Kind of Books Their Children Are Reading

After that brief detour to Earth, and that lesson in love, life, and the importance of good eyesight, let's return to Hell. As we are now aware, the woman striding purposefully through the dim recesses of the Mountain of Despair while wearing a severely tattered floral print dress was Mrs Abernathy, formerly known as Ba'al. Mrs Abernathy had been making a daily pilgrimage to the Great Malevolence's lair ever since the attempt to break into the world of men had come to naught. She wanted to present herself to her master, explain to him what had gone wrong, and find a way to insinuate herself into his favour again. Mrs Abernathy was almost as ancient and evil as the Great Malevolence himself, and they had spent eons together in this desolate place, slowly creating a kingdom out of ash, and filth, and flame.

But now the Great Malevolence, lost in his grief and madness, was apparently refusing to see his lieutenant. Mrs Abernathy was cut off from him, and the demon was troubled by this; troubled, and, yes, frightened. Without the protection and indulgence of the Great

Malevolence, Mrs Abernathy was vulnerable. Something had to be done. The Great Malevolence had to be made to listen, which was why Mrs Abernathy kept returning to this place, where foul creatures watched from the shadows in amusement at the sight of one of the greatest of demons, the commander of Hell's armies, reduced to the status of a beggar; a beggar, what's more, who seemed troublingly keen on wearing women's clothing.

Oddly enough, Mrs Abernathy, having initially been distinctly unhappy at being forced to take on the appearance of a lady in her forties, had grown to like wearing floral print dresses and worrying about her hair. This was partly because Mrs Abernathy had until quite recently been neither male nor female: she had simply been a distinctly horrible 'it'. Now she had an identity, and a form that wasn't mainly teeth, and claws, and tentacles. Ba'al might originally have taken over Mrs Abernathy's body, but something of Mrs Abernathy had subsequently infected Ba'al. For the first time there was a use for a mirror, and nice clothes, and make-up. She worried about her appearance. She was, not to put too fine a point on it, vain.[8] She no longer even thought of herself as Ba'al. Ba'al was the past. Mrs Abernathy was the present, and the future.

[8] Lest anyone starts getting offended on behalf of women everywhere, let me just stress that vanity is not unique to the fairer sex. 'Vanity', according to the poet and essayist Jonathan Swift (1667–1745), 'is the food of fools:/ Yet now and then your men of wit/ Will condescend to take a bit.' Vanity can best be defined as taking too much pride in yourself, and the opposite of pride is humility, which means seeing yourself as you are, and not comparing yourself to other people, even bad ones or, indeed, other demons in dresses, should you happen to be a dress-wearing demon yourself.

As she descended deeper and deeper into the mountain, she was aware of the sniggers and whispers from all around her. The great bridge along which she walked was suspended over a gaping chasm so deep that, if you were to fall into it, you would keep falling for ever and ever, until at last you died of old age without ever nearing the bottom. Metal and chains held the bridge in place, linking it to the inner walls of the mountain. Set into it were countless arched vaults, each hidden in shadow, and each inhabited by a demon. The vaults stretched upwards and downwards, as far as the eye could see and farther still, until the flaming torches set haphazardly into the walls, the sole source of illumination to be found in the chasm, became as small as stars before at last they disappeared entirely, swallowed up by the gloom. Here and there beasts peered from their chambers: small imps, red and grinning; fiends of fire, and fiends of ice; creatures misshapen and creatures without shape, formless entities that were little more than glowing eyes set against smoke. There was a time when they would have cowered from her presence, fearful that even by setting eyes on her they might incur her wrath. Now, though, they had begun to mock her. She had failed her master. In time his cries would cease, and he would remember that she should be punished for her failings.

And then, what fun they would have!

For now, though, the wailing continued. It grew louder as Mrs Abernathy drew closer to its source. She saw that some of the demons had stuffed coal in their ears in an effort to block out the sound of their master's grief, while others appeared to have been driven as mad as he was and were humming to themselves, or banging their heads repeatedly against the walls in frustration.

At last the vaults were left behind, and there were only sheer dark walls of stone. In the murk before her a shape moved, detaching itself from the shadows the way that someone might detach a shoe from sticky tar, tendrils of blackness seeming to stretch from the entity back into the gloom as though it were part of the darkness, and the darkness part of it. It stepped beneath the flickering light of a torch and grinned unpleasantly. In aspect it resembled a vulture, albeit one with somewhat human features. Its head was pink and bare, although the light caught the tiny bristles that pocked its skin. Its nose was long and fleshy, and hooked like that of a bird of prey, joining a single lower lip to form a kind of beak. Its small black eyes shone with inky malevolence. It wore a dark cloak that flowed like oil over its hunched shoulders, and in its left hand it held a staff of bone, topped with a small skull; that staff was now extended before Mrs Abernathy, blocking her progress.

The creature's name was Ozymuth, and he was the Great Malevolence's chancellor.[9] Ozymuth had always

---

💀 [9] The chancellor is the secretary and adviser to a ruler, or a king. It's a risky profession, as rulers with great power often tend to react badly to people who try to tell them what to do, or who suggest that they may be wrong about something. Thomas Becket (1118–70), the chancellor to Henry II of England, was hacked to pieces by knights after he and the king differed over how much power the king should have over the church. Famously, Henry VIII of England had his chancellor, Thomas More (1478–1535), beheaded because More didn't approve of the king's desire to divorce his first wife, Catherine of Aragon, in order to marry the younger and prettier Anne Boleyn. Eventually, Henry VIII hated Ba'al, even before Ba'al began calling itself Mrs Abernathy and wearing odd clothing. Ozymuth's power lay in the fact that he had the ear of the Great Malevolence. If demons wanted favours done, or sought promotion, then they had to approach the Great Malevolence through Ozymuth, and if their favour was granted or they received the promotion that they sought then they in turn owed Ozymuth a favour. This is the way that the world works, not just Hell. It's not nice, and it shouldn't happen, but it does, and you should be aware of it.

'You may not pass,' said Ozymuth. A long pink tongue poked from his beak and licked at something invisible upon his skin.

'Who are you to tell me what I may or may not do?' said Mrs Abernathy, disdain dripping like acid from her tongue. 'You are our master's dog, and nothing more. If you don't show me some respect, I will have you taken to pieces, cell by cell, atom by atom, and then reassembled just so I can start over again.'

Ozymuth sniggered. 'Each day you come here, and each day your threats sound emptier and emptier. You were our master's favourite once, but that time is gone. You had your chance to please him and you threw it away. If I were you, I would find a hole in which to hide myself, and there I would remain in the hope that

---

ended up having Anne Boleyn beheaded too. The lesson to be learned here is not to work for any kings named Henry who seem to have a fondness for lopping off heads. It's a good idea to watch how they take the tops off their boiled eggs: if they do it with too much ferocity, then it might be a good idea to apply for a job somewhere else.

our master might forget I had ever existed. For when his grief ceases, and he remembers the torment that you have caused him, being taken to pieces will seem like a gentle massage compared to what he will visit upon you. Your days of glory are over, "Mrs Abernathy". Look at you! Look at what you have become!'

Mrs Abernathy's eyes blazed. She snarled and raised her hand as if to strike Ozymuth down. Ozymuth cowered and hid his face beneath his cloak. For a moment they stayed like that, these two old adversaries, until a strange sound emerged from under Ozymuth's cloak. It was laughter, a hissing demonstration of mirth like gas escaping from a hole in a pipe, or bacon sizzling in a pan.

'*Tssssssssss*,' laughed Ozymuth. '*Tssssssssssssss*. You have no power here, and if you strike me then you strike our master, for I am his voice, and I speak for him. Leave now, and give up this senseless pilgrimage. If you come here again, I will have you taken away in chains.'

He raised his staff, and the small skull glowed a sickly yellow. From behind him, two enormous winged beasts appeared. In the dim light they had looked like the images of dragons carved into the walls, so still were they, but now they towered above the two beings on the walkway. One of them leaned down, revealing its reptilian skull, its lips curling back to expose long, sharp teeth of diamond. It growled low and threateningly at Mrs Abernathy, who responded by smacking it on the nose with her bag. The dragon whimpered and looked embarrassed, then turned to its companion as if to say

'Well, you see if you can do any better.' The other dragon just shrugged and found something interesting to stare at on the nearest wall. That bag, it thought, was a lot heavier than it looked.

'You have not heard the last of this, Ozymuth,' said Mrs Abernathy. 'I will rise again, and I will not forget your insolence.'

She spun on her heel and began to walk away. Once again, she was aware of the sound of the Great Malevolence's cries, and the whispers from demons, seen and unseen, and the hissing of Ozymuth's laughter. She endured the long walk through the bowels of the Mountain of Despair, seething with hurt and humiliation. As she passed through the entrance and back into the desolate landscape of Hell, a voice spoke from somewhere around the level of her shoe.

'Have a nice day, now,' said Edgefast's detached head.

Mrs Abernathy ignored him, and moved on.

As Ozymuth watched the retreating figure his laughter slowly ceased. A second form appeared from the shadows, tall and regal. The torches cast light upon his pale features, imperious and cruel. His long black hair was braided with gold, and his clothing was of rich, red velvet, as though blood had been woven into cloth. His cloak, also red, billowed behind him even when he was still, like a living extension of its wearer. He reached out a bejewelled claw and stroked absent-mindedly at one of the dragons, which purred contentedly like a large, scaly cat.

'My Lord Abigor,' said Ozymuth, lowering his head in a gesture of utter subjection, which was a very wise idea when in Duke Abigor's presence, as people who forgot to lower their heads around Duke Abigor often found their heads being lowered for them, usually by having them removed from their shoulders with a large blade.

It is said that Nature abhors a vacuum, but so too does power. When someone falls out of favour with a leader, a queue will quickly form to take that person's place. Thus it was that when Mrs Abernathy failed the Great Malevolence, a number of powerful demons began to wonder how they might take advantage of her misfortune to promote themselves. Of these, the most ambitious and conniving was Duke Abigor.

'What say you, Ozymuth?' said Abigor.

'She is stubborn, my Lord.'

'Stubborn, and dangerous. Her persistence troubles me.'

'Our master will not see her. I have made sure of it. With every chance I get, I whisper words against her into his ear. I remind him of how she failed him. I stoke the fires of his madness, just as you asked of me.'

'You are a loyal and faithful servant,' said Abigor, his voice heavy with sarcasm. Abigor made a note to himself to have Ozymuth banished at the first opportunity once he achieved his goal, for anyone who betrays one master cannot be trusted not to betray another.

'I am loyal to the Great Malevolence, my lord,' replied Ozymuth carefully, as though Duke Abigor had spoken his doubts aloud. 'It is better for our master if his lieutenants do not fail him. Or dress in inappropriate women's clothing,' he added.

Abigor stared at the predatory visage of the chancellor. Abigor was not used to being corrected, however gently. It made him even more intent upon disposing of Ozymuth as soon as he could.

'I will remember you when I come to power,' said Abigor, and he let the double meaning hang in the air. 'Our time draws near. Soon, Ozymuth, soon ...'

Abigor faded back into the shadows, and then disappeared. Ozymuth released a long, ragged breath. He was playing a dangerous game, and he knew it, but if he distrusted Duke Abigor, then he hated Mrs Abernathy more. He gripped his staff and headed deeper into the Mountain of Despair, wincing as the howls of his master grew louder. At the entrance to the inner chamber, he paused. In the gloom his keen eyes espied the massive shape of the Great Malevolence, curled in upon himself in grief.

'It is I, my master,' he said, poison dripping from every word. 'I bear you sad tidings: your faithless lieutenant, Mrs Abernathy, continues to speak ill of you ...'

CHAPTER IV

In Which We Reacquaint Ourselves with Nurd, formerly 'Nurd, The Scourge of Five Deities', Which Was All Something of a Misunderstanding, Really

From a Perfectly Modest cave in the base of a Not Terribly Interesting mountain in a Nothing To See Here, Move Along Now part of Hell, there came the sound of tinkering. Tinkering, as you may be aware, is essentially a male pursuit. Women, by and large, do not tinker, which is why it was a man who originally invented the garden shed and the garage, both of which are basically places to which men can retreat in order to perform tasks that serve no particularly useful purpose other than to give them something to do with their hands that does not involve eating, drinking, or fiddling with the remote control for the television. Very occasionally, a useful invention may result from tinkering, but for the most part tinkering involves trying to improve pieces of machinery that work perfectly well already, with the result that they stop doing what they were supposed to do and instead do nothing at all, hence requiring more tinkering to fix them, and even then they never work quite as well as they did before, so they have to be tinkered with some more, and so on and so on, until eventually the man in question dies, often after being severely beaten by his wife with a malfunctioning kettle, or a piece of a fridge.

Inside the cave was a car. At one point, the car had been a pristine Aston Martin, perfectly maintained by Samuel Johnson's father, who had kept it in the garage behind their house and only drove it on sunny days. Unfortunately the car had been one of the casualties of the demonic assault on Biddlecombe. Without it, there might not have been a Biddlecombe at all, or not one that wasn't overrun by hellish entities. Samuel's dad hadn't seen things that way, though, once he found out that his car was missing.

'You mean it was stolen by a demon?' he had asked, staring at the empty space in his garage that had until recently been occupied by his pride and joy. Samuel had watched his dad as he searched behind stacks of old paint and bits of lawnmower, as though expecting the car to jump out from behind a tin of white emulsion and shout 'Surprise!'

'That's right.'

It was Samuel's mum who had answered. She seemed quite pleased that her husband was upset at the loss of his car, mainly because Samuel's dad had left them to go and live with another woman while expecting his abandoned wife and son to look after his car for him, which Mrs Johnson regarded as being more than a little selfish.

It wasn't quite true that the car had been stolen. In fact Samuel had given the keys to the demon Nurd so that he could drive it straight down the mouth of the portal between Hell and Biddlecombe, thus collapsing it and preventing the Great Malevolence from escaping into our world. Samuel had nevertheless been grateful to his mother for clouding the truth, even if he felt that it was unfair on Nurd to describe him as a thief.

That same Nurd was now standing with his arms folded, staring at what had once been Mr Johnson's Aston Martin but was now Nurd's. The car had passed through the portal relatively unscathed, which came as a nice surprise to Nurd who had half expected that he and the car would be ripped into lots of little pieces and then crushed into something the size of a gnat's eyeball. He had also been relieved to find that the pools of viscous, bubbling black liquid dotted throughout Hell were wells of hydrocarbons and other organic compounds: or, to put it another way, every one of those pools was a miniature petrol station waiting to be put to use.

Unfortunately the petroleum mix was somewhat crude, and the landscape of Hell had not been designed with vintage cars in mind. Doubly unfortunately, Nurd knew next to nothing about how internal combustion engines worked, so he was ill-equipped to deal with any problems that might arise. Nurd fancied himself as a good driver, but since driving in Hell required him to do little more than point the car in a given direction, put his foot down, and avoid rocks and pools of crude oil, Nurd was not as expert behind the wheel as he liked to think.

But sometimes fortune can smile unexpectedly on the most unlikely of faces, and Nurd's, being green and shaped like a crescent moon, was unlikelier than most.

For being particularly annoying, Nurd had been banished to one of Hell's many wildernesses by the Great Malevolence. To keep Nurd company, the Great Malevolence had sent with him Nurd's assistant, Wormwood, who looked like a big ferret that had recently been given a haircut by a blind barber with a pair of blunt scissors. Now Wormwood was many things – irritating, funny-smelling, not terribly bright – but, most unexpectedly, he had proved to have an aptitude for all things mechanical. Thus, aided by a manual that he had found in the boot of the Aston Martin, he had taken responsibility for the maintenance and care of the car. It went faster than before, drove more smoothly, and could turn on a penny.

Oh, and it now looked like a big rock.

Nurd knew that Mrs Abernathy and her master, the Great Malevolence, would not exactly be pleased that their plan to create Hell on Earth had been foiled. Neither of them seemed like the forgiving type, which meant that they'd be looking for someone to blame. The Great Malevolence would blame Mrs Abernathy, because that was the kind of demon he was, since she was supposed to have been in charge. Mrs Abernathy, in turn, would be searching for someone else to blame, and that someone had last been seen hiding under a blanket and driving a vintage car into Hell. Nurd wasn't sure what would happen if Mrs Abernathy ever got her claws on him, but he imagined that it might involve every atom in his body being separated from the next, and then each one being prodded with a little pin for eternity, which didn't appeal to him at all.

So he had made two decisions. The first was that it would be a very good idea to stay on the move, because a moving object was harder to target.[10] It might also, he felt, be wise to disguise the car, which is why they had acquired a frame made from bits of wood and gauze and metal, and painted it to resemble a big boulder, albeit a boulder that could go from nought to sixty in under seven seconds.

At the moment, though, Wormwood was peering beneath the bonnet of the car and fiddling with some bit of the engine that only he could name. Nurd could probably have named it too, if he was bothered, which he wasn't, or so he told himself. After all, he was the brains of the operation, and therefore couldn't be going around worrying about carburettors and spark plugs and getting his hands dirty. It never struck him that Wormwood, as the individual who actually understood something of how the car worked, might have had more of a claim to being the brains than Nurd, but that's

[10] Interestingly, this might be viewed as a variation on a principle of physics known as Heisenberg's Uncertainty Principle, which states that there is no way to accurately pinpoint the exact position of a subatomic particle – a very small particle indeed – unless you're willing to be uncertain about its velocity (its speed in a given direction), and there is no way to accurately pinpoint the particle's exact velocity unless you're willing to be uncertain about its position. It makes sense, when you think about it: on a very basic level you can't tell exactly where something very, very small is if it's moving. To do that, you'd have to interfere with its motion, thus making your knowledge of that motion more unclear. Similarly, observing its velocity means that the precise position will become more uncertain, so that even the act of observing a very small particle changes its behaviour. Actually, Heisenberg's Uncertainty Principle is a bit more complex than that, but that's the essence of it. Still, if you're asked if you understand Heisenberg's Uncertainty Principle, just say that you're not sure, which will be considered a very good scientific joke at the right party.

often the way with people who don't like getting their hands dirty. You don't necessarily get to be king by being bright, but it does help to have bright people around you.[11]

'Have you worked out the problem yet?' asked Nurd.

'It's the ignition coil,' said Wormwood.

'Is it really?' said Nurd, who tried not to sound too bored, and failed even at that.

'You don't know what an ignition coil is, do you?' said Wormwood.

'Is it a coil that has something to do with the ignition?'

'Er, yes.'

'Then I do. Do you know what a big stick capable of leaving a lump on your head is?'

'Yes.'

'Good. If you need to be reminded, just continue giving me lip.'

Wormwood emerged from beneath the bonnet and wiped his hands on his overalls. That was another thing: on the front of the car manual there had been a photograph of a man wearing overalls and holding a tool of some kind. On the left breast was written his name: Bob. Wormwood had decided that this was the kind of uniform worn by people who knew stuff about engines, and had managed to make himself a set of patchwork overalls from the contents of his meagre bag of clothes.

---

[11] And if they get too bright and start wondering if they might not make rather good kings themselves, then you can have them killed. That's pretty much Rule One of being a king. You learn that on the first day.

He had even stitched his name on them, or a version of it: 'Wromwood'.

'It's the copper wire on the windings,' said Wromwood – er, Wormwood. 'It's taken a bit of a battering. It would be good if we could find some replacements.'

Nurd turned and stared out from the mouth of the cave. Before them stretched a huge expanse of black volcanic rock, which made a change from the huge expanse of grey volcanic rock that had until recently been the site of their banishment. The sky was dark with clouds, but tinged permanently with a hint of red, for there were always fires burning in Hell.

'We're a long way from copper wire, Wormwood,' said Nurd.

Wormwood joined his master. 'Where are we, exactly?'

Nurd shook his head. 'I don't know, but –' He pointed to his right, where the fires seemed to be burning brighter, the horizon lost to clouds and mists. – 'I'd guess that somewhere over there is the Mountain of Despair, which means that we want to go –'

'Somewhere else?' suggested Wormwood.

'Anywhere else,' agreed Nurd.

'Are we going to have to keep running for ever?' asked Wormwood, and there was something in his voice that almost caused Nurd to hug him, until he thought better of it and settled for patting Wormwood half-heartedly on the back. He wasn't sure what one might catch from hugging Wormwood, but whatever it was he didn't want it.

'We'll keep on the move for now,' he said. He was about to add something more when a shadow passed over the stones before him. It grew smaller and smaller as whatever was above them commenced a circling descent.

'Douse the light!' said Nurd, and instantly Wormwood quenched the flame of the torch, leaving the cave in darkness.

A red figure dropped to the ground within a stone's throw of the cave, its great bat wings raised above its back. It was eight feet tall and had the body of a man, but a forked tail curled from the base of its spine, and two twisted horns protruded from its bald head. It knelt and ran its claws over the rocks before it, then raised them to its nose and sniffed warily. A long forked tongue unrolled from its mouth and licked the ground.

'Oh no,' said Wormwood. He thought that he could almost see the marks of rubber upon the rocks where Nurd had been forced to give the car a little too much gas in order to get them closer to the cave.

The creature on the rocks grew very still. It had no ears, merely a hole on either side of its head, but it was clearly listening. Then it turned its head, and they glimpsed its face for the first time.

It had eight black eyes, like those of some great spider, and mandibles at its jaws. Its nostrils were ragged perforations set in a snout of sharp bone. Nurd saw them widen and contract, glistening with mucus. For a moment the creature stared straight at the mouth of the cave in which they were hiding, and they saw the muscles in its legs tighten as it prepared to spring. Its mandibles clicked, and its jaws made a sucking noise as though it could already taste prey, but instead of exploring further its wings unfolded to their fullest expanse and it shot into the air. The sound of flapping reached their ears, but slowly began to fade as the creature moved away, heading north in the direction of the bright flames.

'Did it see us?' asked Wormwood.

'I think it found the rubber from the tyres,' said Nurd. 'I don't know if it realized we were nearby. If it did, why didn't it come after us? Anyway, we have to go.'

'Was it –?'

'Yes,' said Nurd. 'It was one of hers.'

He sounded tired, and frightened, even to himself. They had been running and hiding for so long that sometimes he thought it might almost be a relief if they were caught, at least until he began thinking about what might happen to them *after* they were caught, for the prospect of being slowly disassembled at the atomic level and then prodded for a very long time usually dispelled such thoughts of giving up. But eventually they would make a serious mistake, or some misfortune would befall them, and then Mrs Abernathy's wrath would rain down upon them. The only consolation for Nurd was that Samuel Johnson was safe on Earth. He missed his friend terribly, but Nurd would willingly have sacrificed himself to keep Samuel safe. He just hoped that it wouldn't come to that, for Nurd liked all of his atoms just where they were.

CHAPTER V

In Which We Encounter Mr Merryweather's Dwarfs – or Elves – and Rather Wish We Hadn't

There are few things more soul-sapping, Mr Merryweather concluded wearily, than being stuck in a van with a bunch of truculent[12] dwarfs. The van in question bore the legend 'Mr Merryweather's Elves – Big Talent Comes in Small Packages'. Alongside the legend was a picture of a small person wearing pointy shoes and a cap with a bell on the end. The small person was grinning happily, and did not look at all threatening, and hence bore no resemblance to the actual contents of the van. Indeed, were one to look closely at the legend about elves and talent and whatnot, one might have noticed that the word 'Elves' had recently been painted over what appeared to be the word 'Dwarfs'.

We'll come to the reasons for the change in our own good time, but to give you some idea of just how difficult Mr Merryweather's dwarfs were currently

---

💀 12 'Truculent' is a lovely word. It essentially means to be very self-assertive and rather destructive. This perfectly described Mr Merryweather's dwarfs, who could have given lessons in aggression to Vikings.

being, a family of four was at that moment passing the van on the motorway, and the two children, a boy and a girl, had pressed their noses against the car window in the hope of catching a glimpse of an elf. Instead, they caught a glimpse of a small chap's bottom, which at that same moment was sticking out of one of the van's windows.

'Dad, is that an elf's bum?' asked the little boy.

'Elves don't exist,' said his father, who hadn't noticed the van or, indeed, the bum. 'And don't say "bum". It's rude.'

'But it says on the van that they're elves.'

'Well, I'm telling you that elves don't exist.'

'But, Dad, there's a bum sticking out of the window of the elf van, so it has to be an elf bum.'

'Look, I told you: don't use the word "b—"'

At which point the boy's dad looked to his right and was treated to the sight of a pale bottom hanging in the wind, alongside which were a number of small people making faces at him.

'Call the police, Ethel,' he said. He shook his fist in the general direction of faces and bottom. 'You little horrors!' he shouted.

'Nyaahhhh!' shouted a dwarf in return, and stuck his tongue out as the van sped away.

'See, I was right,' said the driver's son. 'It was an elf. And a bum.'

Inside the van, Mr Merryweather was trying to keep his eyes on the road while ignoring all that was going on in the back.

'Cold out there,' said Jolly, the leader of the group, as he pulled his bottom from the window and made himself look decent again. The rest of his companions, Dozy, Angry, and Mumbles, took their seats and began opening bottles of Spiggit's Old Peculiar. The air in the van, which hadn't smelled particularly pleasant to begin with, now took on the odour of a factory devoted to producing unwashed socks and fish heads.[13] Curiously, this very strong, and very unpleasant, beer appeared to have little effect on the dwarfs apart from exaggerating their natural character traits. Thus Jolly became jollier, in a drunken, unsettling way; Angry became angrier; Dozy became sleepier; and Mumbles – well, he just became more unintelligible.

'Oi, Merryweather,' called Angry. 'When do we get paid?'

Mr Merryweather's hands tightened on the wheel. He was a fat, bald man in a light brown check suit, and he always wore a red bow tie. He looked like someone who should be managing a bunch of untrustworthy dwarfs, but whether he looked that way because of what he was, or he was what he was because he looked that way, we will never know.

'Paid for what?' said Mr Merryweather.

☠ [13] Spiggit's Old Peculiar had recently been the subject of a number of court cases relating to incidents of temporary blindness, deafness, and undesirable hair growth on the palms of the hands. Due to a loophole in the law, it was allowed to remain on sale but it was required to have a warning label on the bottle, and anyone buying the ale had to sign a one-off agreement promising not to sue in the event of any injury caused by drinking it, up to and including death. Spiggit's had decided to make the best of this and its advertising slogan now read: 'Spiggit's – Ask for the Beer with the Biohazard Symbol!'

'For today's work, that's what for.'

The van swerved on the motorway as Mr Merryweather briefly lost control of the wheel, and of himself.

'Work?' he said. '*Work?* You lot don't know the meaning of work.'

'Careful!' called Dozy. 'You nearly spilled my beer.'

'I. Don't. *Care!*' screamed Mr Merryweather.

'What did he say?' asked Jolly. 'Someone was shouting, so I didn't hear.'

'Says he doesn't care,' said Dozy.

'Oh, well that's just lovely, that is. After all we've done for him—'

The van came to a violent skidding halt by the side of the road. Mr Merryweather stood and shook his fist at the assembled dwarfs.

'All you've done for me? All. You've Done. For Me. I'll tell you what you've done for me. You've made my life a misery, that's what. You've left me a broken man. My nerves are shot. Look at my hand.'

He held up his left hand. It trembled uncontrollably.

'That's bad,' agreed Jolly.

'And that's the good one,' said Mr Merryweather, holding up his right hand, which shook so much he could no longer hold a pint of milk in it, as it would instantly turn to cream.

'Abbledaybit,' said Mumbles.

'What?' said Mr Merryweather.

'He says you're having a bad day, but once you've had time to calm down and rest, you'll get over it,' said Jolly.

45

Despite his all-consuming rage, Mr Merryweather found time to look puzzled.

'He said that?'

'Yep.'

'But it just sounded like "abbledaybit".'

'Ed,' said Mumbles.

'He says that's what he said,' said Jolly. 'You're having a bad—'

Mr Merryweather pointed his finger at Jolly in a manner that could only be described as life-threatening. Had Mr Merryweather's finger been a gun, Jolly would have had a small column of smoke where his head used to be.

'I'm warning you,' said Mr Merryweather. 'I'm warning you all. Today was the last straw. Today was —'

Today was to have been a good day. After weeks, even months, of begging, Mr Merryweather had got the dwarfs a job that paid good money. It had even been worth repainting the van, and altering the name of the business. At last, everything was coming together.

Mr Merryweather's Elves had previously been known as Mr Merryweather's Dwarfs, as the changes to the van's lettering suggested, but a series of unfortunate incidents, including some civil and criminal court actions, had required that Mr Merryweather's Dwarfs maintain a low profile for a time, and then quietly cease to exist. These incidents had included a brief engagement as four of Snow White's seven dwarfs at a pantomime in Aldershot, an engagement that had come to a sudden end following an assault on Prince

Charming, in the course of which he was fed his own wig; two nights as mice and coachmen in *Cinderella*, during which Buttons lost a finger; and a single performance of *The Wizard of Oz* that ended with a riot among the Munchkins, a flying monkey being shot down with a tranquillizer dart, and a fire in the Emerald City that required three units of the local fire brigade to put out.

And so Mr Merryweather's Dwarfs had been re-invented as Mr Merryweather's Elves, a cunning ploy that, incredibly, had somehow managed to fool otherwise sensible people into believing this was an entirely different troupe of little men, and not the horrible bunch of drunks, arsonists, and monkey shooters who had almost singlehandedly brought an end to pantomime season in England. Elves just didn't seem as threatening as dwarfs, and as long as Mr Merryweather kept the dwarfs hidden until the last possible moment, and ensured that they were, for the most part, clean and sober, he began to believe that he just might get away with the deception.

That day, Mr Merryweather's Elves had begun what was potentially their most lucrative engagement yet: they were to feature in a music video for the beloved boyband BoyStarz to be filmed at Lollymore Castle. If all went well, the dwarfs would appear in future videos as well, and perhaps join BoyStarz on tour. There would be T-shirt sales; there was even talk of their own TV show. It seemed, thought Mr Merryweather, too good to be true.

And like most things that seem too good to be true, it was.

First of all, they didn't want to do it, even before they knew what 'it' was.

'I have a job for you lot,' he told them. 'A good one and all.'

'Eh, it wouldn't involve being a dwarf, would it?' asked Angry.

'Well, yes.'

'What a shocker. You know, it's not as if we wake up every morning and think, "Oh look, we're dwarfs. Didn't expect that. I thought I was taller." No, we're just regular people who happen to be small. It doesn't define us.'

'What's your point?' asked Mr Merryweather wearily.

'Our point is,' said Jolly, 'that we'd like to do something where being a dwarf is just incidental. For example, why can't I play Hamlet?'

'Because you're three foot eight inches tall, that's why. You can't play Hamlet. Piglet, maybe, but not Hamlet.'[14]

'Less of that,' said Jolly. 'That's what I'm talking about, see? That kind of attitude keeps us oppressed.'

That, thought Mr Merryweather, and the fact that you all drink too much, and can't be bothered to learn lines, and would pick your own pockets just to pass the time.

'Look, it's just the way the world works,' said Mr Merryweather. 'It's not me. I'm trying to do my best, but you don't help matters with your behaviour. We can't even do *Snow White and the Seven Dwarfs* in panto this year because you fought with Mrs Doris

---

☠ [14] See what I did there? Comedy gold.

Stott's Magnificent Midgets, so we're three little people down. Nobody wants to watch Snow White and the Four Dwarfs. It just doesn't sound right.'

'You could tell them it's a budget production,' said Angry.

'We could double up,' said Dozy.

'You can barely single up,' said Mr Merryweather.

'Careful,' said Dozy.

After they'd bickered and argued for another half-hour he had eventually managed to tell them about the job, and they had reluctantly agreed to earn some money. Mr Merryweather had climbed behind the wheel and thought, not for the first time, that he understood why people liked tossing dwarfs around, and wondered if he could convince someone to toss his dwarfs, preferably off a high cliff.

They had arrived at Lollymore Castle, not far from the town of Biddlecombe, early that morning. It was cold and damp, and the dwarfs were already complaining before they even got out of the van. Still, they were given tea to warm them up, and then dressed in the costumes that had been specially made for them: little suits of armour, little coats of chain mail, light-weight helmets.

Then they were handed swords and maces, and Mr Merryweather had sprinted from the van to stop them killing someone.

'For crying out loud, don't give them weapons,' he said, grabbing Jolly's arm just in time to stop him from braining an assistant director with a mace. 'They might, er, hurt themselves.'

He patted Jolly on the head. 'They're only little fellas, you know.' He hugged Jolly in the manner of a friendly uncle embracing a much-loved nephew, and received a kick in the shin for his trouble.

'Gerroff,' said Jolly. 'And give me back my mace.'

'Look, don't hit anyone with it,' hissed Mr Merryweather.

'It's a mace. It's *for* hitting people with.'

'But you're only supposed to be pretending. It's a video.'

'Well, they want it to look real, don't they?'

'Not that real. Not *funeral* real.'

Jolly conceded that Mr Merryweather had a point, and the dwarfs went to inspect the castle as the director pointed out their 'marks', the places on the battlements where they were supposed to stand during filming.

'What's our motivation?' asked Angry. 'Why are we here?'

'What do you mean?' said the director. 'You're defending the castle.'

'This castle?'

'Yes.'

'Is it ours?'

'Of course it's yours.'

'I beg to differ. The steps are too big. I nearly did myself an injury climbing up those steps. Almost ruptured something, I did. If we'd built this castle, we'd have made the steps smaller. Can't be ours. Makes no sense.'

The director pinched the bridge of his nose hard and closed his eyes.

'Right then, you captured it from somebody else.'

'Who?' asked Jolly.

'Capsmodwa?' said Mumbles.

'That's right,' said Angry. 'Did we capture if from smaller dwarfs? We're dwarfs – er, elves. I can't even see over the battlements. How are four of us supposed to have captured this castle? What did we do, raid it in instalments?'

'Perhaps it was just abandoned, and you took it over.'

'You can't do that. You can't wander into places without a by-your-leave just because someone's popped out for a pint of milk or a bit of a battle, and then call it home. It's not right. They'd have you up in court, you know. That's illegal entry, that is. That's six months in jail. And I should know.'

The director opened his eyes, grasped Angry by his chain mail, then lifted him from the ground so that he and Angry were on eye level.

'Listen to me,' said the director. 'This is going to be a very long, very wet day, and, if I have to, I will drop you from these battlements as an example to your friends of what happens when people start questioning the logic of a video in which a boy band with perfect teeth and blond highlights attempts to capture a castle from a bunch of little people wearing plastic armour. Do I make myself clear?'

'Abundantly,' said Angry. 'Just trying to help.'

The director put him down.

'Good. Now, I'm going to go down there, and we're going to start filming. Clear?'

'As crystal,' said Angry, Dozy, and Jolly.

'A1,' said Mumbles.

The dwarfs watched the director descend to the castle gate, then tramp angrily across the mud to the assemblage of tents and vans that constituted the video set.

'He's obviously very artistic,' said Angry. 'They're like that, artistic people. They go off at the slightest thing. Them, and wrestlers.'

'Why did they give us plastic armour and real swords?' asked Dozy.

'Dunno,' said Angry. 'Doesn't say much for his battle strategy.'

'Nice castle, though.'

'Oh, yes. Lovely workmanship. Knew what they were doing, these old builders.' Angry tapped his sword approvingly on a battlement, and watched as a chunk of it sheared off and almost killed a lighting technician below.

'Sorry,' said Angry.

He saw the director glaring at him, and raised his sword.

'A bit fell off,' he shouted in explanation. 'We can fix it later,' then added to his colleagues: 'Very shoddy, that. Bet a French bloke built this castle. Wouldn't have that in an English castle. Built to last, English castles. It's why we had an empire.'

But the others weren't listening. Instead, they were gazing slack-jawed at the sight of BoyStarz, who had just emerged from the caravan that was their dressing room. Even by the standards of the average boy band, Boystarz looked a bit soft: their hair was perfect, their skin unblemished, their teeth white. They seemed to be struggling under the weight of their armour, and one of them was complaining that his sword was too heavy.

The director accompanied them to within a few feet of the castle walls, and introduced them to the dwarfs.

'OK, these are the BoyStarz,' he said, and at the mention of their band name some deep-seated instinct kicked in, aided by many months of training involving beatings, bribes, and threats of starvation, and each of the four young men did a little dance.

'Hi,' said the first, 'I'm Starlight.'

'And I'm Twinkle.'

'I'm Gemini.'

'And I'm Phil.'

The dwarfs looked at the fourth member, who wasn't as pretty as the rest, and seemed a bit lost.

'Why is there always one bloke in these boy bands who looks like he came to fix the boiler and somehow got bullied into joining the group?' asked Jolly.

'Dunno,' said Dozy. 'Can't dance much either, can he?'

Which was true. Phil danced like a man trying to shake a rat from his leg.

'We're supposed to hand our lovely castle over to this lot?' said Angry. 'It'd be like surrendering it to powder puffs.'

'No,' said Jolly softly. 'No, there's such a thing as pride, as dignity. We can't have this. We just can't.'

'What are they saying?' Twinkle asked the director nervously. 'They look frighteningy.'

'I want to go home,' said Starlight. 'I don't like the little men.'

'The ground feels funny, and it smells like poo,' said Gemini.

'And I'm Phil,' said Phil.

The director was already backing away. He didn't care for the look in the elves' eyes. He didn't care for it at all.

Hey, he thought, they're not elves. They're dwarfs. They're not Mr Merryweather's Elves, they're Mr Merryweather's –

Dwarfs!

He was already running, four terrified boy band members at his heels, as the first rocks began to rain down on them, for Mr Merryweather's Elves were intent upon defending Lollymore Castle, even if they had to take it apart brick by brick to do so.

CHAPTER VI

In Which Samuel is Reunited With Boswell, and We Learn Why One Should Not Trust a Mirror

As such tales will do, the story of how Samuel Johnson had managed to ask a letter box on a date had made its way around the entire school by the time the bell rang to send everyone home.

'Oi, Johnson!' Lionel Hashim shouted at him as he made his way to the school gates. 'I hear there's a very good-looking traffic light over on Shelley Road. You could ask it to go to the cinema with you. Don't try to kiss it though. It might go red!'

Funny, thought Samuel. Really funny. His bag, and his heart, felt very heavy.

Outside the gates, Samuel's pet dachshund, Boswell, was waiting. Boswell had the worried air of one who suspects that bad news is imminent, and its arrival has only been delayed by the fact that it's looking for some more bad news to keep it company. A series of frown lines creased Boswell's brow, and at regular intervals he would give a sigh. He was a familiar sight around the town of Biddlecombe, but particularly at the school, for Boswell was Samuel Johnson's faithful companion, and was always present to greet his master when the bell struck four.

Boswell had always been a somewhat sensitive, contemplative dog.[15] Even as a puppy, he would regard his ball warily, as though waiting for it to sprout legs and run off with another dog. He displayed a fondness for the sadder types of classical music, and had been known to howl along to Mozart's Requiem in a plaintive manner.

But recent events had given Boswell good cause to think that the world was an even stranger and more worrying place than he had previously thought. After all, he had witnessed monsters emerging from holes in space, and had even been injured by one as he attempted to save his master from its clutches. One of his legs had been broken, and ever since he had walked with a slight limp. Being a dog, although a very clever one, Boswell wasn't entirely clear about the nature of what had occurred during the invasion. All he knew was that it had been very bad, and he didn't want it to happen again. Most of all, he didn't want anything to happen to Samuel, whom he loved very much, and so each

---

☠ [15] The English writer Horace Walpole (1717–97) suggested that 'this world is a comedy to those that think, a tragedy to those that feel'. Unfortunately, since most of us both think *and* feel, we are destined to spend a lot of our time on Earth not being certain whether to laugh or cry. Laughter is probably better, but you don't want to be one of those people who laugh all of the time ('Look, that chap over there's just fallen off a cliff! Ah-ha-ha-ha-ha-ha!') because you'll appear uncaring, or insane. Similarly, if you cry all of the time then you'll look like a sissy, or a professional mourner, and you'll start to smell damp. Best to settle for a wry smile, then, the kind that suggests you're able to endure the slings and arrows of outrageous fortune with a degree of grace while still being able to shed a discreet tear at sad films, and funerals. Incidentally, Horace Walpole looked a bit like a horse in a wig, and was once accused of driving the poet Chatterton to suicide. He was, therefore, probably a 'world as tragedy' kind of person.

morning, regardless of the weather, Boswell would trot along beside his beloved master as Samuel walked to school, and would be waiting for him when he emerged from school at the end of the day. A flap in the front door of the house meant that he could come and go as he pleased. Boswell's duty was to protect Samuel, and he intended to fulfil it to the best of a small dog's ability.

That day Boswell detected a change in Samuel's usually sunny disposition. While some dogs might have made an effort to cheer up their master under such circumstances, perhaps by chasing their tail or showing them something that smelled funny, Boswell was the kind of dog that shared his master's mood. If Samuel was happy, then Boswell was content. If Samuel was sad, Boswell stayed quiet and kept him company. In this, Boswell was wiser than most people.

And so the boy and his dog, each bearing some of the weight of the world upon his shoulders, made their way home, and had anyone taken the time to give them more than a passing glance they might have noticed that both the boy and the dog kept their heads down as they went. They did not look in shop windows, and they avoided puddles. They did not seem to want to see themselves. It was as if they were frightened of their own reflections, or scared of being noticed.

People still occasionally shot funny looks at Samuel and indeed Boswell, but not as often as they used to, or perhaps it would be more accurate to say that the funny looks they shot were of a general kind – 'He's an odd kid, and his dog makes me feel sad' – rather than the specific kind, such as, 'There's Samuel Johnson and his dog, who were involved with all of that demonic business that I'd rather not remember, thanks very much. Actually, now that I see them again, I feel a bit angry at them because I don't want to be reminded of what happened, but by their presence here they remind me of it anyway, so I think I'll just blame them for everything instead of the demons because it's easier to be angry at a small boy and a smaller dog, and less likely to result in me being eaten, or whisked off to Hell, or some similarly horrible consequence.'

Or words to that effect.

Samuel had almost ceased to notice the reactions of other people to his presence, but that was not why he and Boswell kept their heads down. It was true to say that they did not want to be noticed, but it was not their neighbours in Biddlecombe who worried them. The individual who concerned them was much further away.

Further away, yet strangely close.

Most of us do not think very hard about the nature of mirrors. We see the reflection of a room, or of ourselves, in a glass and we think, 'Oh, look, it's the couch', or 'Oh, look, it's me. I thought I was thinner/ fatter/ better-looking/ uglier/ a girl.'[16] But it's not your couch, and

---

💀 [16] If you're bored some time, and want to puzzle your parents:
1) Fill a small plastic glass with a little water.
2) Lift said glass as if to drink from it.
3) Bypass your mouth and instead touch the glass to your forehead.
4) Spill a little of the water down your face.
5) Tell your parents that you thought you were taller.
6) Take a bow. Ask people to tip their waitress. Tell them you'll be here all week.
7) Leave.

it's not you. It's a version of you, which is why the artist René Magritte could paint a picture of a pipe and write beneath it, in French, *'Ceci n'est pas une pipe'*, or 'This is not a pipe'. Because it's not a pipe: it's an *image* of a pipe. As Magritte himself pointed out: 'Could you stuff my pipe? No, it's just a representation. So if I had written on my picture, "This is a pipe", I'd have been lying!'

The painting in question, from 1929, is called *The Treachery of Images*. ('Treachery', meaning to trick or deceive, is another great word, especially if you roll that first 'r' on your tongue and really stretch it out: 'Trrrrrrreachery!' you can shout, in a demented way, while waving a sword and alarming the neighbours.) In other words, you can't trust images, because they're not what they pretend to be.

Samuel had become very familiar with this concept, and not in a good way. He had begun to suspect that mirrors were very strange indeed, and that, far from simply providing a reflection of this world, they might in fact be a world of their own.[17] He felt this because very occasionally he would glance at a mirror, or the window of a shop, or some other reflective surface, and would see a figure that should not have been there. It was the figure of a no-longer-quite-beautiful woman in a floral dress. It was Mrs Abernathy.

For Mrs Abernathy, Samuel had decided, walked in the world of mirrors. She couldn't get back into this world, but somehow she could see into it by moving behind the glass. Samuel had caught glimpses of her in the mirror of his bathroom cabinet, in the glass of his front door, even once, most peculiarly, on a spoon, where she was distorted and upside down. She seemed to prefer to come at night, when the windows were dark and the reflections clearer in the glass, as though the clarity of her own image in turn made the world at which she gazed easier to discern.

And each time her eyes were filled with a blue light, and they burned with her hatred for Samuel.

*　　*　　*

[17] Actually, we have a tendency to take our reflection for granted at the best of times, when it's really quite extraordinary. When you see your reflection in a window at night, perhaps with a city visible through the glass beyond, it's because ninety-five per cent of the light striking the window has gone straight through while five per cent has been reflected, hence the ghostly image of your face. This proves the particle nature of light, but what's troubling is that the five per cent of reflected particles of energy, or photons, is reflected for no particularly good reason that we can understand, indicating the possibility of randomness at the heart of the universe. There's a one in twenty chance that a photon will be reflected instead of transmitted, which means that we can't know for certain how a given photon will behave. This is very troubling for scientists. If you want to give your science teacher a nervous breakdown, ask why this happens.

Samuel's mother greeted him from the kitchen as he opened the front door and dumped his bag in the hall.

'Hello, Samuel. Did you have a good day?'

'If, by good, you mean embarrassing and soul-destroying, then, yes, I had a good day,' said Samuel.

'Oh dear,' said his mum. 'Sit down at the table and I'll make you a nice cup of tea.'

What was it about mothers, wondered Samuel, that led them to believe all of the problems of the world could be solved with a nice cup of tea? Samuel could have walked in with his head under his arm, blood spurting from his neck and his back quilled with arrows, and his mother would have suggested a nice cup of tea as a means of salving his wounds. She would probably even have tried to rub some tea on his severed head in an effort to stick it back on his shoulders.

But the funny thing was that, more often than not, a cup of tea and a consoling word from your mum were enough to make things at least a little better, so Samuel sat down and waited until a steaming mug of tea was placed in front of him. It really did smell good. He could almost feel it warming his throat already. Today had been bad, but perhaps tomorrow would be better. Tea: our friend in times of trouble.

'Oh bother,' said Samuel's mother. 'We're out of milk.'

Samuel's forehead thumped hard against the kitchen table.

'I'll go,' he said.

'There's a good lad,' said his mum. 'I'll have a fresh

cup waiting for you when you get back. Will you get some bread while you're at it? I don't know: even with your dad gone, we're still getting through as much food as ever.'

Samuel winced. He wasn't sure which hurt more: to hear his mother grow sad when she talked about his dad's absence, or to hear her remark upon it so casually. His mother seemed to notice his discomfort, for she moved to him and enveloped him in her arms.

'Oh, you,' she said, kissing his hair. 'I don't mind you eating. You're a growing lad. And your dad and I, well, we're talking, which is something. I'm not as angry with him as I was, although I'd still hit him over the head with a frying pan given half the chance. But we're OK, you and I, aren't we?'

Samuel nodded, his eyes closed, taking in the comforting smell of flour and perfume from his mother's dress.

'Yes, we're OK,' he said, although he wasn't sure if it was true.

His mother pushed him gently away, and held him at arm's length. She looked at him seriously.

'There's been no more, um, *strangeness*, has there?' she asked.

'You mean demons?'

Now it was his mother's turn to look uncomfortable.

'Yes, if that's what you want to call them.'

'That's what they were.'

'Now, I don't want to get into an argument about it,' said his mum. 'I'm only asking.'

'No, Mum,' said Samuel. 'There's been no more

strangeness.' Not unless you include glimpses of a woman with her face stitched together, staring out from mirrors and glass doors. 'There's been no more strangeness at all.'

CHAPTER VII

In Which We Pay a Visit to Mrs Abernathy's House. Which Is Nice. Not.

Before we go any further, a quick word about Evil.
Evil has been in existence for a very long time, long
enough to be part of the birth of everything billions
and billions of years ago following the Big Bang that
brought this universe into being. Unfortunately, for a
while after the Big Bang there wasn't much for Evil to
do because there wasn't a great deal of life about, and
what life there was consisted of little single-celled organisms which had quite enough to be getting along with
just trying to become multi-celled organisms, thank you
very much, without having to worry about being unkind
to one another for no good reason as well. Even when
these multi-celled organisms grew incredibly complex,
and became sharks, and spiders, and carnivorous
dinosaurs, they still didn't provide much amusement
for Evil. These beasts operated on instinct alone, and
their instinct was simply to eat, and thus to survive.

But then man came along, and Evil perked up a bit,
because here was a creature that could choose, which
made it very interesting indeed. Being good or bad are
not passive states: you have to decide to be one or the

other. Evil did everything it could to encourage people to do bad instead of good, and because it was clever it disguised itself well, so that people who did bad things found ways to convince themselves that they weren't really bad at all. They needed more money to be happy, and hence they stole, or they cheated on their taxes; and then they told lies to hide what they'd done, because they were kind of sorry for it, but not sorry enough to admit what they'd done, or to stop doing it. In the end, most of it came down to selfishness, but Evil didn't mind. You could call it what you wanted, as far as Evil was concerned, just as long as you kept on being bad.

And Evil wasn't just busy in this universe, but in a lot of others too, for ours was but one in a great froth of universes known as the Multiverse, each one its own expanding bubble of planets and stars. You might think that this would require Evil to spread itself a little thinly, because there can only be so much Evil to go round, but you'd be surprised what Evil can do when it puts its mind to it. On the other hand, no matter how hard Evil tries, it can never quite match up to the power of Good, because Evil is ultimately self-destructive. Evil may set out to corrupt others, but in the process it corrupts itself. That's just the way Evil is. All things considered, it's better to be on the side of Good, even if Evil occasionally has nicer uniforms.

Mrs Abernathy, who was very evil indeed, sat in a high chamber in her palace, a terrifying constuct of spars and sharp edges carved from a single massive slab of shiny black volcanic rock, and stared intently at the shard of glass before her. She had 'borrowed' it a long,

long time before from the Great Malevolence, for he had many such shards, and she had convinced herself that one more or less would make no difference to him. They were his windows into the world of men, each revealing to him some part of the existence that he hated, yet also, in the pit of his being, secretly craved. He would watch the sun set, and lakes turn to gold. He would see children grow up to have children of their own, and become old among those whom they loved, and who loved them in turn. He would gaze upon husbands and wives, brothers and sisters, upon puppies, and frogs, and elephants. He would even gaze upon goldfish in bowls, and hamsters who ran around inside wheels to distract themselves from their tiny cages, and flies struggling in the webs of spiders, and he would envy each and every living thing its freedom, even if it was only the freedom to die.

For so long, Mrs Abernathy had shared her master's desire to turn the Earth into a version of Hell, but something had changed. What that something was might be guessed from the fact that the windows of her dreadful lair, which in its way had long been nearly as awful as the Great Malevolence's Mountain of Despair, but considerably smaller, and with better views, had been decorated with net curtains. The curtains were black and, upon closer inspection, seemed to have been used at some point to catch horrible mutated fish, as the remains of a few were still caught in its strands, but at least someone was making an effort. A long table constructed entirely of tombstones now had a yellow vase at its centre, a vase, furthermore, that bore a pattern of dozing cats. Admittedly, the vase was filled with ugly blood-red flowers that hid sharp teeth inside their petals, and those teeth would have made short work of any real cats that made the mistake of falling asleep within snapping distance, but it was a start, just like the curtains, and the doormat that read 'Please Wipe Your Cloven Hooves!', and the jar of pot-pourri made from the husks of poisonous beetles and scented with stagnant water.

What Mrs Abernathy had discovered, even if she refused to admit it to herself, was that if you go to a place intent upon changing it, then sometimes that place may end up changing you instead. She had returned to Hell, but she had brought back a little of the human world with her, and now she was being altered in ways she did not fully understand.

Mind you, she still hated Samuel Johnson, and his dog. Just because she wanted to make her lair a bit prettier, and maybe spent a few minutes longer than before on making sure her hair was just right before she went out, didn't mean that she wouldn't tear them both limb from limb at the first opportunity. Thus it was that she watched them through the fragment of glass as they trudged from the house, the boy's head low, the dog intent upon his master. Samuel looked unhappy, she thought. That was good. She liked it when he was unhappy. She willed him to look up, to catch a quick sight of her in one of the windows as he was passing. It always gave her pleasure to see him react with fear when she appeared, even if she couldn't do him any real harm, not yet, but he seemed intent upon not noticing her.

She stretched out a pale hand and stared at her fingers. The nails were red, and slightly chipped. She would have to paint them again, once she managed to get a decent supply of suitable blood.

From above her head came the sound of wings flapping. The chamber narrowed into a steeple-like structure at its centre that protruded high above the surrounding plains. At its peak was an opening that now darkened as a figure entered and began to descend. Her Watcher had returned.

When Mrs Abernathy had fallen out of favour with the Great Malevolence, many of those demons who had previously been loyal to her had sought new masters. After all, if someone had failed the Great Malevolence so dreadfully that he had cut her off entirely, refusing even to stare upon her face, it could only be a matter of time before he decided that ignoring her was insufficient punishment, and something more imaginative might be called for. In that case, he might decide that he wanted to stare upon her face again after all, but only if the face had first been removed and nailed to a wall, with the other parts of her body arranged alongside it in an interesting if unconventional manner. When that happened, as most of the cleverer demons seemed to think was increasingly probable, then any of those who had remained close to her were likely to end up in a similar position, except slightly lower down the wall.

In a sense, demons were the embodiment of the law of conservation of matter, which states that matter cannot be created or destroyed, but only transformed from one state to another.[18] When applied to demons, this meant that they could not die, but could still be transformed into various alternative painful versions of existence, and their torments could be made to last an eternity. Nobody wants to spend eternity with his face pinned to a wall and his severed legs crossed underneath his chin, like some ghastly coat-of-arms, so the general wisdom in Hell was that it was unwise to be involved with Mrs Abernathy, because Mrs Abernathy was doomed and would, in turn, doom all those around her.

But there were creatures that had remained loyal to her: some because they were too stupid to know better, some because they hoped that Mrs Abernathy might discover a way to improve her situation, and some because they were as cruel and vicious and intelligent

---

[18] Albert Einstein, aided by the earlier work of Cockcroft and Walton, proved that matter can be changed to energy, and energy to matter, as in an atomic explosion. Thus, it's really the law of conservation of energy *and* matter. But one of the forgotten pioneers in this area is the Frenchman Antoine-Laurent Lavoisier (1743–94), who, in his spare time, became fascinated by the possibility that all of the bits and pieces of stuff on Earth – lions, tigers, budgerigars, trees, slugs, iron, and the like – were parts of a single interconnected whole. He and his wife Marie Anne began rusting pieces of metal in a sealed apparatus, then weighing them along with the air that was lost. They found that the rusted metal, rather than weighing less than before, or the same, in fact weighed *more*, because the oxygen molecules in the air had adhered to the metal. In other words, matter was changing from one form to another, but not disappearing. Lavoisier met a terrible end: he had offended a frustrated scientist, Jean-Paul Marat, and during the Reign of Terror (1793–4) that followed the French Revolution, Marat, who was prominent in the Reign, got his revenge: Lavoisier was tried, sentenced and then beheaded, all in one day. When a plea for mercy was entered on his behalf, the judge responded: 'The Republic has no need of geniuses.' The next time that you burn a match, spare a thought for Lavoisier.

as she was, and couldn't find a better employer, even in Hell. The Watcher appeared to be one of those. It was strong, and tireless, and seemed unquestioningly faithful to its mistress, even if it was a bit disturbed by the changes that had taken place in her appearance recently. It had grown used to serving a monstrous, tentacled demon many times its own height, not a small, blond woman in a print dress. Still, you had to be open to new experiences, that was its philosophy, as long as those new experiences sufficiently resembled the old ones in terms of hurting other creatures.

The Watcher was pleased with itself, and it knew that Mrs Abernathy would in turn be pleased with it. But before it could begin to speak, its mistress spasmed. Her arms shot out from her sides and her back arched. Her mouth gaped and her eyes opened wide. Beams of blue light shot from her jaws, her ears, and the sockets of her eyes. Smaller splinters of energy erupted from every pore of her skin, and she hung suspended in the air like a blue sun.

And the Watcher regarded her, and knew that it had made the right choice.

Mrs Abernathy had been patient: one could not exist for so long without learning the value of patience. She had endured the rejection of the Great Malevolence, continuing to make her regular pilgrimage to his mountain when others laughed at her, reminding them all that she would not be forgotten. When she was not traipsing back and forth between her palace and her master's home, she had been waiting. She had waited for her

Watcher to find traces of the vehicle that had entered the portal and caused it to collapse, dragging them all back to Hell. She had waited for those moments when Samuel Johnson might inadvertently glance in a mirror and find her staring back at him, relishing his fear. She had waited for her chance to avenge herself upon him. But, most of all, she had waited for the humans to do what she knew they most assuredly would do.

She had waited for them to turn on their great Collider once again.

CHAPTER VIII

In Which We Wonder Just How Smart Really Smart People Sometimes Are

Scientists are a funny lot. Oh, they do many great and wonderful things, and without science we wouldn't have all kinds of useful stuff like cures for diseases, and light bulbs, and nuclear missiles, and deadly germ warfare, and . . .

Well, best not go there, perhaps. Let's just say that science has, in general, been very beneficial to humanity, and many scientists have exhibited considerable bravery in the course of their work, although occasionally the more sensible among us might, if given the opportunity to witness some of their experiments, think to ourselves, 'Ooh, I wouldn't do that if I were you'[19], which is why we're not scientists and will never discover anything very interesting, although neither will we accidentally poison ourselves by ingesting the contents of a thermometer.

[19] Alexander Bogdanov (1873–1928), for example, experimented with blood transfusions, possibly in an effort to discover the secret of eternal youth. Regrettably, some of the blood was infected with malaria and tuberculosis, and he promptly died. Meanwhile Karl Scheele (1742–86), the discoverer of tungsten and chlorine, among other chemical elements, liked to taste his discoveries. He survived tasting hydrogen cyanide but not, alas, mercury.

And so, deep in a tunnel near Geneva in Switzerland, a group of scientists was looking a bit anxiously at a switch, while around them the Large Hadron Collider once again went about its very important business. The Collider, for those of you who don't know, was the largest particle accelerator ever built, designed to smash together beams of subatomic protons at enormous speeds – 99.9999991 per cent of the speed of light – and thereby make all kinds of discoveries about the nature of the universe by recreating the conditions that occurred less than a billionth of a second after the Big Bang that created it about 13.7 billion years ago. Unfortunately, when last turned on, the Collider's energy had been harnessed by Mrs Abernathy in order to open a portal between our world and Hell, which was when all the trouble had started. Since then the Collider had remained resolutely switched off, and the scientists had done a great deal of work to ensure that the whole portal to Hell business would never, ever happen again. Promise. Pinky promise. Pinky promise with sugar on top.[20]

☻ [20] Actually, the Collider experiment had been plagued by many difficulties in addition to the unfortunate scientists/demons interface, including a mishap caused by a bird dropping a piece of baguette into the machinery, so that one prominent scientist even suggested it was being sabotaged from the future in order to prevent it being turned on and sucking the planet into a big black hole, or transforming it to ash. On the other hand, those of us who hadn't spent too long hanging around with scientists, and who got out of the house occasionally, thought that the idea of sabotage from the future seemed to be pushing it a bit. Then, strangely, a man was arrested at the Collider who claimed to have come from a future where there were Kit-Kats for everyone, with the precise purpose of sabotaging the experiment. Mind you, he also claimed that his time machine was powered by a kitchen blender, so he may not have been playing with a full deck of cards, if you catch my drift.

'Is anything happening?' said Professor Stefan, CERN's head of particle physics. He sounded both nervous and impatient. Professor Stefan had been present when all that nasty demonic business had happened, and a lot of people had pointed the finger of blame at him, which he felt was a bit unfair as he hadn't *known* that the gates of Hell were going to open because of his nice, shiny particle accelerator. If he had –

Oh dear, that was the thing of it. If he had known, he probably would still have allowed the Collider to be switched on. They'd gone to all that trouble to build it, and had spent all that money: $7 billion, at the last count. They couldn't very well just lock the door, put the key under the mat, leave a note for the milkman cancelling their order, and go back to doing whatever it was they had been doing before the Collider was suggested. That would just be silly. And there would have been no guarantee that the gates of Hell would open anyway, because nobody was sure if Hell even existed. It would be like saying, 'Don't turn that thing on. The Easter Bunny might pop out!' or, 'A fairy's wings might drop off!', or, 'A unicorn might fall over.' That wouldn't be science. That would be nonsense.

On the other hand, the scientists now knew that a) Hell, or something similar to it, did exist; b) it was full of creatures that didn't like them very much, although it wasn't just scientists they didn't like but everything that existed on Earth; and c) somehow the Collider had provided these creatures with a way of poking their heads into our world and eating people.

The general consensus among those who knew about CERN's involvement in the near-catastrophe, and who didn't particularly want to be eaten by demons – thanks very much, ever thought of trying a salad? – was that it probably wouldn't be a very good idea to go turning the Collider on again. The scientists argued that they'd figured out what the problem was (kind of), and they were certain (sort of) that nothing like what had happened before would ever happen again (or probably would never happen again, within a given margin of error. What margin of error? Oh, tiny. Hardly worth bothering about. What, you want to see the piece of paper on which I've made that calculation? What piece of paper? Oh, this piece of paper. Well you can't because – munch, munch – I've just eaten it. So there.)

Eventually they decided that it might just be OK to turn on the Collider again, but the scientists had to be very careful, and if it looked like something bad involving creatures with claws and fangs and bad attitude was about to occur they were to turn off the Collider immediately and go and inform a responsible adult. The scientists were reasonably confident that this would not be necessary, as they had worked hard on what was thought to have been a source of potential weakness. The joints holding the machine's copper stabilizers were discovered not to be strong enough to withstand the forces being unleashed against them – 500 tons per square metre, or the equivalent of five jumbo jets at full throttle being pushed against each square metre – but now the stabilizers had been reinforced, and all was believed to be well.

But the changes and corrections that the scientists had made to the Collider had also enabled them to increase its energy levels. The energies involved in its collisions were measured in terra electron volts, or TeV, with each TeV being equivalent to a million million electron volts. When the first 'incident' had taken place, the Collider was sending twin beams of 1.18 TeV each around its ring, giving collision energies of 2.36 TeV. The new, improved Collider was set to more than double the collision energy to 7 TeV, the first big step toward its routine capacity of 14 TeV.

Which was how the scientists came to be standing around looking at the switch with fingers crossed and lucky rabbits' feet in hand while Professor Stefan enquired if anything had happened yet, and Professor Hilbert, his assistant, who was very curious about all of the Hell and demons stuff because it proved his theory that there were universes out there other than our own, sucked his pencil and wondered if he should confess that he was rather hoping the portal might open again nearby as he'd missed it last time.

'Nothing unusual,' said Professor Hilbert, trying not to sound disappointed.

Professor Stefan let out a deep breath of relief. 'Thank goodness,' he said. 'Everything's going to be fine from now on.'

The other scientists glared at him, because that's just the kind of thing that people say before the roof collapses, the floor cracks, and everything goes to Hell in a handcart, in this case potentially quite literally, assuming someone had remembered to bring along a handcart, but Professor Stefan didn't notice. Neither did he pay any attention to the fact that Professor Hilbert had sidled away, and had disappeared into a small room marked 'Broom Closet – Janitor's Use Only'.

'See,' said Professor Stefan, who just didn't know when to stop tempting fate, 'I told you there was nothing to worry about.'

The broom closet that Professor Hilbert had entered was no longer really for brooms. Instead, an array of monitoring equipment had been set up, and two technicians were staring intently at a pair of screens. Between the screens was a speaker, currently silent.

'And?' said Professor Hilbert.

'It all seems to be working as it should,' said the first technician, whose name was Ed. He was staring at an image that resembled a spider encased in a wire tube dotted with bits of brick.

'I agree,' said his companion, Victor. Behind them was an unfinished game of Battleships, which Professor Hilbert pretended not to notice. 'There is a marginal energy loss, but that could be a joint again. Anyway, it will be contained within the vacuum.'

'Are you sure?'

'No, but it must be. I mean, where else could it go? We've examined every inch of the Collider. Its integrity is now beyond doubt.'

'Really?' said Professor Hilbert. 'I seem to remember that's what was said last time.'

'Well, we were wrong then,' said Ed, with the

certainty of someone who is convinced he knows where his opponent is hiding a submarine and an aircraft carrier, if only he might be allowed to return to the game. 'But we're right now.'

He smiled amiably. Professor Hilbert did not smile back.

'Keep an eye on it,' said Professor Hilbert, as he made for the door. 'And if I catch you playing Battleships again, you'll wish you really were on a sinking aircraft carrier . . .'

Mrs Abernathy slumped to her knees. The beams of blue light withdrew into her body, but her eyes retained a blue glow. It had been there ever since the collapse of the portal, but now it was more intense. She trembled for a moment, then was still. Slowly, a smile spread across her face.

The Watcher had not moved. At last it understood. Yes, Mrs Abernathy had been changed by her time in the world of men, and she had brought back aspects of it with her to Hell: curtains, and vases, and doormats; print dresses, and blond hair, and painted nails.

But it was also she who had first recognized the importance of the Collider experiment. The primal forces involved in the creation of the universe were also present in the most ancient of demons. The recreation of those forces on Earth had formed a connection between universes that she and the Great Malevolence could exploit. The collapse of the portal, and the consequent failure of their invasion, seemed to have severed that connection for ever, but now that appeared not to be so. The connection between worlds remained, but only through her. She had been the first one through the portal, and had held it open initially through sheer force of will. Some small part of the Collider's energy was still being accessed by her. She had to draw upon it slowly and carefully so as not to alert those responsible for the Collider, for she did not want them to shut it down. It would not be enough to stage another invasion, but in time it might be. It was not even enough to enable her to cross over from her world to theirs, for a powerful old demon like herself would require enormous energy to move between universes. But it would be sufficient to pull a human being from their world into hers, and she knew just the human being she wanted. She would drag Samuel Johnson to Hell and present him to her master as a prize. Then she would reveal the secret of the blue light to him and he would love her again.

As she rose to her feet, the Watcher began to speak. It told her of strange tracks in the dirt, of a black substance on rocks, of the smell of fumes and burning in the air. When it was finished she touched its head with her hand, and it bowed low with gratitude.

'All good things come to those who wait,' said Mrs Abernathy. 'All good things . . .'

She began to laugh, a terrible sound. It echoed around the chamber, carried across the plains, and was heard by the demons who had abandoned her. Some fled, fearing her vengeance for their betrayal, but others prepared to return to her, for if Mrs Abernathy was laughing then circumstances had changed, and they might yet profit from it. Foul beings emerged from holes in the ground and caves in black mountains, from pits of ash and pools of fire. They crawled, wobbled and slimed their way from their hiding places, and slowly began to make their way back to her.

CHAPTER IX

In Which Mr Merryweather's Elves Embark on a New Adventure

Mr Merryweather's elves were making good time on the motorway. There had been some initial problems with driving the van, since the only one of them who had a licence was Jolly, and his legs were even shorter than those of his fellow dwarfs and therefore had no chance at all of reaching the brake or the accelerator. This problem was solved by gluing a bottle of Spiggit's Old Peculiar to each of the van's pedals with extra strong adhesive, so Jolly simply had to step on a bottle cap to speed up or slow down.

The dwarfs had been feeling somewhat glum since Mr Merryweather had stomped off down the road, muttering and waving his fists, and vowing never again to work with anyone who couldn't look him in the eye without standing on a chair. Say what you wanted to about Mr Merryweather – and the dwarfs had said virtually everything about him that they could, including a number of insults that would be unprintable in a guide to swearing for sweary sailors – he had at least found them work, and he had stood by them following various incidents of assault, arson and, on one occasion, conspiracy to overthrow an elected government. Without him they were going to struggle to find jobs, and avoid arrest.

Mumbles and Dozy stared mournfully into their glasses of Spiggit's. Even though the van's suspension was suspect and made drinking from a glass difficult, it was generally considered unwise to drink Spiggit's directly from the bottle.[21] In the first place, it was un-civilized, as ale always tasted better from a glass. In the second place, Spiggit's tended to have an odd, cloudy residue that lurked at the bottom of every bottle, rather like one of those strange creatures that live in deep trenches on the sea bed, waiting to snap at the unwary. Jolly had once drunk some of that residue as an experi-ment.[22] The immediate effect was to cause him to seek the comfort of a toilet for so long that it was suggested he might like to take out a mortgage on it. Three months later, as he told anyone who would listen, his insides still weren't right, for somewhere in his digestive organs Spiggit's Old Peculiar continued to ferment away merrily, as the beer had the kind of long life more usually associated with lethal radiation. He was still prone to attacks of temporary blindness, an occasional inability to remember his own name, and explosive

[21] Actually as we have established, it was generally considered unwise to drink Spiggit's at all.

[22] Well, I say 'experiment', but his fellow dwarfs simply sat on him and poured the sediment down his throat, then quickly stepped back to watch what happened. While this is still technically an experiment, it also qualifies as torture, as does almost anything involving the involuntary ingestion of Spiggit's Old Peculiar.

burping, which had led to one of the incidents of alleged arson after he belched a little too close to a naked flame.

So Mumbles, Angry, and Dozy held on tightly to their glasses of ale (particularly since Spiggit's, if spilled on skin or clothing and allowed to remain there for more than five seconds, tended to burn) and wondered how they were going to be able to afford to eat, or drink, without Mr Merryweather to help them. There was a certain urgency to this, as they had only twelve cases of Spiggit's left in the back of the van, along with two boxes of crisps and a couple of sandwiches that appeared to be on the turn. It had been suggested that they dump the two boxes of crisps in order to make room for more beer, but wiser counsel had prevailed, and they had dumped just one of the boxes of crisps, and kept the sandwiches.

'That's the end of us,' said Angry. 'I'll have to go back to my old job.'

'What was that?' said Dozy.

'Not having a job.'

'Take up much time, did it?'

'All day. I had weekends off, though.'

'Well, you would. You'd exhaust yourself otherwise.'

'What about you?'

Dozy shuddered. 'Doesn't bear thinking about. Children's television.'

'No!'

'Yes. Remember that show, *Beefy and the Noodles*?'

'The one set in the bowl of soup?'

'That's the one. I was Percy Pea.'

'Don't remember you saying much.'

'I was a pea. Peas are among your quieter vegetables on account of there not being much air in those pods. You can't get a carrot to shut up, and don't get me started on broccoli. I hated being a pea. And the suit smelled funny. The previous Percy Pea died in it.'

'Really?'

'Contracted something from the soup. We spent hours in that soup. It was horrible. Anyway, he caught a disease from the soup, and he died, but they didn't find out until after the weekend. They thought the suit was empty, so they just pushed him back into his pod and left him there. That suit never smelled the same after.'

'It wouldn't, would it?' said Angry. 'You can't leave a dead person in a pea suit for a weekend and not expect it to smell a bit. Stands to reason. A day, maybe: you can get rid of a day's dead smell, but not a weekend's. What about you, Mumbles, what did you do?'

'Vovos,' said Mumbles.

'Oh,' said Angry.

'Missed that,' said Dozy.

'He says he did voiceovers,' said Angry, who tried to hide his confusion by looking more confused. 'You know, for commercials, and movie trailers, and the like.'

There was a pause while the dwarfs took this in.

'Nice work if you can get it,' said Dozy eventually.

'Have to have a talent for it,' said Angry, who had developed an extra wrinkle in his forehead as he tried to figure out the precise trajectory of Mumbles's career path.

'Anglebog,' agreed Mumbles.

'Indeed,' replied Angry, neutrally. 'Good pronunciation would be the key.'

'What about you, Jolly?' said Dozy. 'What will you do?'

'Do?' said Jolly. 'Do? Listen to you lot. We're not finished yet. We've been through worse times than this. We've been arrested, deported, and almost sold into slavery. You have to be optimistic. I guarantee that opportunity lies around the next bend.'

He was so convincing that they raised their glasses and cheered.

Opportunity did not, in fact, lie around the next bend. What did was a police car, in which Constable Peel and Sergeant Rowan of the Biddlecombe constabulary were checking the speeds of cars and drinking tea from a flask.

'Lovely tea, this,' said Sergeant Rowan. 'How do you get it to taste like that?'

'Honey,' said Constable Peel.

'Fantastic. Never would have thought of it.'

'Honey,' Constable Peel continued, 'and ... elves. With beer.'

Sergeant Rowan sniffed his tea. 'No, I don't get any hint of elves or beer. Honey, yes, but not little people.'

'That's not what I meant, Sarge. There are elves in that van. And they're drinking beer.'

Sergeant Rowan squinted at the side of the van as it passed, and saw glasses of beer being raised in little hands. 'Mr Merryweather's Elves,' he read aloud. He thought for a moment. No, it couldn't be. Not that bunch. Completely different. Admittedly, it did look like the same van. It even looked like the same—

Dwarfs.

'Constable, stop those dwarfs!'

Dozy shifted on his seat. 'Can we stop somewhere? I need to go to the bathroom.'

'Yeah, and I wouldn't mind some food,' said Angry. 'I'm famished.'

'There's no service station around here, lads,' said Jolly. 'Still, that's the exit for Biddlecombe. We can find somewhere there.'

He pulled off the motorway, not noticing the police car that was in pursuit, and quickly found himself on Shirley Jackson Road, which led to the centre of Biddlecombe. As he drove along he passed an ice-cream truck, and a small boy with a dachshund on the end of a leash. Jolly liked small dogs. Being the height that he was, he had to be careful around big ones.

Now there were blue lights in his rear-view mirror, and in his wing mirror. Funny, there seemed to be blue light everywhere. That was—

'Missed!' shouted Mrs Abernathy. 'I missed him.'

She was staring intently at the shard of glass in which she had been monitoring the progress of Samuel Johnson and his little mutt. She had focused all of her energy upon it, intent upon bringing him to her, and instead a vehicle of some kind had got in her way. She concentrated again, feeling already that some of her power had ebbed.

'Careful,' she whispered to herself. 'Careful . . .'

She raised her hands as if the boy were already before her and she was about to clutch his throat, and twin bursts of blue light streaked from her fingers and through the glass. She was aware of an impact of some kind in the world of men, the force of which made her blink hard. When she opened her eyes Samuel Johnson was still in Biddlecombe, except now he had stopped walking and was looking around in bewilderment.

Samuel was puzzled. He could have sworn that, just moments before, a van carrying boozy little men had been about to pass him, but it now seemed to have disappeared. Then a police car had approached him, and that had vanished too. And hadn't there been an ice-cream van nearby? He'd been considering buying a cone for himself, even if the weather was still a bit cold. Perhaps he was working too hard, or he needed to get his glasses changed.

There was something spinning on the road before him. As he drew closer to it it grew still. It was a bottle of Spiggit's Old Peculiar. A faint blue light danced around the cap, causing it to burst and spray beer all over the road. There was more blue light on the bumper of the car beside him, and on the garden gate to his left, and in a puddle of oil on the ground, a puddle in which he could see himself reflected, and Boswell.

And Mrs Abernathy.

'Oh no,' said Samuel, as Mrs Abernathy extended her hands for the final time. Streams of blue light shot from her fingertips and erupted from the puddle, enveloping Samuel and Boswell. For a second there was only a terrible coldness, then suddenly every atom in Samuel's body felt as though it were being torn from its neighbour, and he was falling, falling into blackness and beyond.

CHAPTER X

In Which Mr Merryweather's Dwarfs Make an Unpleasant Discovery

It was Dozy who woke first. He was called Dozy because of his ability to take a nap at any time. He could nap on rollercoasters, on a sinking ocean liner, or while his toes were being set on fire – all of which he had actually done. Dozy was the kind of bloke who could take a nap while he was already taking another nap.

He stretched his arms and yawned. He felt as if his body had been stretched on a rack, disassembled, and then reassembled by someone who wasn't particularly worried about whether or not all of the bits were in the right place. Under similar circumstances most people might have wondered why this might be, but Dozy had been drinking Spiggit's Old Peculiar for some time, and was used to waking up feeling that way.

He looked out of the window and saw what appeared to be immense white sand dunes stretching before him. He scratched his head as he tried to remember where it was they were supposed to be going when – well, whenever it was that whatever it was happened. Had they a seaside engagement? Dozy quite liked the sea.

He decided to leave everyone else sleeping and stretch his legs.

The sky above his head was filled with dark clouds tinged with red, so he figured that it was either sunrise or sunset, and it looked like there might be rain on the way. He took a deep breath, but he couldn't smell the sea. He couldn't hear the sea either. Dozy tried to remember if there was a desert anywhere in the vicinity of Biddlecombe, and decided that there wasn't. There was a beach nearby, at Dunstead, but it was mainly stones and old shopping carts, and not like this at all. The sand beneath his feet was very white, and very fine. That sky was odd, though. The clouds kept changing shape and colour, so that at times the sky appeared to be filled with faces tinged fireplace orange and chimney red. If he hadn't known better, he'd have said that it was on fire. There was certainly a smell of burning in the air, and not nice burning either. It smelled as though someone had left a great many steaks on an enormous barbecue for far too long, and then allowed them to rot.

He began to climb the nearest dune in the hope of getting his bearings, whistling as he went. There were more dunes. He climbed another, then another. When he reached the top of the third dune he stopped whistling. He stopped doing anything at all, really, except staring.

Stretched before him, all the way to the flaming horizon, were desks, and at the desks sat small red men with horns on their heads. Each of the desks had a hole on one side, through which other small red men were feeding pieces of something white that emerged from the far side of the desks as fine white sand. A third group of small red men moved back and forth between the desks, loading the sand into buckets and carrying it away, while the little seated men carefully noted the details of the operation in big books.

To his right, at a much larger desk, sat a tall man in a black cloak with scarlet lining. Unlike the little fellows below his skin was very pale, and his horns were larger and seemed to have been polished to a bright sheen. He had a thin moustache on his upper lip, and a beard that came to a pronounced point at the end of his chin. It was the sort of beard worn by someone who is Up To No Good, and doesn't care who knows it. It was a beard that conjured up images of Dastardly Schemes, of women being Tied To Train Tracks and orphans being Deprived Of Their Inheritances. It was a beard that screamed 'I'm A Wrong 'Un, And Make No Mistake About It'.

On the desk, close to where the bearded gentleman's black, pointed boots were currently crossed, there was a sign that read: A. Bodkin, Demon-In-Charge.

Dozy noted that A. Bodkin, Demon-In-Charge, was reading a newspaper called *The Infernal Times*.[23] The headline read:

☠ [23] There usually isn't very much to read in *The Infernal Times*: the weather is always hot with a chance of fireballs; everybody is either miserable, angry, or tormented; and your favourite football team is in the process of losing its most recent match because, in Hell, *both* teams always lose. And keep losing. To a controversial penalty decision. In extra time. And extra time goes on for ever.

GREAT MALEVOLENCE CONSIDERING NEXT MOVE
'Victory Will Be Ours,' says Chancellor Ozymuth.
'Anyone who doubts this will be dismembered.'

A smaller substory announced:

ACTION TO BE TAKEN AGAINST MRS ABERNATHY
'Someone has to take responsibility for the failure of
the invasion,' says Chancellor Ozymuth, 'and I've
decided it should be her.'

This Chancellor Ozymuth seems to be getting around,
thought Dozy. He might not have been the brightest
of dwarfs, but he was developing the uncomfortable
suspicion that all was not quite right here.

'Morning,' he said, then thought about it. 'Afternoon.
Er, Evening?'

A. Bodkin looked to his left to where Dozy was
standing. He puffed his cheeks and blew air from his
mouth in the bored, world-weary manner of middle
managers everywhere whose lot in life is to be disturbed
just when they're about to reach the good bit of something, and therefore never get to experience the good
bit of anything, which makes them even more bored
and world-weary.

'Yes?' said A.Bodkin. 'What is it?'

'Just wondering what all those blokes are doing.'

A.Bodkin lowered his newspaper.

'Blokes? *Blokes?* They're not "blokes": they're highly
trained demonic operatives, not just some imps-come-
lately with lunch boxes and an attitude. Blokes. Tch!'

A. Bodkin returned to his newspaper, muttering about unions, and toilet breaks, and demons being lucky to have a job.

'Yes, but what are they doing?' repeated Dozy.

A.Bodkin rustled his newspaper in an 'I'm very busy and don't want to be disturbed' way then, realizing that the short annoying person by his desk was not about to depart, lowered the paper again resignedly and said:

'Well, it's obvious, isn't it? They're grinding the bones of the dead.'

'Grinding?' said Dozy.

'Yes.'

'Bones?'

'Yes, yes.'

'Dead?'

'Yes. They're hardly going to grind the bones of the living, are they? That would just be messy.'

'Right,' said Dozy. He put his hands in his pockets and kicked idly at the sand, then remembered that it was not sand after all and apologized to it. 'It's nice to have a trade, I suppose.'

He sucked at his lower lip and thought for a moment. 'Where is this, exactly?' he asked.

'Oh, you're not lost, are you?' said A. Bodkin. 'Not another one. I mean, how hard can it be to get this right? You're bad, you die, you come to Hell, you get processed, we find you a job somewhere. You'd think, after all this time, the chaps in Head Office would have this down to a fine art. Tch! I mean, really. Well, you'll just have to make your own way to Central

Processing. I'm far too busy, um, supervising to help you.'

He raised his left arm and examined an hourglass on his wrist to indicate just how busy he was. Sands poured from the upper glass into the lower one, but the level of the sands in the upper glass didn't get any lower, and the level in the lower glass didn't get any higher.

'Just one small thing,' said Dozy. 'Tell you the truth, two small things. Smallish. Actually, not small. Bit big, to be honest.'

He laughed nervously.

'Go on, then,' said A. Bodkin. 'But this had better be the end of it. You're distracting me from my work. Production has already decreased in the time that we've been talking. If I don't keep an eye on this lot, I'll have protests, people asking for tea breaks and time off to visit their aunties or go to the dentist. Look at them: they're already on the verge of revolt!'

Dozy looked at the lot in question. They looked about as likely to revolt as A. Bodkin was to mind a baby without stealing its pram.

'That business about being dead,' said Dozy. 'What did you mean by that, exactly?'

'Oops, sorry,' said A. Bodkin, who didn't look sorry at all. 'You mean you didn't know. Tragic, just tragic.' He stifled a giggle. 'Well, frankly, you're dead. No longer alive. Faithfully departed. If there's a bucket nearby, then you've kicked it. If you were a parrot, you'd have dropped off your perch. And the second thing?'

'Huh?' said Dozy, who was still trying to come to

terms with the first thing, which he hadn't liked the sound of at all. 'Oh, you mentioned something about Hell.'

'Yes?'

'That would be – why?'

'Because that's where you are: Hell.'

'*The* Hell?'

'Are you aware of any other?'

'No, but I didn't think Hell was real.' Mr Merryweather's elves had missed the excitement of the invasion from Hell due to hangovers. Very long, very bad, memory-destroying hangovers.

'Now you know better. Happy?'

'No, can't say that I am. I don't *feel* dead.' He pinched himself. It hurt.

A. Bodkin looked at him in a curious manner.

'You know, you don't *appear* dead either,' said A. Bodkin. 'Most dead people tend to look slightly dead: you know, pale, missing a limb or two, bullet holes, blood, *bleh*.' A. Bodkin let his tongue loll from his mouth and made the whites of his eyes show in a reasonable impression of someone whose best days are behind him and no longer has to worry about brushing his teeth in the mornings. 'But you don't look like that at all.'

Dozy was already backing away. 'Nice talking to you,' he said. 'Good luck with all of the bone stuff. Be seeing you again. Byee-ee!'

He trotted back down the dune. He looked over his shoulder just once, to see A.Bodkin tugging at his beard in a thoughtful way that boded ill for someone.

Dozy started running.

CHAPTER XI

In Which Samuel Arrives, and Nurd Departs

Samuel felt Boswell licking his face. He tried to brush the dog away, but Boswell seemed insistent that he wake up. Samuel didn't want to. His limbs ached, and his head hurt. He wondered if he might not be coming down with something.

Then he remembered: disappearing vans; a blue light; Mrs Abernathy's face in a puddle . . .

Mrs Abernathy.

He opened his eyes.

He was lying on his side by the bank of a dark, muddy river that flowed sluggishly in the direction of a copse of crooked trees. Beneath his cheek was hard ground topped with sparse, blackened grass. He raised himself to his knees, and Boswell yipped with relief. Samuel gathered his dog into his arms and stroked him, all the while looking around and trying to get some sense of where he was. He had a memory of falling, and being aware that he was falling, but when he tried to stop himself he just fell faster. There had been a moment of compression and severe pain, and then nothing.

Above him were black clouds broken by veins of burning red. It was like looking into the heart of a volcano, and he experienced a sensation of dizziness as, briefly, up became down, and down became up, and he had a vision of himself kneeling at the bottom of a great sphere suspended in a furnace. He had to fight the urge to fall back and hold on to the ground. Instead he hugged Boswell tighter and said, 'It's OK, it's all OK,' but he was trying to convince himself as much as the animal.

Mrs Abernathy had done this, he knew, which meant that they could only be in one place: Hell. Somehow she had wrenched them from their world into hers, and that could only be for one purpose: she wanted revenge. Already, she would be looking for them.

Although he was now just thirteen, and no longer considered himself a child, Samuel wanted to cry. He wanted his mother; he wanted his friends. Back in Biddlecombe, when he had faced Mrs Abernathy's wrath, he had done so surrounded by familiar places, and with the support of those whom he loved, and who loved him in return. Here he was alone, except for Boswell, and it says much about the kind of boy Samuel was that, even in the midst of his own fear and sorrow, he wished he had remembered to let go of Boswell's lead before he was transported. His loyal dog had no business being here, yet Samuel was also not a little grateful that Boswell had in fact come with him, for there was at least one other being who was on his side in this terrible place.

No, that wasn't entirely true. Boswell was not the only one who cared about him. There was another. The question was: how could Samuel find him?

Wormwood tapped Nurd on the shoulder.

'Master, why have we stopped?'

The car, still disguised as a rock, had been making good progress across the Vale of Fruitless Journeys, as Nurd put as much distance as possible between themselves and the cave in which they had been hiding. The Vale was formed of massive slabs of brown stone on which the car left no tracks. To the west (or maybe it was to the south, such concepts as direction having little or no meaning in a place where reality struggled to maintain a grip on itself) they ended at the Forest of Broken Forms, where those who had been vain about their looks, and dismissive of those whom they didn't consider as pretty as themselves, were condemned to spend their lives as ugly trees. But that way was too close to the Mountain of Despair for Nurd's liking, and so they had proceeded in another direction, or what they hoped was another direction given that Hell had a habit of confounding such expectations, so that you might head off away from Point A with the best of intentions only to find yourself rapidly back at Point A without ever having veered from a straight line. Ultimately, they wanted to reach the Honeycomb Hills, where they could hide themselves before the Watcher or, worse, its mistress, came hunting for them.

But now Nurd had brought the car to a halt and was

staring into the distance in the troubled manner of someone who thinks he may have left the gas on even though he can't remember ever owning a gas oven.

'Master?' said Wormwood, by now growing concerned.

Nurd's brow furrowed, and a single tear rolled down one of his cheeks as he whispered softly:

'Samuel?'

Mrs Abernathy was not the only denizen of Hell who had been changed by experiencing the world of men at first hand. Nurd too had been altered. To begin with, he was a little kinder to Wormwood than he had been before, and not only because Wormwood knew how to keep the car running. During the long period of his banishment, Nurd had spent a lot of time moping, complaining, and generally bemoaning his lot in life. When he wasn't doing that, he was usually hitting Wormwood on the head for being annoying. But since his return to Hell he had started to view Wormwood as, for want of a better word, a friend. Admittedly he might have preferred a friend who wasn't as prone to waving a finger under Nurd's nose and inviting him to look at what had just been excavated from some orifice of his body, but beggars can't be choosers.

Similarly, Nurd had abandoned any ideas of ruling another world or becoming a serious demon; not that he'd ever been very keen on that to begin with, but he had now dispensed with his self-invented title 'Scourge of Five Deities' and had decided not to go looking for any other demon's job[24] as he was much happier not bothering anyone at all.

But, crucially, Nurd had also brought back with him a deep psychic and emotional connection to Samuel Johnson, the first person who had ever been kind to Nurd, and the first friend that Nurd had ever made. Had they lived in the same world, they would have been inseparable. Instead they were divided by time, and space, and the difficulties of crossing between worlds and dimensions. Despite all of those obstacles, each had held the memory of the other in his heart and there were times as they slept when it seemed to them that they spoke to each other in their dreams. Not a day went by when one did not think of the other, and such feelings have a way of transcending the barriers that life may put in the way of people. An invisible energy linked these two beings, the boy and the demon, just as it connects all those who feel deeply for another, and the nature of that link had suddenly been altered for Nurd. He felt it more intensely than ever before, and he knew at once that Samuel was near. He was in this world, in this foul place where all things were said to reach the end of hope. But that was no longer true, for Nurd now had hope of better times, of a better way of existing, and it was Samuel who had given it to him.

[24] Not even the jobs of the really lame demons like Watchtower, the demon of people who ring the doorbell just as you're about to serve dinner; Eugh, the demon of things found dead in soup, with additional responsibility for flies in ointment; Bob, the demon of things that float when you don't want them to; Glug, the demon of things that sink when you don't want them to; and Gang and Agley, the demons responsible for disrupting the best-laid plans of mice. Mice really hate them. If it wasn't for them, mice would rule the world.

Yet if Samuel was here, then it could not be of his own will. Nothing came to Hell willingly. Even the entities trapped there wished to be elsewhere, or to cease to exist at all, for that would be infinitely preferable to an eternity spent in this realm.

Mrs Abernathy had been hunting, unknowingly, for Nurd, the mysterious driver of the car that had brought an end to her master's hope of escape, but Nurd knew that Samuel was the greater prize she sought. Somehow she had found a way to bring him here. For all Nurd knew, Samuel might already be her prisoner, and he had a terrifying vision of his friend, chained and bound, being brought before the Great Malevolence himself, there to be punished for his part in all that had occurred. But even if Samuel were not yet in Mrs Abernathy's clutches, there were plenty of other foul beings in Hell who would relish the chance to taste a human child. Someone would have to save Samuel, and that someone was Nurd.

Except Nurd didn't have much experience of saving anyone, apart from Nurd himself, and he was having enough difficulty keeping himself from becoming Mrs Abernathy's prisoner without trying to prevent the capture of someone else. He also didn't consider himself particularly bright, or brave, or cunning. But like most people who think that way, Nurd was a lot smarter, and braver, and cleverer than he realized. He simply hadn't been given much opportunity to prove it to himself, or to others.

'Master?' asked Wormwood, for the third time, and on this occasion he received an answer.

'Samuel is here,' said Nurd. 'We have to find him.'

Wormwood didn't look surprised. If his master said that Samuel, whom Wormwood had never met but about whom he'd heard a great deal, was somewhere in Hell, then Wormwood was happy to believe him. On the other hand Wormwood did look a bit startled when Nurd turned the car 180 degrees so that it was facing in the direction from which they had just come.

'Er, Master,' he said. 'You told me that way lay misery, torture, poor food, and certain dismemberment at the hands of Mrs Abernathy.'

'I did indeed, Wormwood, but only Mrs Abernathy could have brought Samuel here, so wherever she is, that's where he will be too.' He put his foot down and gunned the engine. The car lifted slightly, like a horse yearning for the start of a big race. Then Nurd released the brake and they were off.

Wormwood looked at his master in awe. The old Nurd had been cowardly, self-serving, and determined to avoid personal injury at all costs. This new Nurd was courageous, selfless, and apparently keen to have his limbs separated from his body as soon as possible.

On reflection, thought Wormwood, as they sped towards their destiny, I think I preferred the old one.

CHAPTER XII

In Which Dozy is the Bearer of Bad News

Jolly was just waking up when Dozy got back to the van.

'S'matter,' said Jolly, rubbing his forehead in a pained manner. 'What did we hit?'

From the back of the van Dozy heard assorted mutters, yawns, and unpleasant bodily noises as Angry and Mumbles emerged from the land of Nod.

'Listen to me carefully,' said Dozy. 'Precisely which exit did you take from the motorway?'

'Huh? The Biddlecombe exit. I mean, we agreed.'

'And that's what the sign said? Biddlecombe?'

'Yes, Biddlecombe.'

'It didn't say, like, "Hell", by any chance, did it?'

Jolly looked at him suspiciously, and sniffed his breath. 'Have you been drinking already? You know, it's all very well having one or ten to help you sleep, but at least wait until you've had your cornflakes before you start knocking them back in the morning. You'll have a liver like the sole of a shoe, mark my words.'

'I haven't been drinking,' said Dozy. 'Something is very, very wrong.' And he pointed through the front windscreen at the great expanse of pale dunes that stretched before them.

Jolly stared at the vista for a moment before climbing from the van, Dozy, Angry, and Mumbles close behind. Jolly pursed his lips and did a full circuit of the van, looking hopefully for some sign of a church spire, or a chip shop, or a pub.

'Nah, that can't be right,' said Jolly. 'We must have taken a wrong turning somewhere.'

'Where, Purgatory?' said Dozy. 'We're in Hell.'

'It's not that bad,' said Angry. 'It's a trifle toasty, I'll admit, but don't let's get carried away here.' He knelt, picked up a handful of fine sand, and watched it slip through his fingers. Mumbles did the same.

'Look, we must be near the sea,' said Angry. 'It's sand.'

'No, it's not,' said Dozy.

'Course it is. What else would it be?'

'Smesand,' said Mumbles, lifting a handful of grains to his nose and sniffing them warily.

'That's right,' said Dozy. 'It doesn't smell like sand. That's because it's not sand.'

'What is it, then?' asked Jolly.

Dozy crooked a finger at them in a 'follow me' gesture, and they did.

The four dwarfs lay on the side of one of the dunes, their heads peeping over the top, and watched as the imps fed bones into the sides of their workbenches.

'They're bones,' said Angry. 'We're lying on bits of bone. Quite comfortable, actually. Who'd have thought it?'

'Whose bones are they?' said Jolly.

'Dunno,' said Dozy. 'That bloke over there seems to be in charge, but I don't think he knows either.'

They regarded A. Bodkin curiously. He was talking on an old black rotary dial telephone.

'He's a nutjob,' said Jolly. 'That phone doesn't have a wire attached to it.'

'I don't think that matters,' said Dozy. 'I get the feeling that normal rules don't apply here.'

They continued to watch A. Bodkin, who was becoming quite animated. Although they couldn't hear clearly all of what he was saying, it was apparent that he was troubled by Dozy's unexpected appearance beside his desk, and the fact that Dozy did not appear to be dead.

'So he's a demon,' said Angry.

'Yes,' said Dozy.

'And all that lot are demons too.'

'Imps, apparently, but I think it amounts to the same thing.'

'Then this *is* Hell.'

'That's what I've been trying to tell you.'

'How did we end up in Hell? What have we ever done to anyone?'

There was silence as the other three dwarfs gave Angry's brain a chance to catch up with his mouth.

'Ohhhhhh,' said Angry, as all the reasons why they might justifiably be in Hell came flooding back like rubbish at high tide. He shrugged his shoulders. 'Fair enough, I suppose. I don't remember dying, though. I thought that was supposed to be part of the deal.'

'Maybe it's like Jolly said,' offered Dozy. 'We might have hit something and died in the crash.'

'But I don't think we did hit anything,' said Jolly. 'The van seemed fine. More to the point, I feel fine. If I was dead, I'm sure I'd be feeling poorly. And I'd probably smell a bit. Well, a bit more.'

'So we're not dead, then,' said Angry. 'And if we're not dead, this can't be Hell.'

'I don't know,' said Dozy. 'A. Bodkin over there seemed very sure.'

'He was probably just pulling your leg,' said Angry. 'He looks like the kind of bloke who'd think something like that was funny.'

Suddenly a great pillar of pale fire appeared beside A. Bodkin's desk, stretching from the sands right up to the black clouds above. Its appearance was so unexpected that even the imps at their desks briefly stopped converting bones to dust in order to watch what was happening.

A woman's face appeared in the flames, her eyes twin orbs of the brightest blue.

'She looks familiar,' said Jolly. 'I've seen her somewhere before.'

'She was on the front page of his newspaper,' said Dozy. 'Something about being in trouble.'

'But I didn't see his newspaper,' said Jolly.

'Shhh,' said Angry. 'I want to hear.'

As it turned out, hearing what the woman had to say wasn't going to be a problem. Her voice, when it emerged, sounded like thunder. It was so loud that it hurt the dwarfs' ears.

'BODKIN,' said the woman. 'WHAT HAVE YOU FOUND?'

'Here, turn it down, love,' said Jolly. 'The chap's only standing next to you.'

A. Bodkin looked confused. 'Mrs Abernathy,' he said. 'I wasn't expecting to hear from you.'

'I'M SURE THAT YOU WEREN'T,' said Mrs Abernathy. 'NEVERTHELESS, HEARING FROM ME YOU ARE. YOU REPORTED AN INTER-LOPER. WAS IT A BOY? TELL ME.'

'To be honest, much as I'd love to help you, I'm not sure that I can answer your question. This really needs to go through official channels.'

Mrs Abernathy's face darkened. Her lips peeled back, exposing teeth that began to grow longer and sharper as they watched. Her face swelled, and she was at once both a woman and a monster, although it was still the woman that appeared the more terrifying of the two.

'Oops, said the wrong thing there, mate,' said Jolly. 'He'll be telling her it's men's business next, and that she shouldn't worry her pretty little head about it.'

'Nah, he couldn't be that stupid,' said Angry.

'Mrs Abernathy,' said A. Bodkin. 'I really must insist: this is a matter for the Senior Council of Demons. Er, that is, the Council of demons that are, um, entirely fixed in their concept of, um, demonality in the non-female sense.'

'I take it back,' said Angry. 'He is that stupid.'

But A. Bodkin, having decided to put his foot in his mouth, was now determined to eat it, possibly with an order of socks on the side. 'You must understand that since your, ahem, transformation and subsequent, ah, fall from favour, senior management has informed us that you are no longer to be included in the decision-making process.' A. Bodkin smiled his most patronizing smile, which was very patronizing indeed. 'I'm sure that you have far more important matters to attend to,' he continued, 'such as –'

'And he's going for broke,' said Angry.

'Oh dear,' said Jolly, shielding his eyes with his hands. 'I can hardly bear to watch.'

'– beautifying yourself, for example,' continued A. Bodkin, 'or making something pretty for—'

The precise purpose of the something pretty in question was lost in a torrent of white-hot fire that shot from Mrs Abernathy's mouth and engulfed the unfortunate A. Bodkin, consuming him entirely and leaving only a pair of smoking black boots in his place.

The pillar of fire moved, turning to face the ranks of seated imps.

'NOW, WOULD ANYBODY ELSE LIKE TO SUGGEST THAT I MIND MY OWN BUSINESS?' said Mrs Abernathy.

Thousands of heads shook simultaneously.

'WOULD SOMEONE PREFER TO TELL ME IF A BOY WAS SEEN HERE, A BOY WITH A DOG?'

Two rows from the front, one of the imps raised a hand.

'YES?'

'Please Miss, it was the size of a boy, Miss, but it wasn't a boy, Miss,' said the demon.

'Ooh, tattle-tale,' said Dozy. 'If he didn't have all his pals behind him, I'd deck him for that.'

'WHAT DO YOU MEAN?'

'It was a little man, Miss. Mr Bodkin didn't think he was dead, Miss, so he reported him, Miss.'

'AND THIS LITTLE MAN WAS ALONE?'

'Yes, Miss. Far as Mr Bodkin could tell, Miss.'

'VERY GOOD. WHAT'S YOUR NAME?'

'I don't have a name, Miss. I'm just a demon imp, third class, Miss.'

'WELL, CONSIDER YOURSELF PROMOTED. FROM NOW ON, YOU MAY CALL YOURSELF B. BODKIN. THE DESK IS YOURS.'

'Oh, thank you very much, Miss. I'll be a very good B. Bodkin, Miss, mark my words.'

The imp rose from its workbench and trotted up to the main desk as the pillar of fire narrowed and then disappeared entirely. It slipped its feet into A. Bodkin's smoking boots. Slowly it began to increase in height, and its appearance started to change. Within seconds it bore a startling resemblance to the original A.Bodkin, right down to the nasty little beard and the superior manner.

'Right, back to work, you lot,' said B. Bodkin. 'The show is over.'

He settled himself into his new seat, put his feet on the desk, and picked up the newspaper. With a collective shrug of resignation, the rest of the imps returned to the grinding, carrying, and recording of bits of bone.

'Did you see that?' said Angry. 'What this place needs is a good workers' revolution.'

'You can organize the masses another time,' said Jolly as the dwarfs slid down the dune and headed for their van. 'We need to find a way to get home. I remember now where I saw that woman. It was back in Biddlecombe. She appeared on my windscreen, and then there was a blue flash, and next thing I knew we were here.' He paused, and scratched his chin. 'And there was a boy with a dachshund.'

He looked back in the direction from which they had come, as though expecting to see that pillar of flame rising high above them and that dreadful woman's voice asking about a boy and his dog. Slowly, Jolly began shuffling pieces of the puzzle around in his brain.

'I wonder,' he said. 'I wonder, I wonder, I wonder . . .'

CHAPTER XIII

In Which We Meet a Ram, and Some Old Friends are Reunited

Samuel had overcome his fear and, Boswell's lead in hand, had decided to seek cover. As the nearest shelter was the forest of crooked, leafless trees, that was where he and Boswell aimed for. Boswell shivered as they drew near to the forest, and plonked his bottom down firmly on the ground. As far as Boswell was concerned nothing in this land smelled good, sounded good, or looked good, but this forest felt particularly unpleasant.

'Come along, Boswell,' said Samuel. 'I don't like this place much either, but it really isn't a good idea for us to be out in the open where anyone can see us. And not just anyone, if you know what I mean.'

Boswell twitched his ears and lowered his head. His life had once been so normal: wake up, go outside for a sniff and a wee, have a bite to eat, play for a while, have a nap, wake up, and repeat. Had he heard the phrase 'a dog's life' used in the sense of one's existence being a bit harsh, he would have been slightly worried. As far as Boswell was concerned, a dog's life was absolutely fine. It was humans who made things compli-cated; humans, and those nasty creatures with horns, and big teeth, and a stink of burning about them. His senses were flooded with the scent of those creatures now. This was their place, and Boswell loathed it.

Samuel tugged on the lead and, reluctantly, Boswell trotted along beside his master. The branches of the trees met above their heads, as though they were reaching out to one another for consolation, their extremities tangling. Their bark was pitted with hollows that looked like eyes and mouths, faces contorted in expressions of agony. He heard the leaves whispering as though a breeze had briefly blown through them.

But there was no breeze, and there were no leaves.

'Boy,' said a soft voice. 'Boy, help me.'

'Boy,' said another, this time the voice of a woman. 'Free me.'

'Boy ...'

'Boy ...'

'... help me ...'

'No, me, help me ...'

'Boy, I've been here for so long, for so very long ...'

The mouths in the trees stretched and opened, and the eyes twisted in their wooden sockets. The branches moved, stretching for him. One snagged his jacket. Another tried to pull the lead from his hand.

'Boy, don't leave us ...'

'Boy, listen to us ...'

Behind him the forest closed, the trees forming an impenetrable wall through which he could not retreat. Samuel picked Boswell up, shielding him beneath his jacket, and started to run, even as branches cut his face and tore his trousers and tried to trip him as he passed.

They should not have come here. He had made a mistake, but they could not go back. Samuel kept his head down, barely able to see where he was going, and all the time the voices kept calling him: pleading, threatening, promising. Anything at all, he could have anything he desired, if only he would make the pain stop.

A presence appeared in front of him, and a voice said 'Back!'

The trees instantly grew silent and were still. Samuel looked up to see a hunched animal with a distorted mouth, blunt teeth, and ancient, twisted horns protruding from its head, which was bearded with shaggy white fur. It took Samuel a moment or two to see that it was a ram of sorts, but one that had learned to walk on two legs. Its upper hooves had mutated, lengthening to form two pairs of bony fingers, in one of which it held a long staff. Its coat was matted and filthy, and smelled of damp and smoke.

From deep in the forest came another voice, sinister and male.

'What right have you to claim him?' it said.

The branches of the trees parted like courtiers before a king, and Samuel was confronted by an enormous gnarled oak with a complex root system that reminded him uncomfortably of serpents writhing. This was the tree that had spoken. It had two holes in its trunk for eyes, and a twisted gash for a mouth, from which a reeking gas emerged as it talked. It stank of rotting vegetation, and worse: the slow decay of the non-vegetative.

'What right have you?' said the ram in reply. 'He's just a boy.'

'He could help us. He could free us.'

'And how could he do that? You are afflicted things. He cannot help you.'

'Give him an axe, and let him cut us down. Let him reduce us to splinters and sawdust.'

'And then? Do you still believe that mortal rules apply to you? The Great Malevolence would simply start again, reconstituting you into even more grotesque forms for his amusement. That will not bring your pain to an end. It will merely increase it.'

'Then give us the boy, that he might keep us company. We can gaze upon his beauty, and remember what we once were.'

The ram laughed, a low, bleating sound. 'Give him to you so that he can rot slowly in your insides, more like, allowing you to visit some of your anger on him. He is lost, but not forsaken. He does not belong here, and he does not belong to you.'

The great oak seemed to snarl, and Samuel saw deep into the racked, tortured soul of it.

'We will not forget this, Old Ram,' it said. 'Our roots grow longer, our branches sharper. We draw ever nearer to you, and soon you will wake in your hovel to find yourself surrounded by us, and our arms will draw you to us, and your pain will be a source of amusement for us in this miserable place.'

'Yes, yes, yes,' said the ram dismissively. 'Old Ram has heard it all before. You're trees, in case you hadn't noticed. You grow so slowly that even the Great Malevolence himself has ceased to find your misery amusing. Keep staring into your pools of stagnant water, and recalling what you once were. The child has no more business with you.'

He nudged Samuel with his stick.

'Come, my boy,' he said. 'Leave them to their mutterings.'

Samuel did as he was told, but as he went he could not resist looking back at the great oak; for a moment he could have sworn that he saw its roots emerge from the ground. But then the forest closed around it, and he could see it no longer.

Meanwhile, Mr Merryweather's elves, or dwarfs, or however they currently chose to describe themselves, had encountered a serious problem.

Somebody had stolen their van.

'And you're sure this is where you left it?' said Angry. 'You know, a lot of these dunes look alike.'

'Don't take that tone with me,' said Jolly. '*We* left it here. All of us. Not just me. And of course this is where we left it: you can see the tyre marks.'

'Were the keys still in the ignition? Very unwise to walk away and leave the keys in the ignition. Invitation to thieves, that is.'

If a volcano could have assumed the form of a small human being, and had then been photographed on the verge of eruption, it would have looked not unlike Jolly at that moment. When he spoke, though, he was remarkably calm. Dangerously so, one might have thought.

'Yes,' he said. 'I left the keys in it.'

'So that was a bit careless, wasn't it?'

'Well, it might have been – IF SOMEONE HAD DRIVEN IT AWAY!'

The dwarfs looked at the space that had, until recently, been occupied by a bright yellow van decorated with a painting of a happy little person who bore no resemblance at all to themselves, even at the best of times, of which this was definitely not one. There were four marks in the dust where the van's tyres had stood, but there were no tracks indicating the direction in which it might have gone. Simultaneously all four dwarfs raised their heads, shaded their eyes with their hands, and examined the brooding skies above in the hope of catching a glimpse of their vehicle.

'I can't believe someone's nicked the van,' said Dozy. 'I mean, it's not like we left it on a council estate with the doors open. It's a desert. What kind of lowlifes do they have around here, anyway?'

'It's Hell,' Angry pointed out glumly. 'It's probably full of the kind of people who'd nick your feet if your legs weren't attached to them.'

'Suppose so,' said Dozy. 'Still, that's how a place gets a reputation for being unwelcoming to visitors.'

'Leaseraneem,' said Mumbles.

'You're right,' said Jolly. 'There never is a copper around when you need one.'

Which was slightly ironic, given that a) Mr Merryweather's dwarfs were not the sort to court the attention of the police at any time; and b) generally it was not Mr Merryweather's dwarfs who needed the help of the police, but other people who needed it to protect them from Mr Merryweather's dwarfs.

At this point, as if on cue, a police patrol car appeared on top of a nearby dune, its blue lights flashing.

'Blimey,' said Jolly. 'They're efficient around here, I'll give them that.'

Angry squinted at the car as it made its way carefully down the side of the dune.

'You know, I could be wrong, but those coppers don't half look familiar.'

The car drew to a halt. Its doors opened. From one side stepped Sergeant Rowan, and from the other Constable Peel. Both of them scowled at the dwarfs, and on their faces was etched the memory of incidents of assault; drunkenness; unauthorized taking of vehicles, including an ambulance and a bus; arson; breaking and entering, specifically into Biddlecombe's Little World of Animal Wonders, and the removal of a penguin and two ferrets from same; using a penguin and two ferrets as dangerous weapons; and last, but by no means least, stealing a policeman's helmet, namely Constable Peel's, and allowing a penguin and two ferrets to use it as a public convenience. What these incidents had in common was that they had all involved, to some degree or another, one or more of, that's right, Mr Merryweather's dwarfs.

'Oh no,' said Jolly, as his brain registered the two policemen, and all of the unfortunate memories associated with them. 'It's true: this must be Hell.'

CHAPTER XIV

In Which the Forces of Law and Order Assert Themselves

Sergeant Rowan and Constable Peel were deeply, deeply unhappy. To begin with, they had been hauled through an interdimensional portal, which had hurt a lot. Then they had recovered consciousness just in time to see a pink-skinned demon with three heads, too many eyes, and a mouth in its stomach steal the loudspeaker from their roof before running away while wearing it as a hat on its middle head. Then a smaller demon carrying a bucket of white sand had passed them, waved, and disappeared over the top of a dune. He had been followed by another, and another, and another, all of them identical and all of them carrying buckets of white sand. Attempts to engage them in conversation, including such beloved opening gambits as 'Who are you?', 'Where is this?', and 'What are you doing with that bucket?' had met with no reply.

'You know what, Constable?' said Sergeant Rowan, as the never-ending procession of demons passed, each one greeting them with a cheery wave.

'I don't want to know what, Sarge.'

'What?'

'I mean that I don't want to hear what you're about to say, because I know what you're about to say, and I know it's not something I want to hear. So, if it's all the same to you, I think I might just put my fingers in my ears and hum a happy tune.'

And he did just that, until Sergeant Rowan made him stop.

'Now, lad, don't let's be overdramatic,' said Sergeant Rowan. 'We have to face up to the truth here.'

'I don't want to face up to the truth. The truth's nasty. The truth's walking up that dune holding a bucket. The truth has three heads and stole our loudspeaker.'

'Which means?'

Constable Peel looked as if he was about to cry.

'You're going to tell me that the portal's opened again, and all kinds of horrible creatures are pouring out.'

Sergeant Rowan smiled at him. 'I wasn't going to tell you that at all, lad.'

'Really?'

'No, that's not what's happening here.'

'Are you sure?'

'Virtually certain.'

'Oh!' said Constable Peel. He smiled with relief. 'Oh, thank goodness. Phew, don't I feel foolish?'

'I'll bet you do, lad.'

'There was I, worrying that the portal had opened, and monsters were going to pop out of it and try to eat us, and the dead were going to come alive again, and, you know, all that kind of thing. Silly old Peel, eh?'

'Silly old you,' said Sergeant Rowan. 'Monsters aren't going to come pouring through the portal.'

'That's a load off my mind,' said Constable Peel, then thought about what he had just heard. 'But what about the one that stole our loudspeaker, and the little red blokes with the buckets?'

'They didn't come through the portal. None of them did.'

'Why not?'

'Because they're already here. It's we who have come through the portal, Constable, not them. We're in Hell.'

All things considered, thought Sergeant Rowan, Constable Peel had taken the news remarkably well, once he'd stopped raving and calmed down. They had taken the decision to get away from the steady train of bucket-toting, polite, but relatively uncommunicative demons and find someone who might be able to answer a straight question, which is how they had come across four dwarfs standing on a flat patch between dunes, scratching their heads and staring at the sky. Both policemen had recognized them instantly, and their moods had immediately brightened. They might have been in Hell, but they weren't alone, and if there were four individuals that Sergeant Rowan and Constable Peel would like to have seen consigned to Hell more than Mr Merryweather's dwarfs, then they hadn't met those people yet, and probably never would.

'Hello, hello, hello,' said Sergeant Rowan, watching

with pleasure as the four dwarfs looked for a means of escape, and found none. 'What have we here, then?'

'Why, I believe it's the fabled Mr Merryweather's Dwarfs, Sarge,' said Constable Peel.

'Is it really? My, my. Correct me if I'm wrong, Constable, but would they be the same dwarfs who stole your helmet and allowed two ferrets to do their business in it?'

'Two ferrets *and* a penguin, Sarge,' Constable Peel corrected.

'Oh yes, the penguin. I'd almost forgotten about that penguin. Phil, wasn't it?'

'That's right, Sarge. Phil the Penguin. Filled my helmet and all.' He smiled at his own little joke. The thought of getting some revenge on Mr Merryweather's dwarfs was cheering him up no end.

Sergeant Rowan looked around. 'So we have the dwarfs, but where is Mr Merryweather?' He turned his attention back to the dwarfs, and pointed at Jolly. 'You, Mr Jolly Smallpants, you're the leader of this motley crew, but where's the ringmaster?'

'He abandoned us,' said Jolly.

'Hardly blame him,' said Sergeant Rowan.

'He doesn't love us any more,' said Dozy.

'Wonder that he ever did,' said Sergeant Rowan.

'Prifowig,' said Mumbles.

'Whatever,' said Sergeant Rowan.

'We're only little people,' said Angry. He put on his best sad face, made his eyes large, and tried unsuccessfully to force a tear from them. 'We're very small and we're all alone in the world.'

His fellow dwarfs bowed their heads, peered up from beneath their brows, and introduced some trembling to their lips.

'No, you're not alone in the world,' said Sergeant Rowan, his words heavy with consolation. He put his hand on Angry's shoulder. 'You've got us now. And you're under arrest.'

CHAPTER XV

In Which Something of the Nature of this World is Revealed Through Old Ram

Old Ram led Samuel and Boswell through weeds and briars, hacking a path with his staff when the way was blocked. What trees there were appeared smaller here at the edge of the forest. Old Ram had described them as 'new arrivals'. While they still had faces on their trunks, they were confused rather than angry and hateful, and their branches were too small and weak to present a threat.

'Ugly things grow quickly here,' explained Old Ram. 'Each time Old Ram walks, Old Ram has to cut his way through afresh. The forest sets itself against him, but Old Ram will not let it win.'

A stone hovel shaped like a beehive came into view. It had slit windows, and a narrow entrance that was blocked by a door woven from twigs and branches. A thin finger of smoke wound its way upward from a hole in the roof. Above them the dark clouds collided and dispersed, sending flashes of white and red and orange across the sky. As in the forest, Samuel believed that he could discern faces in the clouds, their cheeks billowing, their mouths screaming thunder, forming, swirling, and re-forming in a great tumult of noise and light.

Old Ram followed the boy's gaze.

'They were people once, just as the trees were,' he said. 'The skies are filled with the souls of the angry, turned to storm clouds by the Great Malevolence, so that they can fight and rage for eternity.'

'And the trees?'

'The trees are the souls of the vain. Everything here is given a purpose, a role to play. The Great Malevolence offers each soul a choice: to join his ranks, and become a demon, or to become part of the essence of this world. Most choose to join him, but those in the skies and those in the forest were too wrathful or too self-absorbed to serve even him, and so he found a suitable punishment for them.'

'Those poor people,' said Samuel, and Boswell whined in agreement.

Old Ram shook his head. 'You have to understand that only the very worst end up here: the ones whose anger made them kill, and who felt no sorrow or guilt after the act; those so obsessed with themselves that they turned their backs on the sufferings of others, and left them in pain; those whose greed meant that others starved and died. Such souls belong here, because they would find no peace elsewhere. In this place, they are understood. In this place, their faults have meaning. In this place, they belong.'

Old Ram opened the door, and indicated that Samuel should enter. Samuel paused on the threshold. He was old enough to know that he shouldn't trust strangers, and Old Ram was a very strange stranger indeed. On the other hand Old Ram had saved both Samuel and Boswell from the trees, and they needed help from someone if they were to avoid Mrs Abernathy and find a way home.

Samuel entered the dwelling. It had no furniture, no pictures, no signs of habitation at all except for the lingering odour of Old Ram himself, and the fire that burned in a hollow in the dirt floor. Black wood was piled beside it, ready to the added to the blaze.

'It's . . . very nice,' said Samuel.

'No, it isn't,' said Old Ram, 'but it's polite of you to say so. You may find this odd from one trapped in this kingdom of fire, but Old Ram feels the cold. Old Ram is never hungry, never thirsty, never tired, but Old Ram is always, always cold, so Old Ram keeps the fire burning. Old Ram feeds it with branches from the forest. When there are no fallen branches to be found, Old Ram breaks them from young trees. Old Ram needs his warmth.'

'Is that why the trees hate you so much?' asked Samuel. 'Because you cut their branches?'

'They hate everything,' said Old Ram, 'but most of all they hate themselves. Still, Old Ram has given them much reason to resent him, that's true. If nothing else, tormenting them offers Old Ram something to break the monotony.'

He sat down by the fire, crossing his hind legs beneath him and stretching his forelegs before him to warm his hooves. Samuel and Boswell sat opposite, and watched Old Ram through the flames.

'What did you do to end up here, if it's not rude to ask?' said Samuel.

Old Ram looked away. 'Old Ram was a bad shepherd,' he said. 'Old Ram betrayed his flock.'

And he would say no more.[25]

Samuel was tired and hungry. He searched in his pockets where he found a biscuit and a small apple. It wasn't much. Despite what Old Ram had said about lacking an appetite, Samuel offered him a bite of each, but Old Ram ignored the biscuit entirely, instead sniffing at the apple.

'Old Ram remembers apples,' he said, sadness in his voice, and in his pale eyes. 'Old Ram remembers pears, and plums, and pomegranates. Old Ram remembers . . . everything.'

'You can have a little, if you like,' said Samuel.

Old Ram seemed tempted, but then drew back, as though suspecting Samuel of some plot to poison him.

---

[25] From this we may surmise that Old Ram was a priest or church minister of some kind. Who knows, he may even have been a pope, for there have been some very dodgy popes over the years. Alexander VI, who was one of the infamous Borgias, and was pope from 1492–1503, sired at least seven children and was described as being similar to a hungry wolf. Benedict IX (who reigned at various points from 1032–48) was pope on three occasions, but surrendered the papacy on two of them in exchange for lots of gold before being hounded out of Rome in 1048. Finally, Stephen VI (896–97) disliked his predecessor, Formosus, so much that he had the corpse dug up and put on trial. Found guilty, Formosus had his garments removed, two fingers cut off, and was then reburied. But Stephen, who was still angry at Formosus, ordered him to be dug up again and Formosus's body was thrown into the Tiber. Stephen probably would have sent divers to find the corpse so he could do something else to it if he hadn't been strangled himself in 897, suggesting that Stephen wasn't much to write home about either when it came to being a pope.

'No, Old Ram doesn't want any. Old Ram isn't hungry. Eat, you and your little dog. Eat.'

Old Ram folded his arms and stared into the fire, lost in his own thoughts. Samuel gave the biscuit to Boswell, then ate the apple himself, Boswell not being much of a fan of fruit.

'How can we get back to our own world?' asked Samuel, when he had finished the apple and grown tired of the silence. Boswell, he noticed, had fallen asleep with his head on his lap. He stroked the dog, who opened his eyes, wagged his tail once, then went back to sleep.

'You can't,' said Old Ram. 'Nothing ever leaves here. Not even the Great Malevolence himself can leave, and he's tried.'

'But they managed to break into my world. If it was done once, it can be done again.'

Old Ram's mouth curled into what might have been a smile.

'Mrs Abernathy,' he said. He bleated his laughter. 'A demon obsessed with being human is a demon no longer. She has fallen from power. Another will take her place, unless she can find a way to make up for her failure.' He glanced slyly at Samuel. 'How did you come here, boy?'

Samuel began to tell him everything, then stopped. 'There was light, a blue light. It flashed as I was walking home with Boswell, and I woke up here.'

'And you saw nothing more, only a light?'

'That's all,' Samuel lied. He chose not to mention his knowledge of Mrs Abernathy to Old Ram. He could not have said why, but he was sure that it would not be a good idea.

Old Ram nodded his head and was silent again. The stone hive was uncomfortably warm, and the smoke was making Samuel drowsy. His eyelids grew heavy. He saw Old Ram watching him, and felt the intensity of the creature's regard, but he was so tired. He lay down and closed his eyes, and was soon fast asleep.

Samuel dreamed. He dreamed that Old Ram was standing over him, and scattering dust upon the flames. There was a sour, acrid smell, and then a face appeared in the fire, black-eyed and insect-jawed. In the dream, Old Ram said: 'Where is your mistress?' and the creature in the fire responded with a series of clicks and hisses that Old Ram seemed to understand.

'When she returns, tell her that Old Ram has a prize for her. Old Ram is tired of this exile. Old Ram wants a place of honour at her table. As she rises again, so shall Old Ram. Tell her this.'

The face in the flames disappeared, and Old Ram sat down again. That was Samuel's dream. But when he opened his eyes the sour smell was still in his nostrils, and Old Ram was not sitting in quite the same place that he had occupied before Samuel fell asleep.

'Rest more,' said Old Ram. 'You'll need your energy. Old Ram will take you to someone who may be able to help you, but first we must wait.'

'Why must we wait?'

'It's too dangerous to travel now. Later, it will be safer.'

Samuel stood, and Boswell stood too.

'I think Boswell and I should leave,' he said. 'We've stayed here long enough.'

'No, no,' said Old Ram. 'Please, sit. Old Ram has things to tell you, important things. You must listen.'

But Samuel was already leading Boswell to the door, although he did not turn his back on Old Ram. Old Ram scrambled upright, and in the light of the fire his eyes took on a red glow.

'You must stay!' he said. 'Old Ram must rise again!'

Thunder roared in the skies above, and lightning flashed, as though the fighting souls had heard Old Ram's cry, but Samuel thought that he discerned another sound hidden beneath the great tumult: a grinding, moaning noise like a mighty engine in motion.

Old Ram moved. He grabbed his staff and swung it at Samuel, barely missing the boy's head.

'Nobody leaves!' shouted Old Ram. 'Nobody leaves until the Dark Lady arrives!'

He made as if to swing the staff again, but instead spun it in his hooves and used it to trip Samuel, who fell heavily to the floor. Boswell snapped and barked, but now Old Ram was standing above them, the staff held high, ready to bring it down on Samuel's skull.

And then the staff was snatched from Old Ram's hooves and disappeared through the hole in the roof, drawn upwards by a snakelike length of wood. The hut began to collapse: stones tumbled down from the ceiling, and fissures appeared in the walls. Black roots and branches thrust their way through, winding themselves around Old Ram's body and neck and legs. The door exploded inwards, and Samuel saw the face of the Great Oak grinning and leering in the gap.

'Old Ram,' said the tree. 'I warned you. We were tormented enough without you adding to our misery. Now we will add to yours instead.'

Old Ram struggled in its grasp, but the ancient tree was too strong for him. More stones dislodged themselves, and an opening appeared close to where Samuel lay. As quickly as he could, he held Boswell under his left arm and pushed himself through the hole. Outside he got to his feet and ran until he came to a boulder which was big enough for him to hide behind. Only then did he risk a look back at the house.

The Great Oak towered above the scattered stones of Old Ram's dwelling, its branches swinging wildly, its roots twisting and curling. Old Ram was held high above the ground, his frightened face close to the Great Oak's features. The Great Oak was laughing at him, and taunting him. Behind it the contorted trees swayed and cried as the Great Oak took its prize and returned to the forest, and the fire in the ruins turned to ash and went out for ever.

CHAPTER XVI

In Which Hell Gets Stranger, and the Scientists Grow More Curious

Not for the first time, Mr Merryweather's dwarfs and the forces of law and order were having a disagreement.

'You can't arrest us,' said Jolly.

'I beg to differ,' said Sergeant Rowan. 'I can, and I have.'

'But someone's nicked our van. It hardly seems fair to arrest us when somewhere out there is a criminal driving a stolen van.'

'But there are four criminals right here,' said Sergeant Rowan. 'A dwarf in the hand is worth two in a van, or words to that effect.'

'Er, Sarge,' said Constable Peel.

'Not now, Constable. I'm enjoying my moment of triumph.'

'It's important, Sarge.'

'So is this.'

'No, really important.'

Sergeant Rowan, still keeping a firm grip on Jolly's collar, turned to Constable Peel and said, 'All right, then, what is—'

He stopped talking. He looked around.

'Constable, where's our car?' he said.

'That's just it, Sarge. It's gone. Someone's nicked it.'

Sergeant Rowan returned his attention to the dwarfs, who all held up their hands in gestures of innocence that, for the first time ever, they actually meant.

'Wasn't us,' said Angry.

'Serves you right,' said Jolly. 'I told you there was a thief about.'

'Nobody saw anything?' said Sergeant Rowan.

'We was too busy being arrested, Sarge,' said Dozy. 'Our rights was being infringed.'

'Nojidell,' said Mumbles.

'Absolutely,' said Angry. 'You have no jurisdiction in Hell. The minute you felt our collars, it was assault. We're going to sue.'

Sergeant Rowan raised a fist in a manner suggesting that, if he was going to be sued for something, he planned to make the most of it and add charges of inflicting serious bodily harm to a dwarf to his list of offences.

'Calm down, calm down,' said Jolly. 'This isn't helping anyone. Look, we all want the same thing here, right? We want to find our vehicles, and get home.'

Dozy's face suddenly assumed an expression of grave loss. 'The booze!' he said.

'What?' said Constable Peel.

'The last of the Spiggit's: it was in the van. It's gone. Oh, the humanity!'

Dozy fell to his knees and started to sob, moving

Constable Peel sufficiently to pat him on the back and offer him a paper tissue.

'There, there,' he said. 'It was probably for the best. Makes you mad, that stuff. And blind.'

Dozy began to pull himself together. Constable Peel helped him to his feet. Together, they listened to 'How Much Is That Doggie in the Window?' being played badly on what sounded like bicycle bells.

'I think all of that beer is making me hear things too, Constable,' said Dozy.

'No, I can hear it as well, and I've never touched a drop of Spiggit's,' said Constable Peel.

'We can all hear it,' said Sergeant Rowan, as an ice-cream van appeared from around the back of a nearby dune and pulled up alongside them. Seated on its roof was a plastic mannequin wearing a peaked cap and holding a plastic ice cream while grinning manically. Red writing on his cap announced him as 'Mr Happy Whip'.

The driver of the van rolled down his window. He wore very thick glasses, which made him look like an owl in a white coat.

'Hello!' he said. 'Which way is the sea?'

'What?' said Angry.

'The sea: where is it?' The driver squinted at Angry. 'Hey, son, fancy an ice cream? Just a quid. Two quid with sprinkles.'

Angry, who was about to punch the driver for mistaking him for a child, found a more immediate outlet for his rage.

'Two quid with sprinkles? You're having a laugh. What are you sprinkling them with, gold dust?'

'Top quality chocolate, son. Only the best.'

'Listen, I expect to bathe in chocolate if I'm paying an extra quid for it. And stop calling me "son". I'm a dwarf.'

'Right you are, son. Anyway, which way is the sea, there's a good lad.'

Angry looked back at his comrade. 'I'll 'ave him,' he said. 'I mean it. He calls me "lad" or "son" again, and I'll sprinkle him, I swear.'

The remaining three dwarfs, and Constable Peel and Sergeant Rowan, gathered round the van.

'I'll have a choc ice, please,' said Constable Peel.

'Now is not the time, Constable,' said Sergeant Rowan. 'Sir, you would be –?'

'I'm Dan,' said the driver. 'Dan, Dan, The Ice-Cream Man, actually. Changed my name when I bought the van. Thought it might be good publicity.'

'Right, Mr Dan. Do you have any idea where you are?'

'On a beach.'

'No, not quite. It's not a beach.'

'Oh, I thought the tide had gone out,' said Dan.

'Where, on the Sahara?' said Jolly.

'It did seem a bit big,' admitted Dan.

'You're in Hell,' said Sergeant Rowan.

'Nah,' said Dan. 'I'm near Biddlecombe.'

'Not any more. Remember a blue flash? A feeling like every atom of your body was being torn apart?'

'Sort of,' said Dan. 'I thought I'd just taken a funny turn.'

'You did take a funny turn: to Hell. Same thing happened to us.'

Dan thought about this for a while. 'Hell is hot, right?'

'Warm, so rumour would have it,' said Dozy.

'Good place to sell ice cream, then,' said Dan brightly. The dwarfs and the policemen stared at him. It was clear that Dan, Dan The Ice-Cream Man was an incurable optimist. If you told him that his shoes were on fire, he'd have toasted marshmallows on them.

'What did you do before you sold ice cream?' asked Angry.

'I was an undertaker,' said Dan.

'Nice change of pace for you, then.'

'Oh, it's fantastic. I get out. I meet people. I suppose I met people when I was an undertaker as well, but the conversations were a bit one-sided.' He tootled his horn merrily. 'If nobody wants any ice cream, I'll be off, then.'

'Hang on, hang on,' said Sergeant Rowan. 'You don't seem to have grasped the gravity of the situation. You're in Hell. Constable Peel and I have some experience of these matters, and we can say, with a degree of authority, that your time as an ice-cream salesman is going to be very short here, and will probably end with something very large nibbling on you like an ice lolly.'

'You won't like it,' said Constable Peel solemnly. 'It'll hurt.'

'In addition to this, you may have noticed that Constable Peel and I appear to be stranded, and we are therefore forced to commandeer your van in order to unstrand ourselves.'

'Lovely,' said Dan. 'I like a bit of company.'

'What about us?' asked Jolly.

'You can commandeer your own ice-cream van,' said Constable Peel.

'Really? And what do you think are the chances of another ice-cream van coming along any time soon, then?'

'Somewhat slim, I would have said,' said Constable Peel. He did not look unduly troubled by this fact.

'Come on, you can't leave us stuck here. Something might happen to us.'

'That's what I was hoping.'

'That's not very nice of you.'

'You should have thought of that before you encouraged Phil the Penguin to relieve himself in my hat.'

Sergeant Rowan intervened. 'Constable, much as I am tempted to agree with you, I think we have a responsibility as policemen to ensure the safety of civilians, even ones as nasty and criminal-minded as this lot. All right, everybody in the back. I'll take a seat up front with Mr Dan here, and we'll see about getting us home, shall we?'

Everybody did as Sergeant Rowan suggested, because the sergeant just had that way about him. Even though they were trapped in a region that was generally agreed to be the last place in which anyone wanted to end up, with no idea of how they had got there, and no idea of how they were going to get back, they were willing to follow Sergeant Rowan because he had Authority. He had Seriousness.

And he had a big truncheon that he waved meaningfully at the dwarfs in order to encourage them to make the right decision. In these situations, Sergeant Rowan had found, waving a big stick always helps.

Meanwhile, back in that small room supposedly being used for the storage of cleaning products and brooms, Professor Hilbert was engaged in an animated conversation with Victor and Ed. He had just concluded a similar conversation with Professor Stefan, a consequence of a small loss of energy that had occurred shortly after the Collider had been turned on again. Professor Stefan, Hilbert felt, had become slightly hysterical at the possibility that all those demons might start popping up again, although this stemmed as much from his understandable fear of being eaten as from his concern that, if the gateway to Hell did open for a second time, someone would find a way to blame him for it. It had taken all of Professor Hilbert's considerable diplomatic skills to convince Professor Stefan not to close down the Collider again, or not yet. Now, in the broom closet with Victor and Ed, he was using some of his other skills, namely the ones linked to bullying staff in a gentle manner in order to get his way.

Professor Hilbert was a believer in the 'hidden worlds' theory, the idea that there might be universes other than our own somewhere beyond the realm of our senses. He also felt that particle physicists were spending far too much time worrying about the nature of atoms, and refracting light, and other relatively mundane matters related to this world that actually exists, and too little time speculating on the nature of worlds that might exist elsewhere.

Here's the thing: we know that everything we can see around us is made up of some fairly elementary particles, and that various forces, like gravity, help to keep the whole process of existence moving along smoothly without people floating off into the ether or spontaneously collapsing into a muddle of atoms. But suppose that there were other particles, and other forces, operating alongside us, yet which we couldn't perceive because they were beyond the limits of our powers? That would indicate that the cosmos was a great deal more complicated and interesting than it already appeared to be.

In one way, we already know that there are hidden forces at work in our own universe, because only four per cent of the stuff of the cosmos is visible to us. Roughly seventy per cent of what remains is labelled 'dark energy', and is the force causing our universe to expand, sending galaxies racing away from one another. The other twenty-five per cent is called 'dark matter', detectable only by its effect on the mass and gravity of galaxies. Dark matter, then, could be part of the hidden world, and where you have matter you can, in theory, have planets, and life – dark life – assuming that the forces involved are strong enough to hold them all together, as the forces in our own universe are. And what do we know about dark matter? Well, it doesn't cool down, because if it did it would release heat, and we would be able to detect it.

Hmmm. A hidden world. Dark life. Heat. See where Professor Hilbert was going with this? Ed and Victor could, and just in case they were in any doubt he wrote the word in big letters upon a sheet of paper and showed it to them. The word was:

HELL

'Suppose,' said Professor Hilbert, 'that the portal didn't really connect us to Hell at all, because all that stuff about Hell and the Devil is just nonsense. It's a myth. Hell doesn't exist, and neither does this "Great Malevolence". What we could have instead is a dark matter world, filled with dark life, and the only way we can connect to it is through the Collider. If we turn the Collider off, we'll be turning our backs on the greatest scientific discovery of this, or any, age, and endangering the future of the ILC.[26] There's a Nobel Prize in this, mark my words.'

'Will we get the Nobel Prize too?' asked Ed.

'No,' said Professor Hilbert, 'but if I win it I'll give you a day off, and a box of sweeties.'

---

[26] The ILC, or International Linear Collider, was the proposed next stage in the physicists' attempts to understand the nature of this, and possibly other, universes. It would be a straight-line tunnel 31 km long, and in it electrons and positrons (antimatter electrons) would be fired from opposite ends, reaching accelerations of 99.9999999998 per cent of the speed of light before they collided. The collisions would be more precise than in the Large Hadron Collider, and therefore potentially more likely to provide answers to those big scientific questions: What happened in the Big Bang? How many dimensions are there in space? What is the nature and purpose of the different subatomic particles? And what does the Higgs boson, the theoretical particle that gives matter mass and gravity, look like? Which was all well and good, except that the LHC had already cost $7 billion and the ILC was likely to cost nearly as much again. In scientific terms, this is a little like your parents scrimping and saving to buy you the latest computer games console only for you to tell them that there's a new one coming out in six months time, but this one would just have to do until then. Ungrateful lot, scientists . . .

'But what about the energy loss?' asked Victor, who knew that they had about as much chance of sharing in Professor Hilbert's potential Nobel Prize glory as they had of growing feathers and winning first prize at a 'Lovely Parrot' competition.

Professor Hilbert smiled in that mad way scientists have of smiling just before the lightning strikes and the monster made up of bits of dead people comes to life and starts looking for someone to blame for plugging him into the mains and lighting him up like a Christmas tree.

'But that's the best part!' he said. 'We *should* be losing energy!'

'From a vacuum?' Victor did not sound convinced.

'It's like I told Professor Stefan,' said Hilbert. 'We're searching for the Higgs boson, right?'

'Right,' said Victor, thinking, He's lost it.

'And we realize that the Higgs boson may be the theoretical link between our world and the hidden universe?'

'OK.' Really lost it.

'And we're assuming that the Higgs boson, if it does exist, is present somewhere in the aftermath of the explosions in the Collider?'

'Absolutely.' Look at him: nutty as a bag of hazelnut crackers.

'Well, what if the energy loss is natural? What if the Higgs boson is decaying in the Collider, but is decaying into particles of another world: dark matter. The Collider would register the decay as an energy loss, when in fact it's the nature of the particles that has changed. There is no energy loss, because they're still there. We just can't see them.'

Victor stared at him, jaw agape. Professor Hilbert might have been mad, but Victor was starting to suspect that he was *brilliantly* mad, because this was a really, really interesting theory.

'Did you tell Professor Stefan all this?' asked Ed, who felt the same way that Victor did about Professor Hilbert's ambitions, but was happy enough to be a cog in the wheel of this Nobel Prize-winning operation, in part because he was a modest, unassuming sort of chap, and also because he really liked sweeties.

'Most of it,' said Professor Hilbert[27], and Victor and Ed knew that, in Professor Hilbert's mind, there was only ever going to be one name on the citation from

---

💀 [27] Translated from lies to truth, this means 'No, I hardly told him anything at all, and what I did tell him was just enough to enable me to continue to pursue my ultimate goal without having him worry about what suit he might wear to the Nobel Prize ceremony, because he's not going. I'm the only one who is going. Just me. Got a problem with that? No, I didn't think so. It's mine, all mine! Ha-ha-ha-ha-ha-ha-ha!' *Laughter fades to madness. Men in white suits arrive with promises of a nice padded cell, three meals a day in pill form, and no nasty sharp edges upon which you might bang your knee and hurt yourself.*

Similar translations from other areas of life of which you should be aware include: 'The cheque is in the post.' (A cheque may be in the post, but it's not your cheque, and it's not going to your letter box.); 'I'll think about it.' (I don't need to think about it, because the answer is 'No'.); 'You don't look a day older.' (You really don't look a day older – you look ten years older, and that's in dim light.); 'You may feel a small sting.' (Only death will hurt more, and that won't take as long.); and the ever-popular 'It's perfectly safe. It isn't even switched on . . .' usually spoken just before moments of electrocution, the loss of a limb due to incorrect use of a hedge-trimmer, and people being blown up by gas ovens.

the Nobel Prize committee, and he wasn't going to endanger that possibility by sharing too much of what he thought with anyone who might have too many letters after his name.

'So we shouldn't worry about the energy loss?' said Victor.

'No.'

'And you don't think the portal to He—, er, this hidden world is in any danger of opening again?'

'The energy loss isn't remotely comparable to last time,' said Professor Hilbert, which wasn't really answering the question at all.

Ed and Victor exchanged a look.

'Two boxes of sweeties,' said Ed. 'Each.'

Professor Hilbert smiled a shark's smile. 'You drive a hard bargain . . .'

CHAPTER XVII

In Which the True Faces of the Conspirators Are Revealed, and An Ugly Bunch They Are Too

Mrs Abernathy was in her element: she sat in her chamber and listened as an array of demons fawned their way into her presence, attempting to find favour with her once again. Even Chelom, the great spider demon, and Naroth, the most bloated of the toad demons, who had fled after the failure of the invasion, now sought a place by her side once again. She wanted to punish them for their disloyalty, but she restrained herself. It was enough that they were coming back to her, and she needed them. She needed them all. Later, she would violently dispense with some of those who had abandoned her, if only to remind the others of the limits of her tolerance.

Mrs Abernathy's original plan had been to target Samuel and Boswell, and bring them straight to her lair. Unfortunately she had reckoned without a number of factors, including:

a. the difficulty of a targeted acquisition between dimensions
b. an ice-cream salesman
c. a police car
d. a van filled with unknown little people.

She had also exhausted herself bringing them all here, and had fallen into unconsciousness for a time. When she woke, she found that she was unable to locate any of them, at least until the insufferable A. Bodkin had tried to send a message to his superiors, a message that she had intercepted. She now knew roughly the area in which at least some of those whom she had accidentally targeted might be, and by extension where she might find Samuel Johnson, but since this was Hell, which, as we have established, tended to play a little fast and loose with concepts such as direction and geography, it was like being told that a needle is almost certainly in a haystack, and then being shown a very large field filled with very large haystacks. Oh, and the field goes up and down as well as across for very long distances. And it's a bit diagonal as well.

Therefore Mrs Abernathy required help if she was to search for the boy, which was why she had decided against immediately torturing those who had earlier turned their backs on her. Instead she listened to their pleas and their excuses before dispatching them to seek out Samuel Johnson. For the most part they had nothing of interest to tell her anyway, but there were certain exceptions. One of those exceptions was standing before her now. Actually 'standing' might be too strong a word for what it was doing, since it had technically oozed beneath her gaze and had now simply ceased oozing, although assorted substances still dripped from its pores in a way that suggested further oozing could only be a matter of time. It resembled a transparent slug with aspirations to be something more interesting, hampered by the fact that it was, and always would be, made of gelatinous material and about three feet tall, and therefore only of interest to other things made of jelly and slightly smaller than itself. Two unblinking eyeballs were set into what was, for now, its front part, beneath which was a toothless mouth. It wore a black top hat, which it raised in greeting using a tentacle that slowly extruded from its body expressly for that purpose, and then was promptly reabsorbed.

'Afternoon, Ma'am,' it said. 'Happy to see you on the up again, as it were.'

'And you are?' said Mrs Abernathy.

'Crudford, Esq., Ma'am. I work in the Pits of Hopelessness. Don't really fit in, though. Not the hopeless type. I've always been a hopeful sort of gelatinous mass, me. The glass is always half full, that's what I say. When you're made of jelly, and only have a hat to your name, it can only get better, can't it?'

'Someone could take your hat,' said Mrs Abernathy.

'Agreed, agreed, but it wasn't my hat to begin with. I just found it, so technically that wouldn't be much of a reversal, would it?'

'It would if I took it, forced you into it, then slowly roasted you, and it, over a large fire.'

Crudford considered this. 'I'd still have my hat, though, wouldn't I?'

Mrs Abernathy decided that Crudford, Esq. might just have to be made an example of at some point in the near future, if only to discourage such a brightness of outlook in others.

'So what can you do for me until then?' said Mrs Abernathy.

'Well, I can ooze. I've worked hard at it. Laboured my way up from just dripping, through sliming, until I hit on a steady ooze. You could say I've perfected it. But I appreciate that it's a skill of limited applicability in most circumstances, if you catch my drift. Still, onwards and upwards.'

'Mr Crudford, if I stood on you, would it hurt?'

'Yes. You'd get ooze on your shoe, though.'

'It's a price I'm willing to pay, unless you give me a good reason why I shouldn't.'

'Suppose I told you about Chancellor Ozymuth, Ma'am, and how he's been plotting against you,' said Crudford, and he was pleased to see Mrs Abernathy's expression of profound distaste change to one of mild distaste, coupled with a side order of interest.

'Continue.'

'As it happens I was there the last time that you came to visit, when you were trying to see our master, the Great Malevolence. It's one of the advantages of oozing, see: you can ooze just about anywhere, fitting into all kinds of small spaces, and nobody ever notices. Anyway, I was there, and I saw what happened after you'd gone.'

'Which was?'

'Someone emerged from the shadows, and it was Duke Abigor, who congratulated Chancellor Ozymuth on how well he was doing in keeping you away from the Great Malevolence, and on telling our master what a bad sort you are. Completely unjustified, I hasten to add. I mean, you are a bad sort, but in the best possible way. Then Duke Abigor slipped away, and having nothing better to do than a bit more oozing I followed him deep underground, until we came to a meeting room, and they were all there waiting for him.'

'Who was waiting?'

'Most of the Grand Dukes of Hell. They were sitting at a big table, and Duke Abigor joined them at the head of it. They started talking about you. Funny thing is, Ma'am, they're back there again now. Just thought you might like to know. I was hopeful about it, you might say . . .'

Duke Abigor looked very unimpressed, a not inconsiderable achievement given that his standard expression veered towards the unimpressed, even when he was impressed, which wasn't very often.

'Tell me again,' he said, as Duke Duscias quivered before him.

'She has found a way to reach out to the world of men,' said Duscias. 'She pulled something from their world into ours, and now she seeks it.'

Duke Abigor was no fool. You didn't end up with sixty legions of demons at your command by being a dolt. Duscias, on the other hand, was a fool, but he was Abigor's fool, and so Duscias's twenty-nine legions were, to all intents and purposes, also under Abigor's command.

'It's the boy,' said Abigor. 'That is the only reason why she would risk opening up a portal without the knowledge of our master. If she has the boy, she can present him to the Great Malevolence for his amusement, and she will be back at his left hand. Our chance to rule will vanish, and she will move against us.'

'But how?' said Duscias. 'She cannot know of our plot. We have kept ourselves well hidden.'

'Because, you idiot, someone will tell her. If she finds a way to worm herself back into our master's trust, then demons will be falling over themselves to betray one another if it increases their chances of a promotion.'

Other figures began to file into the meeting room, their heads hidden by great black hoods that they let fall to reveal their faces: Duke Guares, commander of thirty legions; Duke Docer, commander of thirty-six legions; Duke Borym, commander of twenty-six legions; and Duke Peros, commander of thirty-six legions. These were the ringleaders, the ones who had staked their reputations, and a potential eternity of pain if they failed, on Duke Abigor's ability to convince the Great Malevolence that he should take over from Mrs Abernathy as the Commander of the Infernal Armies. The problem for all concerned was that Mrs Abernathy had not technically been relieved of her post, since the Great Malevolence had simply refused to see her and was still lost in the madness of his grief. Therefore the dukes were engaged in an act of treason against not only their own general, but against the Great Malevolence himself.

'We should have arrested her long before now,' said Duke Docer, once the situation had been explained to him. 'We left her in peace, and the result is that she has outmanoeuvred us.'

'We couldn't have arrested her,' said Duke Abigor with as much patience as he could muster. Duke Docer was a soldier, and without cunning. He had won every battle in which he had fought by charging forwards and overwhelming his foes by sheer might, and now he spent most of his time looking for new foes so that he wouldn't get bored, even if it meant alienating allies to do so.[28] He wouldn't have known a strategy if it bit him. 'There are too many that we have not yet brought over to our side.'

'But the hordes of Hell have no love for her either,' said Duke Peros. 'Most would be glad if she were gone.'

'They may not care for her, but they care as little for me,' said Duke Abigor. 'They may fear her, and hate her, but she is a force that they know and understand. I am an unknown quantity, as are we all.'

'We are more than two hundred legions strong,' said Duke Docer. 'That is all they need to know and understand.'

'It is not enough!' said Duke Abigor. 'We will not go to war unless we are certain of victory, and we do not know which side the Great Malevolence will support once he emerges from his mourning. If we misstep, then we are in danger of being perceived as traitors, and I do not need to remind you what the punishment is for such a betrayal.'

At this the dukes were silent. They had all seen Cocytus, the great lake of ice far to the north in which traitors were kept frozen for eternity. If they were lucky, their heads might be permitted to protrude from the ice, but as traitors not only to the kingdom but also to

---

💀 [28] Evil, unlike good, is constantly at war with those most like itself, and ambition is its spur.

their master, the Great Malevolence, it was more likely that they would be entirely immersed in the cold and darkness, not a fate any of them desired.

'But the Great Malevolence is ...' Duke Guares searched for the right words, and settled on, 'not well. He may never cease his mourning. What then? Do we let this kingdom that we have hewn from rock and fire fall into decay and strife?'

Duke Abigor eyed Duke Guares warily. Guares was almost as clever as Abigor, and Abigor sometimes wondered if Guares had already guessed Abigor's larger plan. It was true that the Great Malevolence seemed lost to them, but Guares and the others hoped each day that he might recover what passed for his sanity and resume his rule over Hell. Only Abigor wanted the Great Malevolence to remain immersed in his sorrow and his anger. Moreover Abigor wanted that sorrow and anger to grow so much deeper that the Great Malevolence would descend into a fateful madness from which he would never emerge. This was why Abigor had enlisted Chancellor Ozymuth to their cause, for Ozymuth ensured that the Great Malevolence was cut off from all contact with other demons, and Ozymuth whispered in the Great Malevolence's ear that all was lost, lost for ever, and it was Mrs Abernathy's fault that this was so.

'We will track down the boy, Samuel Johnson, before she does,' said Duke Abigor. 'We will find him, and we will lock him away where no one will ever discover him, and deny all knowledge of his whereabouts. Her last hope of earning back her place at our master's left hand will be gone, and we will be able to claim that she is no longer suited to command the Infernal Armies, and a temporary replacement should be appointed as a matter of urgency until our master has found his wits again. You will all put my name forward as the most suitable candidate, and our opponents will have no time to muster a response. If they try to do so, we will wipe them out.'

'And Mrs Abernathy?' said Duke Guares.

Duke Abigor smiled, but such an unpleasant smile that he still looked like an unimpressed demon, albeit one who has just been presented with a head on a plate, and who really likes heads.

'Is she not a traitor? A traitor for failing to achieve the victory we sought in the world of men, a traitor for bringing the boy who caused our defeat to this realm, our realm, and then losing him. She will be tried, and found guilty. We will take her to Cocytus, and we will chain a rock around her neck, and we will throw her through the ice. Let her be frozen for ever as a warning to those who would promise us new worlds, and then disappoint.'

Duke Abigor looked to his co-conspirators, and each of them in turn nodded his agreement. Then one by one they filed from the meeting room, Duke Abigor the last to leave, until all was quiet again.

The silence was disturbed by a soft *glop*.

'Beg pardon,' said Crudford. 'I oozed.'

'Clean yourself up,' said Mrs Abernathy. She had seen and heard everything, crouched behind a crack in the rock wall. The expression on her face was unreadable but Crudford, who was sensitive to emotions, detected fear, and surprise, and disappointment.

And rage: pure, channelled, governed rage.

'Did I do well, Ma'am?' asked Crudford.

'You did very well,' said Mrs Abernathy. 'For this, I'll even find you a new hat.'

Crudford's slimy features parted in a grin. A new hat: it was more than he had dared to hope for.

CHAPTER XVIII

In Which Those Who Will Be of Help to Samuel Begin to Come Together

The Watcher found a quiet cave, where it mulled over what Old Ram had said. Eventually it sought out Mrs Abernathy, but when it tried to speak with her it found her overwhelmed by the attentions of the returning demons as they crowded around her, anxious to make recompense for their lack of faith in her. Their words were a salve to her wounded vanity, and although the Watcher might have fought its way through the mass of stinking bodies in order to reach its mistress, it had not done so. In part this was because it could see the pleasure she derived as they prostrated themselves before her, but there was also a part of the Watcher that still wondered about the boy, and the wisdom of what Mrs Abernathy had done in dragging him to Hell.

In addition, the news that the boy might have been found had almost driven from its mind the discovery of the burnt rubber on the plain; almost, but not quite, for the Watcher had spent the intervening period trying to identify the other smells it had picked up among the rocks, comparing them with the scent memory in its strange, alien brain. The Watcher was an entity apart, even among the many foul and demonic beings that inhabited the various strata of Hell. It had attached itself to what was now its mistress shortly after the formation of Hell itself, and the emergence of the oldest of the demons. No one could recall quite how the Watcher had come into being; its nature was a mystery to all. Not even Mrs Abernathy herself truly understood it: she knew only that it obeyed her will, and when so many others had turned their backs on her, only the Watcher had remained truly faithful.

But the Watcher did not obey her will alone. For as long as it had been in existence, it had reported back to the Great Malevolence himself, for the Great Malevolence trusted no one and nothing, and despite his power he was suspicious of all those around him.[29] But the Watcher had spent so long with Mrs Abernathy that its loyalties had become confused: while it still answered to the Great Malevolence, it did not tell him everything. It could not have said why; it merely understood instinctively that not simply knowledge is power, but *secret* knowledge. So it was that it made its own judgements on what the Great Malevolence needed to be told, and what could safely be hidden from him. In that sense the Watcher was serving two masters, which is never a good idea.

☠ [29] A Scottish proverb says that 'Evil doers are evil dreaders.' In other words, those that do ill, or think ill of others, naturally expect others to do ill to them. Wickedness never rests easily so, in a way, one might almost feel pity for the wicked, for they are destined to live their lives in fear, in a prison of the heart. Or, as the French writer Voltaire put it, 'Fear follows crime, and is its punishment.'

Its situation had been complicated by the Great Malevolence's descent into misery and madness, which meant that, even if the Watcher had wanted to report to him, it could not, for its voice could not be heard above the wailing that filled the Mountain of Despair, and the Chancellor was careful to control all access. Then again, until now there had been little to report: Mrs Abernathy had spent most of her time moving back and forth between her lair and that of the Great Malevolence, seeking an audience that would never be granted, and then brooding over it alone in her chamber until it came time to make the pilgrimage again. When she was not walking, or brooding, she was watching Samuel Johnson in the glass, and hurling curses at him that he could not hear. It was left to the Watcher to try to track down the vehicle that had collapsed the portal, but each time it returned without news Mrs Abernathy's interest in the vehicle seemed to grow less and less, or so the Watcher had thought. Then, when the Watcher had at last returned with evidence of the vehicle's presence, it had been surprised to find that Mrs Abernathy had been plotting quietly all along to open the portal once again, if only to snatch Samuel Johnson from his world and transport him to Hell. She really was a most unusual woman, even leaving aside the fact that she was actually an ancient tentacled demon in disguise, which was one of the reasons why the Watcher's loyalties were split between her and the Great Malevolence.

The Watcher sniffed at the air, recreating the scents it had picked up on the Plain. It had felt presences nearby, watching it, but it was not sure if they were related to the black substance on the rock. Its sunken nostrils twitched.

An old smell, almost forgotten. And another with it: sharper, more pungent. They were familiar, those smells. The Watcher rummaged through its memories, back, back, until it came at last to a pair of cowering figures, its mistress towering above them in her old, monstrous form, banishing them for ever to the Wasteland . . .

Very little surprised the Watcher. It had seen so much that it was almost incapable of surprise. But its realization of who had been responsible for the collapse of the portal nearly caused it to topple over in shock.

Nurd.

Nurd, the Scourge of Five Deities.

Nurd, who barely justified the term 'demon' to begin with, so inept was he at being evil.

Nurd had betrayed them all.

Meanwhile, Nurd and Wormwood were standing on a rise and watching a small van tootling merrily across the Desert of Bones while playing 'How Much Is That Doggie in the Window?' Nurd and Wormwood knew that the piece of music was called 'How Much Is That Doggie in the Window?' because at least four voices were singing along to it, adding 'woof-woof' noises after each mention of the word 'window', and the words 'waggle-waggle' to the bit about 'the one with the waggley tail'.

'What's a doggie?' asked Wormwood. 'And why do they want one?'

'A doggie is a small creature that barks, like Boswell, Samuel Johnson's dachshund,' said Nurd. 'It goes "woof-woof". This one, though, also appears to have a tail that is waggley, which makes it more desirable, I suppose.'

'They do seem to want it very badly,' said Wormwood.

'It doesn't seem like a good idea to go shouting about it, though,' said Nurd. 'The kind of things with waggley tails that live around here tend to have big waggley bodies too, and waggley heads with waggley teeth.'

'If it's from the world of men, then maybe Samuel is in there too.'

Nurd shook his head. 'No, I'd sense him if he were so close.' Nurd strained to read the writing on the side of the van. 'It says something about ice cream on the side. And sweets.'

'Sweets?' said Wormwood.

'Sweets,' said Nurd.

They looked at each other. Their faces brightened, and both said, simultaneously: 'Wine gums!'

Seconds later, they were in hot pursuit of the ice-cream van.

Constable Peel very much wanted to die. More than that, he wanted to die and take four dwarfs with him, and maybe a driver of an ice-cream van for good measure. He'd been listening to 'How Much Is That Doggie in the Window?' for a good four hours now, and was on the verge of insanity.

'Stop singing,' he said to the dwarfs.

'No,' said Angry.

'Stop singing.'

'No.'

'Stop singing.'

'Say "please".'

'Please.'

'No.'

Constable Peel banged on the glass connecting the back of the van to the front compartment, in which Sergeant Rowan and Dan, Dan the Ice-Cream Man were sitting.

'For the last time,' he pleaded, 'there must be some way to turn that music off.'

Dan shrugged. 'I've told you: it comes on automatically with the engine. I haven't been able to work out how to make it stop without messing up the wiring.'

'You're messing up *my* wiring,' said Constable Peel. 'Can't I at least sit up front with you?'

'There isn't really enough room,' said Sergeant Rowan, who didn't like being cramped.

'Then why don't we swap places for a while, and you can sit back here?'

'With that lot singing? I don't think so. It's bad enough up here.'

Jolly made himself another ice-cream cone. He'd already had twelve, but the sometimes bumpy nature of the terrain meant that he had only managed successfully to eat nine, while the remaining three were smeared all over his face and clothes.

'Lovely ice cream, this,' he said, for the thirteenth time.

'Oi, I hope you're paying for all of those,' said Dan.

'I'm putting them on my tab.'

'You don't have a tab.'

'Oh, now you tell me. You should have said before I started eating them all. Bit late now, isn't it?'

'He was right about the chocolate too,' said Dozy, who had taken to eating the sprinkles by the fistful. 'Very high quality.'

Angry and Mumbles began singing about doggies again, at least Angry did. Mumbles could have been singing about dinosaurs and nobody would have been any the wiser. Constable Peel, his patience now at an end, was stretching out his hands to strangle one or both of them when Dan stopped the van, for there was now something to distract them all from the music.

'That's interesting,' said Dozy. He and the other three dwarfs, each munching happily on Dan's livelihood, hopped from the van, closely followed by the two policemen and Dan himself.

Stretched before them were thousands and thousands of little workbenches, each occupied by an imp. Between the desks walked other imps carrying buckets of bone dust. They poured the bone dust into a hole at one end of each desk, the seated imps turned a lever, there was the sound of grinding and then from the other end of the desks emerged clean, intact bones, which the demons with buckets took from them before walking back the way they had come.

'Well, that explains a lot,' said Jolly. 'Sort of.'

There was a larger desk some distance to their right. The dwarfs left the policemen and Dan and made their way over to it. A demon who bore a remarkable resemblance to the recently vaporized A. Bodkin sat at the desk, snoozing. His name plate read 'Mr D. Bodkin, Demon-In-Charge'.

''Scuse me,' said Jolly, tapping D. Bodkin's boot.

D. Bodkin woke slowly, and stared at Jolly.

'Yes, what is it?'

'Do you know where all of this dust comes from?'

'What dust?'

'The dust that makes the bones.'

D. Bodkin looked at Jolly as though Jolly had just asked him why the sky was grey and black with bursts of purple and red flame currently flashing through it. That was just the way things were.

'Is there something wrong with you?' asked D. Bodkin. 'Look around: there's *only* dust. Hardly going to run out, are we?'

The dwarfs started giggling. D. Bodkin, suspecting that he was the butt of a joke he didn't understand, and who didn't care much for humour at the best of times, glowered at them.

'See over that way,' said Angry, 'where all those little demons with buckets are coming from?'

'Yes,' said D. Bodkin.

'You should take a walk over there. There's a bloke who'd love to meet you. Looks a bit like you. Long-lost relative, you might say.'

'Really?'

'Cross my heart. You and him would have a lot to talk about. You're both in the same business, in a way.'

'Well, I will then,' said D. Bodkin. 'I feel like giving the old legs a stretch. Haven't left my desk in, ooooh –'

He glanced at the hourglass on his wrist which, like Mr A. Bodkin's similar model, was designed to funnel sand very efficiently from one glass to another without ever depleting the store in the upper glass, or increasing the store in the lower glass. This watch though, appeared to have stopped, possibly due to a blockage. D. Bodkin looked perturbed. He tapped the glass with a clawed forefinger.

'Funny, my watch doesn't seem to be working.' He gave his wrist a little shake, and said, 'Ah, that's better.'

Angry leaned forward and noticed that the sand from the lower glass was now running upwards into the upper glass, although, as before, neither glass got any emptier, or any fuller.

'You really have been at this desk for too long,' said Angry, glancing back at his fellow dwarfs and twisting one finger slowly by his right temple in the universal indication of someone else's general absence of marbles. 'It'll be good for you to take a break. We'll keep an eye on this lot until you get back.'

'You won't steal anything, will you?' asked D. Bodkin. 'I'll get into terrible trouble if anything goes missing. Budgets, you know. I have to account for every paper clip these days.'

Angry was the picture of wounded innocence. 'I'm hurt,' he said, blinking away an imaginary tear. He fumbled in his pocket for a handkerchief upon which to blow his nose, discovered one, looked at it, decided that the only thing more disease-ridden than this handkerchief was an actual disease, and put it back where he'd found it. 'I'm so hurt that I don't know what to say.'

'That's insulting, that is,' said Dozy.

'We're just trying to brighten up your day,' said Jolly, 'and you go and say something nasty like that about us.'

'We've been the victims of theft ourselves,' said Angry. 'On that subject, you wouldn't have seen a van anywhere – four wheels, picture of a handsome smiling gentleman somewhat like ourselves on the side – would you?'

'No,' said D. Bodkin.

'What about a police car: four wheels, blue lights?'

'No. I'd like to, though. It sounds very interesting.'

'Hmmm,' said Angry. 'Fat lot of good that does us.'

He and the other dwarfs folded their arms and looked expectantly at D. Bodkin. Jolly tapped his foot impatiently.

'Well,' said Jolly, 'we're waiting.'

Eventually, D. Bodkin took the hint.

'I'm very sorry for what I said just now,' he said. He looked embarrassed. The horns on his head glowed bright red. He put his hands behind his back and traced little patterns of shame in the sand. 'I shouldn't have asked if you were going to steal anything. You can't be too careful, you know. After all, this is Hell. All sorts of rotten types end up here.'

'Apology accepted,' said Angry. 'Off you go, then. Tell the other chap we said hello.'

'Righty-ho,' said D. Bodkin, and began following the line of bone-bearing bucket carriers.

The dwarfs waved him off.

'Nice bloke,' said Jolly.

'Lovely,' said Angry, as D. Bodkin disappeared over a dune. 'This world needs more demons like him.'

'Suckers, you mean?' said Jolly.

'Absolutely,' said Angry. 'Complete and utter suckers.'

Back in the van, Jolly counted their loot.

'That's fifteen pencils, one pencil sharpener, a stapler, a rubber, a mug that says "You Don't Have To Be Diabolical To Work Here, But It Helps", and some stamps,' said Jolly.

'You forgot the desk,' said Dozy.

'And the desk,' confirmed Jolly. He stuck his head out of the side of the van and checked on the desk, which they'd tied to the roof of the van with a length of rope they'd found in Dan's boot.

'You're sure he said that you could take them?' said Constable Peel. He was more than a little suspicious, but at least the dwarfs had stopped singing for a while.

'Absolutely. Told us he was quitting. No future in the job. Said we'd be doing him a favour.'

'Well, if you're sure, although I don't know why you think you need a desk anyway.'

'Question not the need,' said Angry. 'If it isn't nailed down, we'll have it. And if it is nailed down, we'll find a way to un-nail it and have that as well.'

Constable Peel's brow furrowed. A cloud of dust seemed to be following them. As it drew closer he saw that it was being preceded by a fast-moving rock.

'Look at that,' he said. He pulled back the glass separating the front of the van from the serving section. 'Sarge, we're being chased by a rock.'

'You don't see a rock rolling uphill very often,' said Angry. 'Very unusual, that.'

'It's gaining on us,' said Dozy.

'Stop the van,' said Sergeant Rowan. Dan did as he was instructed, but kept it neutral and they all listened.

'That's the sound of an engine, Sarge,' said Constable Peel.

'So it is, Constable,' said Sergeant Rowan as the rock pulled up alongside them, its doors opened, and what looked like a ferret with mange jumped out, closely followed by a cloaked demon wearing big boots and an expectant smile on his green face.

'Two bags of wine gums, please,' said Nurd. 'And two cones with sprinkles.'

He waved a small gold coin in the air, just as Constable Peel's head appeared through the service hatch.

'Well, well, well,' said Constable Peel. 'Would you look at who it is?'

Nurd's jaw dropped. Wormwood helpfully picked it up and reattached it.

'Oh, nuts,' said Nurd.

'No,' said Constable Peel, 'but we do have sprinkles . . .'

CHAPTER XIX

In Which We Encounter Some of the Other Unfortunate Denizens of Hell

Samuel and Boswell, frightened and tired, traversed the landscape of Hell. There were great causeways of stone that crossed chasms filled with fire, and dark lakes in whose depths swam nightmarish forms, their fins and tails occasionally breaking the surface as they hunted and were hunted. They saw demons large and small, sometimes in the distance, sometimes up close, but even those upon whose path they stumbled paid them little or no attention. They seemed to assume that if Samuel and Boswell were there, then they were meant to be and were therefore some other demon's concern, not theirs.

But for the most part there wasn't a great deal to see, for Hell looked largely unfinished to Samuel and Boswell. True, the skies above their heads continued to rage, and Samuel sometimes felt that the clouds were looking down and mocking him before resuming their never-ending conflict of noise and light, but vast stretches of Hell's landscape had little or nothing to offer at all.[30] There was just dirt beneath their feet, or cracked stone, or low mounds of short black grass unenlivened by even a single weed.

After a time the ground began to slope upwards, and they ascended a small hill. As they reached the crest they saw arrayed before them an enormous banquet. It covered a table that stretched so far into the distance that Samuel lost sight of it in the dreary white mist always lurking on the horizon, but he could see every kind of food imaginable laid out on it, from breads to desserts and everything in between, with dusty bottles of fine wine interspersed among the bowls and dishes. It was a feast beyond compare, yet although Samuel and Boswell were starving they did not feel their appetites piqued by what they saw. Perhaps it was because the food, regardless of its type, was a uniform dull grey, or because, even as they drew closer, they could detect no smell from it

Or it may have been the behaviour of those seated at the banquet, for chairs stood side by side along the length and breadth of the table, so close that there was no room for anyone else to squeeze in, and they were

[30] Because Hell was huge, and only a fraction of it was occupied, the Great Malevolence had largely given up on trying to decorate every inch of it in a suitable manner. After all, there's only so much time that you can spend putting up big black mountains that loom menacingly, and building great fiery pits in which demons toil, before you start to think, well, why bother? Thus most of Hell is like the spare room in your house, the one your dad keeps promising to turn into his den but instead just fills with boxes of unread books, and old bills, and that exercise bike he bought and now claims doesn't work properly because it's too hard to cycle, although it'll be fine once he gets around to fixing it, and anyway, it cost a fortune, that bike.

Dads: they're just made that way.

all occupied by thin, wasted people who forced food constantly into their mouths, and guzzled wine while their jaws chomped tirelessly, half-chewed meats and grey liquid dripping from their chins and staining their clothes.

Samuel and Boswell were now close enough to the feast to be noticed by the man seated at the head of the table. He wore a dinner jacket with a crooked bow tie. His shirt buttons were open, and a distended belly bulged through the gap, but it was not the belly of a fat person. Samuel had seen poor, hungry people on television, and he knew that chronic malnutrition made the stomach swell. This man was starving, yet he had more than enough food to eat. While Samuel watched, the man tossed aside a half-eaten chicken leg and began chomping on a juicy, if slate-coloured, steak. As one dish was finished a new one appeared, so that there was never an empty plate on the table.

The man spotted Samuel, but he did not stop eating.

'Get away,' he said. 'There isn't enough for anyone else.'

'There's barely enough for us,' said a woman to his left, who was eating caviar with a huge wooden spoon, shovelling the little fish eggs into her mouth. She wore an ornate ball gown, and her head was topped by a white wig dotted with crystals. 'And you haven't been invited.'

'How do you know?' asked Samuel.

'Because if you were invited there would be a chair for you, but there isn't, so you haven't. Now run along. Don't you know that you shouldn't interrupt people when they're eating? You're making me talk with my mouth full. That's rude.'

'And she's spilling some,' said a tall bald man sitting across from her. 'If she doesn't want that caviar, I'll have it.'

He reached for the bowl, but the woman slapped him hard on the hand with the spoon.

'Get your own!' she snapped.

'But the food has no smell,' said Samuel, almost to himself.

'No smell,' said the man in the tuxedo. 'No taste. No texture. No colour. But I'm *so* hungry, always *so* hungry.' He polished off the steak and moved on to a bowl of trifle, using his hand to scoop up mouthfuls of jelly, sponge, and custard. 'I'm so hungry, I could eat you. And your dog.'

And for the first time in a century, for he had been at the table for a very, very long time, the man in the dinner jacket stopped eating, and began thinking. There was a new hunger in his eyes as he examined Samuel the way a chef might examine a pig that has been offered to him by the butcher, sizing it up for the best cuts. Beside him, the woman turned her gaze on Samuel, her mouth open, caviar falling from her tongue. The tall bald man set aside a fish head, and picked up a sharp knife.

'Proper food,' he whispered. 'Fresh meat.'

The words were taken up by the elderly man beside him, and the wizened old lady whose toothless jaws could only suck the meat from bones, and the children dressed like princes and princesses, passed on and on down the table until they, like the distant, starving guests at the feast, were lost in the mist.

'*Fresh meat, fresh meat, fresh meat . . .*'

Samuel picked up Boswell and backed away from the table. The man in the dinner jacket put his hands on the arms of the chair, preparing to rise, but found that he could not stand. He tried to shift his chair, as if hoping to shuffle it towards Samuel, but it would not budge. His hands stretched for Samuel, but Samuel was beyond his reach. The tall bald man with the sharp knife howled in fury, slashing at the air with the blade as though his limbs might somehow extend far enough to cut Samuel's flesh.

The bewigged woman tried to be more cunning. 'Come here, little boy,' she whispered, offering him a grey piece of chocolate. 'I'll protect you from them. I had a little boy of my own once. I wouldn't hurt a child.'

But Samuel was no fool. He stayed out of her reach, clutching Boswell tightly.

'At least leave us your dog,' said the man in the dinner jacket. 'I hear dog is very tasty.'

All along the table voices were raised, shouting threats, promises, bribes, anything that might convince Samuel to approach, or to hand Boswell over, but Samuel just backed away, never taking his eyes from them, fearful that if he did so they might find a way to free themselves from the prison of their chairs. Then, one by one, their appetites got the better of them until the guests resumed their great, tasteless meal, all but the woman with the wig who stared after Samuel, repeating over and over to herself, 'I had a little boy of my own . . .' and only when Samuel was again at the crest of the hill did she turn back to her caviar and lose herself once more in the feast.

Samuel and Boswell moved on. In time they saw a great wooden horse burning; around it sat Greek warriors, lost in melancholy. Samuel approached them warily, but the warriors did not stir and when he tried to speak to them they did not answer.

'What do you want, child?' said a voice, and Samuel turned to see a woman emerge from the sand: first the head, then the body, until she stood before him, grains tumbling from her hair, her hands, her gown. As Samuel looked more closely at her he saw that she had not merely risen from the sand: she was sand, different textures and hues combining to give the impression of clothing, and colour, and life. Only her eyes were not formed from sand: they blazed a deep, fiery red, and Samuel knew that he was staring at a demon.

'This is . . . the Trojan horse, isn't it?' said Samuel.

'It is.'

'And these are the men who used it to gain access to the city.'

'They are. The one who sits apart from the others, the man alone, that is Odysseus.' She spoke his name softly. 'The horse was his idea.'

'But why are they here?'

'Because it was an act of deception. It was not honest, not truthful.'

'But it was clever.'

'A lie may be clever, but it is still a lie.'

'But don't they say that all is fair in love and war? I heard that somewhere.'

'"They"?' Who are "they"?'

'I don't know. Just people.'

'That's what the victorious claim, not the defeated; the powerful, not the powerless. "All is fair." "The end justifies the means". Is that what you believe?'

'I don't know.'

'Is there someone you love? A girl, perhaps?'

'There's a girl that I like.'

'Would you lie to gain her affection?'

'No, I don't think so.'

'You don't think so?'

'No, I wouldn't.'

'And if someone lied to her about you in order to turn her against you, would you feel that was fair?'

'No, of course not.'

'Have you heard it said that sport is war by other means?'

'I haven't, but I suppose it could be true.'

'Do you cheat when you play games?'

'No.'

'Why?'

'Because it's not right. It's not –'

'Fair?'

'No, it's not fair.'

'So all is *not* fair in love, and all is *not* fair in war.'

'I suppose not.' Samuel was troubled. He looked at the warriors, but none of them seemed to have paid any attention to his conversation with the demon. 'It still seems like a harsh punishment,' he said.

'It is,' said the demon, with something like regret in her voice.

'Who decided?' asked Samuel. 'Who decided that they should be here?'

'They decided,' said the demon. 'They chose. Now go, child. Their melancholy is infectious.'

The grains of sand at her eyes formed a tear that shed itself upon her cheek. The demon sank back into the ground, and Samuel and Boswell turned away from the burning horse and continued their journey.

CHAPTER XX

In Which We Meet the Blacksmith

The barren landscape began to change, although not for the better. It was now dotted with objects that seemed to come from another world, Samuel's world: a suit of armour, empty and rusted; a German biplane from World War I; a submarine standing perfectly upright, balanced on its propellers; and a rifle, the largest, longest gun that Samuel had ever seen, so long that it would have taken him an hour or more just to walk around it, made up of millions and millions of smaller guns, all fused together to create a kind of giant sculpture. As Samuel examined it he saw that pieces of the rifle appeared to be alive, wriggling like metal snakes, and he realized that the rifle was still forming, weapons popping into existence in the air around it and slowly being absorbed into the whole.

A huge man appeared from behind the discarded turret of a tank. He wore dirty black overalls and a welder's mask upon his face. In his right hand he held a blowtorch that burned with a white-hot flame. He killed the flame and pushed the mask up so that his face was revealed. He was bearded, and his eyes shone with the same white fire as his torch had, as though he had spent too long looking at metal dissolve.

'Who are you?' he asked. His voice was hoarse, but there was no hostility to his tone.

'My name is Samuel Johnson, and this is Boswell.'

Those white eyes looked down upon the little dachshund.

'A dog,' said the man. 'It's a long time since I've seen a dog.'

He reached out a gloved hand. Boswell shied away, but the hand was too quick. It fastened on Boswell's head, then rubbed at it with a surprising gentleness.

'Good dog,' said the man. 'Good little dog.'

He released his grip on Boswell, somewhat to the relief of the good little dog in question.

'I kept dogs,' he said. 'A man should have a dog.'

'Do you have a name?' asked Samuel.

'I had a name once as well, but I've forgotten it. I have no use for it, for nobody has come here for so very long. Now, I am the Blacksmith. I work with metal. It is my punishment.'

'What is this place?' asked Samuel.

'This is the Junkyard. It is the place of broken things that should never have been made. Come and see.'

Samuel and Boswell followed the Blacksmith beneath the ever-changing gun, and past row upon row of fighter planes and armoured cars, and there was revealed to them an enormous crater, and in it were swords and knives; machine guns and pistols; tanks and battleships and aircraft carriers; every conceivable weapon that might be used to inflict harm upon another person. Like the great gun, the contents of the crater were constantly being added to, so that the whole mass of metal creaked and groaned and clattered and clanked.

'Why are they here?' asked Samuel.

'Because they took lives, and this is where they belong.'

'Then why are you here?'

'Because I designed such weapons, and I put them in the hands of those who would use them against innocents, and I did not care. Now, I break them down.'

'What about the great gun, the one that keeps growing in size?'

'A reminder to me,' said the Blacksmith. 'No matter how hard I work, or how many weapons I break down, still that rifle increases in size. I contributed to the existence of such weapons in life, and I am not permitted to forget it.'

'I'm sorry,' said Samuel. 'You don't seem like a bad person.'

'I didn't think that I was,' said the Blacksmith. 'Or perhaps I just didn't think. And you: why are you here?'

Samuel was still wary of telling the truth about his situation, particularly after his encounter with Old Ram, but something about the Blacksmith made Samuel trust him.

'I was dragged here. A woman – a demon – called Mrs Abernathy wants to punish me.'

The Blacksmith grinned. 'So you are the boy. Even I, in this dreadful place, have heard tell of you.' He fumbled beneath his apron and brought out a piece of newspaper which he handed to Samuel. It was a cutting from an old edition of *The Infernal Times*, and it showed a picture of Samuel beneath two words:

THE ENEMY!

The article that followed, written by the editor, Mr P. Bodkin, detailed the attempt to escape from Hell through the portal, and the failure of the invasion because of the intervention of Samuel and an unknown other who had driven a car the wrong way through the portal. Samuel thought that the article was a little unfair, and only told one side of the story, but then he supposed that the editor of *The Infernal Times* might have found himself in a spot of trouble had he suggested that sending hordes of demons to invade the Earth wasn't a very nice thing to do in the first place.

'I expect she'll be looking for you,' said the Blacksmith.

'I expect so,' said Samuel.

'Well, if she comes this way I won't tell her anything. You can rely on me.'

'Thank you,' said Samuel. 'But I want to get home, and I don't know how.'

The last words caught in his throat. His eyes grew warm, but he fought away the tears. The Blacksmith discreetly looked away for a moment and then, once he was sure that Samuel was in control of his emotions, turned his attention back to the boy.

'It seems to me that if Mrs Abernathy brought you here, then she may have the means of returning you as well.'

'But she won't do that,' said Samuel. 'She wants to kill me.'

'Nevertheless, whatever power she used to drag you here can surely be used to get you back.'

'So I have to face her?'

'You have to find her, or be found by her. After that, you'll have to use your own cleverness to help you.'

'But I'm just a kid. And she's a demon.'

'A demon that you've defeated once before and can defeat again.'

'But I had help that time,' said Samuel. 'I had help from—'

He almost said Nurd's name, but he bit his tongue at the last minute. It was one thing to trust the Blacksmith with his secrets, but another thing entirely to trust him with Nurd's.

'You had help from Nurd,' said the Blacksmith, and Samuel could not conceal his shock.

'How did you know that?'

'Because I've helped him too. I've seen his vehicle. It broke down, and I helped him and his servant, Wormwood, to repair it. Then they insisted upon disguising the car, so I aided them with that as well. Mind you, they seemed intent upon disguising it as a rock, for reasons I still don't fully understand, but he's a strange one, that Nurd. I rather liked him.'

'He's my friend,' said Samuel. 'If he knew I was here, he'd help me.'

'Oh, he knows you're here,' said the Blacksmith.

'How?'

'He can feel you.' The Blacksmith patted his chest,

just where his heart once beat when he lived and perhaps still did, in some strange way. 'Can't you feel him too?'

Samuel closed his eyes, and thought hard. He pictured Nurd in his head, and remembered what they had spoken of in Samuel's bedroom when Nurd had first appeared to him. He recalled Nurd's joy at the taste of a wine gum, and his own surprise that Nurd had never before had anyone whom he could call a friend. He opened his heart to Nurd, and suddenly he had an image of him, an odd, ferret-like creature beside him that could only have been Wormwood, Nurd's hands gripping the wheel of the Aston Martin that had, until recently, been the proudest possession of Samuel's dad.

Then the image changed, and he saw Nurd and Wormwood standing beside –

Hang on, was that an ice-cream van?

Samuel called out to Nurd. He called out with his voice, and his heart. He called out with all the hope that he had left, and all his faith in the automobile-loving demon who was his friend.

He called out, and Nurd answered.

CHAPTER XXI

In Which Nurd Considers Changing His Name to 'Nurd, Unlucky in Numerous Dimensions'

Nurd, the former Scourge of Five Deities, now reformed, wondered how much bad luck a demon could have. First of all, he'd been banished to the Wasteland with Wormwood, where they had spent a very, very long time getting to know each other and wishing that they hadn't. It had been eons of utter monotony, broken only by the capacity of Wormwood's body to produce the most extraordinary odours, and Nurd amusing himself by hitting Wormwood hard on the head with a sceptre in return. Then, in the manner of a great many buses arriving together after you've been standing in the rain for hours waiting for just one, Nurd had found himself sent back and forth through a hole in space and time on no fewer than four occasions, causing his body to be stretched and then compressed in a most uncomfortable manner, as well as being crushed by a vaccuum cleaner, hit by a truck, dropped down a sewer, and then forced to face the wrath of the armies of Hell by undoing the Great Malevolence's plan to invade Earth. What was more he had managed to annoy two policemen, the very same policemen who were now staring at him balefully while surrounded by four hostile-looking dwarfs and a short-sighted ice-cream salesman.

It's just not fair, thought Nurd. All I wanted was a quiet life, and maybe some sweeties and an ice cream.

Constable Peel removed his notebook in an officious manner, licked the tip of his pencil, and prepared to write.

'Ready, Sarge,' he said.

'List of charges,' began Sergeant Rowan. 'Evading arrest. Leaving the scene of a crime, namely an attack on a house of worship by assorted dead people. Soiling a police vehicle.'

'I never did,' said Nurd.

'You made it smell,' said Sergeant Rowan.

'I fell down a sewer.'

'Nevertheless, our car has never smelled right since. Causes Constable Peel here to feel nauseous on a regular basis.'

'And it makes my uniform pong,' said Constable Peel. 'It undermines my authority, having a smelly uniform.'

Nurd was tempted to suggest that the main factor undermining Constable Peel's authority was Constable Peel himself, but decided against it. He was in enough trouble already.

'What else do we have, Constable?' asked Sergeant Rowan.

'Immigration offences?' suggested Constable Peel.

'Right you are. Improper entry. Entering Britain

without a proper visa. Entering Britain without a passport. Illegal alien, you are.'

'I'm not an alien,' Nurd corrected. 'I'm a demon.'

'Don't nit-pick. You were an illegal immigrant.'

'I didn't immigrate,' said Nurd. 'I was sent against my will.'

'You can explain it to the judge,' said Sergeant Rowan. 'Now we get on to the really interesting stuff. Damage to private property. Theft of a privately owned vehicle. Driving without a proper licence. Driving without insurance. Speeding. Theft of a police vehicle. They're going to throw away the key for you, Sonny Jim. They'll put you away for so long that by the time you get out we'll all be living on other planets.'

Nurd folded his arms. He whistled, scratched his pointy chin, then tapped his fingers against it, all of which served to communicate the following message: *Hmmm, I'm thinking here, and I seem to have spotted a fatal flaw in all that you've just told me.*

'Forgive me for pointing this out, officers, but I wasn't aware that you had jurisdiction in Hell. Biddlecombe: yes. Hell: I think not.'

'Got you there, Sergeant,' said Jolly, sticking his oar in and splashing it about merrily. 'Old Moonface is a bit of a jailhouse lawyer.'

'You keep quiet,' said Constable Peel. 'You lot are in enough trouble of your own.'

'Oooh,' said Dozy. 'Make sure you add "stealing ice cream" to our list of charges. We'll get life for that.'

'Listen, you,' said Sergeant Rowan, wagging his finger at Nurd and doing his best to ignore the Greek chorus[31] of dwarfs, 'you have a lot to answer for. You need to come down to the station and explain yourself.'

'You know, I'd actually be happy to do that,' said Nurd. 'Unfortunately, I, like you, am stuck here in Hell, and there are more pressing problems to consider.'

'Such as?'

'You're not the only humans in Hell.'

'What do you mean? Who else is here?'

'Samuel Johnson and his dog.'

Sergeant Rowan frowned. Nurd could almost hear the cogs turning in his brain. The sergeant had been one of the first on the scene after the portal closed, but he'd never managed to find out the full story. He only knew that Samuel had effectively saved the Earth, aided by an unknown person in a stolen Aston Martin who –

Who had bravely driven it into the portal, causing it to collapse.

Sergeant Rowan took a few steps forward and examined the moving rock. More particularly, he examined

---

💀 [31] Plays in ancient Greece always included a group of between twelve and twenty-four actors who would comment on the action on stage, and they were known as the 'chorus'. If you're bored, and fancy amusing your parents (and when I say 'amuse', I mean 'annoy greatly') you can form your own one-person Greek chorus by following your Mum and Dad around the house and giving them a little commentary on their comings and goings. You know: 'Mum takes milk from the fridge. Mum pours milk. Mum puts milk back. Mum tells me to stop talking about her in that weird way.' Or: 'Dad goes to the bathroom. Dad drops pants. Dad rustles newspaper. Dad tells me to go away I or I'll never receive pocket money again.' The long winter evenings will just fly by, I guarantee it.

the wheels of the rock, and then peered into the interior of the disguised car.

'Constable Peel, do you still have your notebook open?' he said.

'Yes, Sarge.'

'You know that page you've just filled with all of the charges against Mr Nurd here?'

'Yes, Sarge. I've written them all down very neatly, in case the judge wants to read them for himself.'

'Tear it out and throw it away, there's a good lad.'

'But—'

'No buts. Just do as I say.'

With considerable reluctance, Constable Peel did as he was told. He tore the page into little pieces and dropped them on the ground.

'Littering,' said a small, cheery voice from somewhere around his belly button. 'That's a fifty-quid fine.'

'Shut up,' said Constable Peel.

'It seems I may owe you an apology, sir,' said Sergeant Rowan.

'No, not really,' said Nurd. 'I did all of the things that you said, or most of them anyway.'

'Well, I think you may have made up for them. Now, what's this about Samuel Johnson?'

And Nurd did his best to explain how he had felt Samuel's presence, and how he believed that it was Mrs Abernathy who had been responsible for dragging Samuel and, by extension, the policemen, the dwarfs, and Dan, Dan the Ice-Cream Man to Hell.

'And what do you suggest we do about that?' asked Sergeant Rowan.

'We find Samuel, and then we try to discover the location of the gateway so we can get you all home,' said Nurd.

'You seem very sure that there is a gateway.'

'There has to be. Even here, certain laws apply. Wherever it is, it has to be close to Mrs Abernathy. I do have one question for you, though?'

'And what's that?' said Sergeant Rowan.

'What is that *terrible* music?'

'It's "How Much Is That Doggie in the Window?"' said Constable Peel glumly.

'Woof-woof,' said Angry, mainly out of force of habit. (He was Pavlov's Dwarf.[32])

'I told you,' said Dan. 'I can't turn it off if the engine is on, and I'm a bit worried about turning the engine off and leaving us stuck here.'

As he spoke Wormwood opened the door of the van, peered beneath the dashboard, and fiddled about a bit. Instantly, the music stopped.

'Thank you,' said Constable Peel. 'Thank you, thank you, thank you. If you didn't look like a rodent, smell funny, and have what I suspect may be a number of easily communicable diseases, I might even hug you.'

💀 [32] Ivan Pavlov (1849–1936) was a Russian scientist who signalled the arrival of his dogs' food by ringing a bell or, occasionally, giving them an electric shock, which wasn't very nice of him. He found that the dogs began producing saliva even before they tasted any food, simply because they'd heard the bell, or received a shock. This is known as 'conditioning'. You have to wonder, though, if the dogs eventually got a bit tired of the shocks and the bells and the absence of food, and made their unhappiness known to Pavlov. This is known as 'biting'.

'Nicest thing anyone has ever said to me,' Wormwood replied. He sniffled, and wiped away a little tear.

'That is a relief,' said Sergeant Rowan. 'Now, where's Samuel?'

Nurd pointed to his left. 'I think he's over there somewhere.'

'Then over there somewhere is where we're going. Lead on, sir.'

Nurd and Wormwood returned to their car, while the policemen and the dwarfs climbed back into the ice-cream van with Dan.

'Hey, what was that song again?' said Dozy, followed quickly by the words 'Ow!' and 'Never mind,' as Constable Peel made his disapproval of such questions felt.

Nurd started the ignition on the Aston Martin and pulled ahead of the van, which was soon rumbling along behind them.

Wormwood tapped Nurd on the arm.

'Look what I found in the van,' he said.

In his hand he held a bag of wine gums.

'If you ever tell anyone I said this, I shall deny it,' said Nurd, 'but, Wormwood, you're a marvel ...'

CHAPTER XXII

In Which We Learn That There Is Always Hope, As Long As One Chooses Not To Abandon It

Samuel's face wore a smile for the first time since he had arrived in that desolate place. He turned to the Blacksmith and said: 'You were right! Nurd heard me. I know he did!'

But instead of congratulating him, the Blacksmith grabbed Samuel and Boswell and threw them behind a Russian T-34 tank that was lying on its side nearby, its tracks shredded and its innards exposed by a hole that had been ripped in its armour. For a moment, Samuel thought that he had misjudged the Blacksmith and, like Old Ram, he was about to betray them, until the Blacksmith whispered to him to be quiet and stay still. Samuel saw shapes moving across the sky, their tattered wings beating, their keen eyes scouring the land below. Then the ground began to tremble, and Samuel heard the beating of hooves, and a voice said, 'Greetings, Blacksmith.'

Samuel peered around the side of the tank, his hand holding Boswell's muzzle to prevent him from barking. Above the Blacksmith loomed a black horse, three times taller than the Blacksmith himself, with the wings of a bat and yellow eyes that glowed like molten gold set into its skull. Black blood dripped from its mouth where it was biting on its bridle, and its hooves struck sparks upon the stony ground. In its saddle sat a demon with two pale horns protruding from his skull, the horns, like those of some great bull, so long and heavy it seemed almost impossible that he should be able to hold his head upright upon his shoulders. His hair was dark and long, his skin very pale, and his eyes bright with a wit and intelligence that made the cruelty writ upon his features seem somehow more terrible. He wore armour of red and gold, and a red cloak that was clasped at his neck with a tusk of bone. The cloak billowed behind him even though there was no wind to carry it, so that it seemed to have a life of its own, to be a weapon in its own right, a shroud that could suffocate and consume. The rider's saddle was heavy with weapons: a sabre, a spiked mace, and an array of knives with ornate, twisted blades.

'My Lord Abigor,' said the Blacksmith. 'I was not expecting such illustrious company.'

Abigor pulled back on the horse's reins, causing it to rear up before the Blacksmith, its monstrous hooves barely inches from his head, but the man did not flinch. Abigor, seeing that his effort to frighten the Blacksmith had proved fruitless, turned the horse and let its front hooves once again touch the ground.

'If I did not know better, I might have said that I detected a tone of mockery in your voice,' said Abigor.

'I would not dare, my lord.'

'Oh, but you would, Blacksmith. Your skill in forging

my weapons only buys you a little tolerance. Be careful how you spend it.'

The Blacksmith hung his head in shame. 'You made me forge them, on pain of greater torment. I would not have done so otherwise.'

'I do recall your misguided attempt at defiance. If I remember correctly, it died when I threatened to sever your toes.'

The Blacksmith's jaw tightened, and Samuel felt his anger. Despite Abigor's fearsome aspect, the Blacksmith was barely restraining himself from an attack. Abigor released his hold on the reins and spread his arms wide, as though daring an assault, but the Blacksmith did not take the bait, and Abigor once again resumed his hold upon the horse.

'I find that pain focuses the mind wonderfully,' continued Abigor. 'Do you need help in that department again, Blacksmith? I would be happy to oblige if I decide that you are withholding information from me.'

The Blacksmith raised his head. 'I don't know what you're talking about, my lord.'

'I seek a boy. He is a trespasser. He can't be allowed to wander freely, and I have reason to believe that he is in this area.'

'I have seen no boy. I have had no visitors since last your lordship came to me.'

'I detect no sense of sorrow that so long has passed without contact between us.'

'I will not lie to you, my lord. You come to me only when you need weapons, and it pains me to forge such implements. It is why I ended up here, and I wish now that I had not been so eager to please men of power in my past life.'

'Regrets, Blacksmith, make poor currency. You can't buy back with them what you most desire.'

'Which would be, my lord?' asked the Blacksmith, sensing that Abigor was waiting for the question to be asked.

'The past,' said Abigor. 'You are being punished for what you have done. Were it so easy to make up for one's failings, then Hell would be empty.'

'And would that be such a bad thing, my lord?'

'Only for its demons, Blacksmith. Without beings like you to humiliate, our existences would be significantly duller.'

Abigor stared at the weapons and devices scattered across the sands. 'And yet what invention you creatures display,' he said, 'what skill, all put to one end: the destruction of those most like yourselves. Sometimes, I wonder if the real demons already rule the Earth.'

'We put our skills to other uses too,' said the Blacksmith. 'We cure. We help. We protect.'

'Do you, now? But which skill does your kind value more: the willingness to help another, or the ability to wipe him out of existence?'

The Blacksmith looked down, unable to meet Abigor's eye. As he did so he saw the tracks left by Boswell and Samuel in the sand. He shifted position slightly so that his body hid them, then slowly he began to move away from Abigor, erasing the marks with his feet as he did so.

'You back away, Blacksmith,' said Abigor. 'Do you fear me so much?'

'Yes, my lord.'

Abigor tapped a clawed finger upon the horn of his saddle.

'You know, I am tempted to doubt your word. You hate me, almost as much as you hate yourself, but I don't think that you truly fear me, and I know that you do not respect me. You are a peculiar man, Blacksmith, but perhaps such strangeness comes with your gifts. And you have seen no sign of a boy, you say?'

'No, I have not,' said the Blacksmith. The traces of paws and footprints were now entirely gone from Abigor's sight. Samuel noticed that the Blacksmith's voice had changed, and he no longer referred to the demon Abigor as 'my lord'.

'But would you tell me if you had, Blacksmith? I have always suspected your loyalties. Sometimes I wonder how you ended up here. I fear there may be a spark of goodness in you, a flicker of conscience, that has not yet been extinguished. One might even call it hope.'

'I have no hope. I left it in my past life.'

Abigor leaned forward. He drew back his lips, exposing perfect white fangs.

'But not your talent for weaponry. There is a war coming, Blacksmith. You may have thought yourself forgotten by others, but the promise of conflict will recall you to them once again. My rivals will seek you out for your skills. What will you do then, Blacksmith?'

'I will turn them down.'

'Will you, now? I think not. Their capacity for inflicting hurt is almost as great as mine. Almost, but not quite. Even if you were loyal to me, which you are not, your loyalty would not be great enough to stand against such pain. So I have decided to demonstrate both my wisdom and my mercy by relieving you of the burden of being forced to betray me in order to end your suffering.'

Abigor drew his sabre, and with a single slashing motion he cut off the Blacksmith's head. The sword rose and fell, rose and fell, over and over until the Blacksmith lay in pieces upon the ground. The Blacksmith's eyes still blinked, and his hands still moved, the fingers clawing at the dirt like the legs of insects. No blood flowed from his wounds, but his face was contorted with agony. From the sky, an imp descended. It picked up the Blacksmith's hands and flew away with them while Abigor stared down at the work of his sword.

'Even were someone to reconstitute you, you could do nothing without your hands. Goodbye, Blacksmith. We will not meet again.'

With that, Abigor urged on his steed. It galloped away, and then its wings began to beat and it rose up into the sky and vanished into the clouds.

Samuel emerged from his hiding place and ran to where the Blacksmith's remains lay.

'You could have told him where I was,' said Samuel. 'You could have told him, and he might have spared you. I'm sorry. I'm so sorry.'

'Don't be,' said the Blacksmith, 'for I am not.'

And as he spoke, his expression changed. He looked puzzled, and his face became filled with a soft glow tinged faintly with amber, like the reflected light of a slowly setting sun.

'There is no pain,' he said. 'It is gone.' He smiled at Samuel. 'I did not betray you. I have redeemed myself. Now, there is peace.'

Slowly, the pieces of his poor, butchered body faded away, and Samuel and Boswell were alone once more.

The Aston Martin and the ice-cream van were hidden beneath the heads of giant green toadstools that had sprouted from an area of damp, noisome earth, a forest of them that extended for miles. Nurd and Wormwood, along with the policemen and the dwarfs, watched as flights of demons passed overhead, some circling and descending, then ascending again once they had examined more closely whatever had attracted their attention on the ground. After a time a great black steed broke through the clouds above and passed among their ranks, their rider urging the demons to ever greater effort. His voice even carried to the odd little group watching him from below.

'Find the boy!' he cried. 'Bring him to me!'

'I don't like the look of him,' said Jolly.

'I don't like the look of any of them,' said Dozy.

'Who's the big lad on the horse, then?' Angry asked Nurd.

'Duke Abigor,' said Nurd. He sounded distracted. This wasn't right. He had to assume that Abigor and his minions were looking for Samuel, but Samuel could only have been brought here by Mrs Abernathy and Duke Abigor and Mrs Abernathy hated each other. Duke Abigor would do nothing to aid Mrs Abernathy, yet now here he was, using his minions to search for the human Mrs Abernathy loathed above all others. It could only mean that Abigor wanted Samuel for his own purposes.

'Whose side is he on?' asked Sergeant Rowan.

'His own,' said Nurd. 'He's looking for Samuel.'

'Why?'

'Perhaps because if he has Samuel, then Mrs Abernathy doesn't. Samuel is her way back to power, and Duke Abigor doesn't want that. Duke Abigor wants to rule. I think that if he could find a way to get rid of the Great Malevolence himself then he'd do it, but he can't, so he'll have to settle for being second-in-command. To succeed, he has to ensure that Mrs Abernathy is out of the picture. That means taking away any hope she has of regaining the Great Malevolence's trust, and her only hope of that is to present him with Samuel.'

Sergeant Rowan looked at Nurd with a new respect. 'When did you get so clever?'

'When I realized that I wasn't as clever as I thought,' Nurd replied. 'We have to move. Samuel is nearby. I'm certain of it.'

But even as he spoke his sense of Samuel's presence began to diminish, and he felt the boy's spirit start to weaken. Something was very wrong, and Nurd willed Samuel to keep going and not to give up.

Hold on, Samuel, he thought. Hold on for just a little while longer . . .

Samuel and Boswell had left behind the crater of weapons, and the memory of the Blacksmith's bravery. In the distance Samuel could see hills. He decided to head in that direction. He and Boswell might be able to find a place to hide there, for they were too vulnerable out here upon the open plain. But he was so tired. He could barely drag one foot along after the other, and he was also carrying Boswell, who was exhausted and had begun limping. Samuel's nostrils burned and his lungs hurt from breathing the noxious air, tinged as it was with the stink of sulphur. His head grew lower with his spirits, for it seemed that his only hope of returning to his own world lay with the very woman he most wished to avoid. He understood the Blacksmith's logic, but he did not want to face Mrs Abernathy again. None of this was fair. He wished that he'd never seen the stupid portal, never tried to save the Earth, never met Nurd.

He shook his head. Where had that thought come from? It wasn't true. Nurd was his friend. How could he think such a thing of a friend? But if Nurd was his friend, then where was he? Samuel had called out to him, but still he had not come. Perhaps Nurd didn't care, and was just like all the rest. Even his father had abandoned him, and his mother had done nothing to prevent it, nothing. What was the point in continuing if even your own parents couldn't be bothered to behave as they should?

He stopped walking. Ahead of him was a vast expanse of pure nothingness, a void that appeared to open blackly before him but was not really black at all, because at least 'black' was something.[33] The hole in time and space into which he and Boswell now stared was a relic of non-existence, the last trace of all that had not been before the Multiverse was created. Looking into it made Samuel's head hurt, because it had no length, or width, or depth. It had no gravity, nor could energy be transmitted through it. What Samuel and Boswell were seeing was not just the end of this dimension, and this universe, but the beginning and end of all universes, and as they gazed upon it they felt a great sadness overcome them; their spirits fell, and their will to continue was finally sapped, for clever young boys and smart, loyal dogs were never meant to face the bleakness of absolute nothingness. Slowly Samuel sank down, Boswell beside him, and together they looked into the void, and the void began to enter them.

💀 [33] When we see colours, what we're really seeing is a certain frequency and wavelength of light hitting our eyes. Photons, which are units of light, have to leave an object in order for us to pick up on pink, or blue, or that strange brown colour only found in damp earth and school uniforms. Without atoms, there can be no photons, and thus no colour, not even black. There is a school of philosophy known as Existentialism which takes the view that life is all a lot of nothing, really, and as a consequence we are all in a state of constant despair. Unsurprisingly, existentialists don't get invited to many birthday parties.

CHAPTER XXIII

In Which Mrs Abernathy Loses Her Temper, and We Meet Up Again with an Unpleasant Personage from Earlier In Our Tale

Mrs Abernathy's voice rose to a shriek. Even the Watcher was taken aback at its volume and intensity.

'*Nurd*?' screamed Mrs Abernathy. 'Nurd? You're telling me that imbecile, that miserable excuse for a demon, is responsible for all this? But I banished him. I sent him to the Wasteland with his idiot servant where he couldn't be a nuisance any more. How could –? How did – ? I mean –'

Probably for the first time ever, words failed Mrs Abernathy. Nurd? But he was so inconsequential, so inept, or so it had seemed. How could she have misjudged him so badly? She began to feel what might almost have been admiration for him, even if it was the kind that came before you began inflicting serious pain on the object of said admiration. The scale of what he had achieved, the great enterprise that he had managed to undo, was almost inconceivable. For a moment, the revelation of Nurd's perfidy drove the Watcher's second piece of news – the message from Old Ram that he had Samuel Johnson nearby – from her mind, but it quickly returned.

'I'll deal with Nurd later,' she said. 'For now, Samuel Johnson is our priority. You should have come to me before now, Watcher. I am disappointed in you.'

Had the Watcher been an entity of a different stripe, it might have felt obliged to protest at the unfairness of this, if only to obscure its other reason for remaining silent. After all, Mrs Abernathy had been variously unconscious, over-concerned with her own vanity, and too keen on finding out the identities of those who were plotting against her to even allow the Watcher into her presence. It wasn't entirely its fault that it had taken so long to relay Old Ram's news to her. But the Watcher was not the kind of entity to complain, and had it done so Mrs Abernathy would not have listened, so it forced such thoughts from its mind even as it wondered if thinking them was enough to make it a complainer after all.

Mrs Abernathy spun on her heel, and the Watcher followed. Behind her lair was a stone courtyard, and in the courtyard a massive crested basilisk[34] stood, saddled and ready. It hissed a greeting at its mistress as she

☠ [34] In mythology, the basilisk was known as the 'King of Serpents' because of its crown-shaped crest. Ascribed to it were variously the capacity to kill with its gaze, its breath, or the sound of its cry. It was even said that if a soldier pierced its skin with a spear, the poison in the basilisk's blood would flow up the weapon and kill its assailant. It was rumoured to be hatched by a rooster from the egg of a toad or serpent, thus providing an interesting variation on the question of which came first, the chicken or the egg. Actually, scientists believe that they have now proved the chicken came first, given that a particular protein in eggshells can only be produced inside a chicken. Mind you, it was probably a very surprised chicken that pushed out the first egg: '*Cluck!* Mavis, dear – *cluck, cluck* – you won't believe what's just fallen out of my bottom . . .'

climbed into the saddle. Spurs of bone emerged from Mrs Abernathy's heels, and she urged the creature towards the Forest of Broken Forms, the Watcher shadowing her from above.

Samuel was no longer angry at his mother. In fact, Samuel could no longer remember what his mother looked like. He knew that he had a mother, once, but he could not picture her in his mind. Likewise his father was a blur, but it didn't matter. Nothing really mattered. The void coursed through him, emptying him of all feelings and memories, turning him into a husk, a hollow being. Beside Samuel, Boswell whined and tried to lick his master's hand, but his strength was seeping from him. The sound caused Samuel to turn. He stared down at the dog and struggled to recall his name. Bos-something? Was that it?

And then even that was gone as the light in his eyes began to die.

Mrs Abernathy's basilisk stopped at the edge of the Forest of Broken Forms, beside the ruins of Old Ram's home. She searched among the stones, half expecting to see Samuel Johnson buried in the rubble, but there was no sign of the boy, or of Old Ram. When she examined the ground, and saw the tracks left by the Great Oak, she knew what had happened here. With the Watcher at her heels, she entered the forest, the trees recoiling in terror, clearing a path for her until she and the basilisk reached the Great Oak. Unlike its smaller brethren, it showed no fear of her. If anything it was

Mrs Abernathy who seemed wary of the massive tree, with its coiling roots and its twisted branches. Mrs Abernathy might have been evil incarnate, and capable of acts of immense cruelty and harm, but the Great Oak was ancient, and strong, and dangerous. The vestiges of its humanity made it so.

The Great Oak was also insane, the result of millennia of misery and racked growth. Its madness rendered it unpredictable, and Mrs Abernathy knew that it would not be beyond the Great Oak's capabilities to try to hurt her, or trap her with its roots and keep her here for its own amusement, torturing her as it had been tortured for so long, avenging some of its pain by visiting pain on another. She knew she was especially vulnerable now that she was no longer under the protection of the Great Malevolence, and she was glad of the Watcher's presence beside her.

'It has been a long time since last you set foot here,' said the Great Oak. 'You were not welcome then, and you are not welcome now.'

'What have you done with Old Ram?'

'No more than he deserved,' said the Great Oak, and its trunk split open beneath its gaping mouth like a vertical wound, revealing a hollow interior in which Old Ram hung suspended by ivy, moaning softly as branches tugged and tore at him, and roots dug into his flesh.

'There was a boy with him,' said Mrs Abernathy.

'Boy?' said the Great Oak. 'I saw no boy.'

And Mrs Abernathy heard the surrounding trees laugh.

'Don't lie to me. Do you have the boy?'

'There is no boy here,' said the Great Oak, and Mrs Abernathy sensed that it spoke the truth.

'Then let Old Ram go,' she said.

'And why should I do that, when I enjoy toying with him so much?'

'I must talk with him, and I can't do that while you're hurting him.'

The ivy uncurled, the roots and branches retreated, and Old Ram was released from bondage. He climbed through the gap in the tree and knelt before Mrs Abernathy.

'Thank you,' he said, stroking her feet with his clawed upper hooves. 'Thank you, kind mistress, thank you.'

'The boy,' said Mrs Abernathy. 'Tell me about the boy.'

'Old Ram was holding him for you, him and his dog. He was sleeping, and he trusted Old Ram. Then Great Oak came and tore Old Ram's home apart, and the boy escaped. Old Ram saw him crawl away, but Old Ram could do nothing to stop him. It is all the fault of the Great Oak. Punish him! Punish him!'

Mrs Abernathy turned to the Great Oak.

'Is this true?'

The Great Oak creaked and rustled. 'Old Ram had hurt us. It was Old Ram who had to be punished. I did not know that the boy was yours. It was . . . my mistake.'

The Great Oak lowered two of its biggest branches, as though they were arms and he was extending them in supplication. Suddenly, they slashed at Mrs Abernathy, smaller branches as sharp as knives radiating from their ends. Its roots erupted from the ground at her feet, twisting around her legs. The Watcher grabbed Mrs Abernathy and tried to take flight, but now the surrounding trees were closing in and there was not room for the Watcher's wings to unfold. Mrs Abernathy's basilisk spat venom, instantly rotting branches and roots, but the trees were too many, and lengths of ivy coiled around the basilisk's mouth, forcing it shut; mud and filth were forced into its eyes, obscuring its lethal gaze. Meanwhile Old Ram cowered in the dirt, his hooves curled over his head, bleating in misery and alarm.

Six thick tentacles erupted from Mrs Abernathy's back, topped with sharp beaks that snapped at the branches and nipped at the roots, but the Great Oak was too strong, and too intent upon hurting Mrs Abernathy now that she was within reach. Slowly, she and the Watcher were being enveloped. Already the Watcher's arms were pinned to its sides, and Mrs Abernathy was concealed from the waist down by twisted roots.

'Come to the Great Oak,' said the old tree. 'Come, and be part of us.'

Mrs Abernathy's eyes began to glow whitely. She opened her mouth and clicked her tongue, and a small blue flame appeared between her teeth. She drew a deep breath into her lungs, then exhaled. Fire burst from her lips, a torrent of light and heat that struck at the heart of the Great Oak, igniting it both inside and out. It roared in pain, and instantly its branches and roots began to retreat, freeing Mrs Abernathy and the Watcher. The

Watcher spread his wings and carried them both
upwards and out of the forest as the other trees bent
away from the flames, crying out in fear as the Great
Oak's struggles sent blue sparks in their direction. The
basilisk freed itself and tore a path through the remaining
trees, and Old Ram fled with it, running on all fours
until he found himself at last beside what was left of
his home, where Mrs Abernathy was waiting for him.

'The boy,' she said. 'Which way did he go?'

Old Ram pointed to his right. 'He was hiding behind
those boulders, and that was the last Old Ram saw of
him, but he could not have gone far. He is a child in a
strange land, with only a dog for company. Let Old
Ram come with you. Old Ram can help you find him.
Old Ram is tired of this place.'

He looked back at the forest as blue flame rose from
its heart, and he shivered.

'And the Great Oak will recover, and will come again
for Old Ram,' he whispered.

Mrs Abernathy strode to her basilisk and mounted
it. As she did so she saw two pale demons circling high
above, drawn by the flames in the forest, and she knew
them to be Abigor's.

'Go where you will,' she said. 'But if anyone asks
you about the boy, deny all knowledge of him. If you
do otherwise, I will hear of it, and I will have you tied
and bound, and let the Great Oak have his way with
you for ever.'

Old Ram nodded, and thanked her again. Mrs
Abernathy and the Watcher waited until Abigor's
demons had descended to the forest before they took

off themselves, travelling fast and true, until the basilisk found the trail of footsteps and paw prints left by Samuel and Boswell.

And they knew that he was near.

CHAPTER XXIV

In Which We Speculate On What, If Anything, Might Be Worse Than Evil

If there is anything worse than evil, it is nothingness. At least evil has a form, and a voice, and a purpose, however depraved. Perhaps some good can even come out of evil: a terrible deed of violence against someone weaker may lead others to act in order to ensure that such a deed is not perpetrated again, whereas before they might have been unaware of the reasons why an individual might behave in such a way, or they might simply have chosen to ignore them. And evil, as we saw with the Blacksmith, always contains within itself the possibility of its own redemption. It is not evil that is the enemy of hope: it is nothingness.

As Nurd felt Samuel's life force ebb away, so too did he come to realize just where the boy was. Even in the grim, blasted regions of Hell, there was only one place that could cause such a loss of self, eating away at all the substance of an individual, all that he loved and hated, all that he was and ever would be. It was the Void, the Emptiness, the Eternal Absence that even the Great Malevolence himself feared. So Nurd kept his foot pressed hard upon the accelerator and found himself pulling away from the ice-cream van, loaded down as it was with dwarfs, policemen, and rapidly dwindling supplies of ice cream. But as he drew closer to Samuel so too was the light in Samuel's soul fading. Nurd felt as though he were trying to reach a candle flame before it flickered for the last time, that he might wrap his hands around it and feed it the oxygen it needed to survive. Nurd knew that if Samuel continued to stare into the Void he would eventually be lost entirely, and nobody would ever be able to bring him back. Samuel and Boswell would become like statues of flesh and bone, with an empty place where their spirits once were (for animals have spirits too, and let no one tell you otherwise). Having endured so much, and having been separated by space and time only to be offered the chance of a reunion at last by Mrs Abernathy's vengeance, Nurd did not wish to see his friend's essence sacrificed to the emptiness that underlay the chaos of Hell.

Faster and faster he drove, until Wormwood put a hand on his arm in warning, for now there were sharp and treacherous stones beneath their wheels. Were they to suffer a puncture or, worse, rupture the engine or break an axle, then Samuel and Boswell would not be saved. Reluctantly Nurd slowed down, while high above their heads unseen eyes watched their progress, and reported it to others.

Samuel was almost entirely still. His eyes did not blink, his lips did not open, and he barely seemed to be breathing. Yet had anyone been watching him, they would have seen one small sign of movement. For even as all that had made him what he was – every memory, every thought, every spark of brightness and eccentricity – was being consumed, his right hand continued to stroke Boswell's fur, and, in response, his dog's tail contributed the barest thump on the ground, but a thump nonetheless. Had Boswell not been present, Samuel would already have ceased to exist, leaving nothing more than the shell of a boy seated on the edge of a dark sea; and if Samuel had not been present, Boswell would have been little more than a stuffed animal withering away. But if a child loves an animal, and is loved in turn, there will always be a connection between them: they are spirits intertwined. And if the Void had feelings, which it clearly did not, it might well have experienced a sense of frustration at its inability to break down the defences of the boy and the dog. Deep inside each of them was a wall protecting the best of themselves, but it was crumbling at last, like a dam finally giving way to the flood, and soon they would be drowned. The movements of Samuel's hand began to slow, and the thumps of Boswell's tail became less frequent, and their eyes grew dim as never-ending night fell upon their hearts.

A hand touched Samuel's shoulder, and gently turned him from the darkness. And Boswell was carefully gathered up, and words of comfort were whispered into his ear.

'Good dog. Loyal dog. Brave Boswell.'

Samuel heard a name being called, over and over, and understood that it was his own.

He looked up and saw four dwarfs, two policemen, and a man dressed in white offering him an ice cream. He saw Boswell being held by what looked like a bald rodent in overalls, and the little dog was licking the rodent's face.

And he saw Nurd. Samuel buried his head against his friend's breast, and for the first time since his arrival in that terrible place he allowed himself to cry.

Old Ram left the forest behind, sulking and muttering his discontent all the way, his gaze focused inward, fixed upon his own sufferings. Sometimes a good turn is the worst that you can do for a certain type of individual, because he will hate you for putting him in your debt. Mrs Abernathy had spared Old Ram any further misery, and had permitted him to leave the place of his banishment, but Old Ram had wanted more: he had wanted influence, and recognition. He had wanted power. Instead he had been left to wander in the wilderness. He began to think that he was now worse off than he had been before. After all, he used to have a roof over his head, and fuel for his fire, but what did he have now? No roof, no fuel, and the cold was seeping into his bones. For this, he blamed Mrs Abernathy.

'She hates Old Ram,' he whispered to himself. 'She thinks Old Ram is worthless, but Old Ram is not. Old Ram was great once, and Old Ram could be great again, but none will give Old Ram the chance that Old Ram deserves. Poor Old Ram! Poor forsaken Old Ram!'

So caught up was he in bitterness that he failed to notice the winged horse alight before him, and the flight of demons that quietly descended behind him. It was only when the horse blew a bad-tempered blast of air through its nostrils in warning that Old Ram looked up to find Duke Abigor staring down at him.

'You are far from home, Old Ram,' said Abigor. 'Were you not banished, and forbidden to leave the precincts of the forest?'

'I was, my lord, but Mrs Abernathy freed me.'

'Did she, now? And why would she do that?'

Old Ram, mindful of Mrs Abernathy's injunction to remain silent about the circumstances of his freedom, said nothing, but Duke Abigor was as clever as he was ruthless. He knew much about Old Ram, and was aware that, like so many who had found themselves damned to the Infernal Regions, his vanity was his weakness. Were Abigor to threaten him, or torture him, Old Ram might simply endure his sufferings with clenched teeth, if only to prove to Abigor that, humbled though he might be, Old Ram had his pride. No, there were easier ways to deal with Old Ram.

'Well, no matter,' said Abigor airily. 'It strikes me only that you don't sound very pleased, even though your long period of exile has come to an end. Surely such generosity of spirit on the part of Mrs Abernathy merits a greater show of gratitude?'

He watched Old Ram twist and writhe, a pantomime of hurt, and envy, and loathing.

'Gratitude.' Old Ram spat the word. 'For what? It cost her nothing, and left Old Ram with nothing. Old Ram tried to help her. It's not Old Ram's fault that—'

Old Ram stopped talking. Mrs Abernathy had

warned him not to speak of the boy, but she wasn't here. Duke Abigor was here though, and Old Ram wondered why that might be. Abigor's presence, thought Old Ram, might be used to some advantage.

'Go on,' said Abigor. 'I'm listening.'

'Old Ram has been alone for a long time, my lord,' said Old Ram carefully. 'Old Ram seeks a master. Old Ram would be a good servant.'

'I already have more servants than I need. You would have to offer me something that no one else can.'

Old Ram's yellow eyes narrowed with cunning.

'Mrs Abernathy made Old Ram promise not to tell, but it may be that Old Ram was wrong to make that promise.'

'Promises are made to be broken,' said Abigor. 'Particularly promises made in the face of a threat.'

'Old Ram has no duty of loyalty to Mrs Abernathy.'

'No, he does not. After all, what fealty do you owe to the one who banished you? The greater fault is hers, not yours. So, what can you offer to prove your loyalty to me?'

'I can offer you news,' said Old Ram, 'news of a human child.'

Mrs Abernathy's basilisk reached the edge of the Void just behind the Watcher, and she quickly turned her mount's head away from the emptiness so that neither of them looked upon it for too long. Even the Watcher kept its head down as it examined the tracks on the ground. Its words echoed in her head.

It is the boy and his dog. They were here. Others came and took them away.

'Others?' demanded Mrs Abernathy. 'What others?'

The Watcher sniffed the ground.

Nurd. And humans. Seven humans.

'Can you track them?'

The Watcher stared out over the stony ground, finding the places in which the stones had been disturbed, distinguishing the marks of wheeled vehicles.

Yes, but they travel fast.

'Then we will travel faster.'

She moved on, not even checking to make sure that the Watcher was following, and so she did not see it pause, its red brow furrowing. All of this was wrong, thought the Watcher. It has all spiralled out of control. My master is mad, and my mistress may be madder still. Something must be done. The bells have been silent for too long. Perhaps the time is coming when they must peal again.

Old Ram's tongue, once loosened, unburdened itself of all its secrets. He told Duke Abigor of the boy, and the attack by the Great Oak, and Mrs Abernathy's appearance in the forest. He told him of how he had seen the boy hide, and the direction in which he must have walked. As he spoke, he saw Abigor's face darken in anger.

'The Blacksmith lied,' said Abigor. 'He must have seen the boy, but he would not speak of it.'

He turned to one of his demons, who had only just alighted, and ordered it to retrieve the remaining pieces of the Blacksmith, that he might punish him further. He asked first for the Blacksmith's severed hands, that he might crush them so the Blacksmith could never use them again, but the sack containing the Blacksmith's hands was empty. A second demon, who had recently been patrolling the skies for signs of the boy, approached them and told Abigor that the Blacksmith had disappeared, for it had passed over the crater of weapons and detected no sign of him. Furthermore, it said that there had been a peculiar smell in the air: the smell of virtue, of decency, of *humanity*. The Blacksmith, in the demon's opinion, was gone for ever. His soul was no longer in Hell.

Abigor stifled his rage. He had always sensed a fault in the Blacksmith, some residue of hope and decency that should have been snuffed out long before, but he could never have imagined that it would be enough to redeem him. The Blacksmith had not merely been a soul filled with regret, he was a soul who had genuinely repented, even with no prospect that it might end his sufferings, for he must surely have believed that he was damned to Hell for eternity. But repentance would not have been enough; a sacrifice would have been required. The boy, Samuel Johnson, had saved the Blacksmith by allowing the maker of weapons to offer himself up on behalf of another, one worthy of the gesture. Samuel Johnson was a Good Soul, for only such a soul could survive in this place; survive, and provide sustenance to the soul of another. The boy was dangerous, more so than even Mrs Abernathy realized. His presence in Hell was a pollutant. He had to be locked away, hidden from sight. He could not be killed: a mortal could not die in Hell. Nothing could. It was a place of endless torment, and endless torment required the absence of death.

A shadow passed over him, and another of his demons alighted by his side. It announced that it had followed two moving carts as they had passed into the stony place that led to the Void, and there it had watched as the boy and his pet were gathered into safety. It had stayed with them for a time until it was sure of the direction that they were taking, before returning to inform its master.

'Quickly!' cried Abigor. 'Rise up, rise up! Apprehend the boy and bring him to me.'

The demons took flight like crows from the noise of a gun. Duke Abigor was about to follow them into the sky when Old Ram tugged at his horse's reins.

'What about Old Ram?' he said. 'Old Ram told you all. What about Old Ram's reward?'

Duke Abigor's horse reared up, and one of its hooves struck Old Ram a blow to the head, sending him sprawling to the ground.

'How can I trust a pitiful creature who would break a promise, and betray one master for another?' said Duke Abigor. 'There is only one reward for a traitor.'

He raised a clawed finger, and Old Ram's world went black for a time. When he awoke he was trapped in ice, with only his horned head above the surface of the great frozen lake of Cocytus that extended as far as the eye could see, the icy whiteness of it broken only by others like himself: traitors all, betrayers of family and friends, of lords and masters.

Old Ram's teeth began to chatter, for Old Ram hated the cold.

CHAPTER XXV

In Which a Familiar Odour Sends the Dwarfs' Spirits Soaring

There were a great many things that Wormwood had never expected to see in the course of his existence – a tree that didn't want to tear him apart, for example, or a demon that just fancied a bit of a chat and a warm hug instead of inflicting misery and hurt and generally making a nuisance of itself – but high on that list, perhaps higher even than Someplace Other Than Hell, was Nurd showing a genuine, positive emotion. But as he watched Nurd and Samuel hug, and heard them begin to chatter at high speed about all that had happened since last they had met, and saw a big, sloppy tear drop from one of Nurd's eyes, slide down his face, and perform a little jump into the air from the end of his chin, Wormwood thought that if such a thing as Nurd weeping for joy was possible, then anything might be.

'Got something in my eye,' said Jolly, as the friends enjoyed their reunion. He gave a little sniff.

'Very moving,' said Angry, dabbing at his nose with a sleeve that had clearly been used for that same purpose a great many times in the past, and consequently resembled a race track for snails.

'Seeing people happy always makes me want an ice cream,' said Dozy. 'Seriously.'

'Arfle,' said Mumbles, in what might have been agreement.

They looked hopefully at Dan, Dan the Ice-Cream Man, who brandished an empty cone at them.

'There isn't any more ice cream,' said Dan. 'You've eaten it all. I didn't think it was possible, but you have. You're monsters, all of you.'

'Oh well,' said Dozy, 'I'll just have to be happy without one, then, but it won't be the same.'

He returned to watching Nurd and Samuel.

'Come along, you lot,' said Sergeant Rowan gently. 'Let's not make it a spectator sport.'

Somewhat reluctantly, because they were sentimental little men despite themselves, the dwarfs turned away.

Samuel and Nurd walked a short distance, Boswell trotting along happily beside them. They sat on a flat stone while each considered what the other had just told him.

'So you've been hiding away all this time?' said Samuel.

'Well, running and hiding,' said Nurd. 'You see, I'm not sure that Mrs Abernathy knows I was the one who collapsed the portal. She knows about the car, of course, but not about me, so Wormwood came up with the idea of disguising it as a rock.'

Samuel looked at the disguised Aston Martin; the rock exterior – actually a sheet of thin metal beaten and painted to resemble stone – was held in place by struts that sat upon the body of the car, with gauze replacing metal in front of the windows so that the driver had a clear view to the front, the sides, and behind him. There was actually a kind of brilliance to the idea, as long as nobody saw it moving. Then again, thought Samuel, this was Hell, and moving rocks might well exist somewhere in its depths, presumably with diamond teeth to help them munch on smaller rocks that couldn't defend themselves.

'But how did you find me?' asked Samuel. 'I mean, Hell is a big place, isn't it?'

'I've heard it said that it's infinite, or if it isn't it's as close to infinite as to make no difference. If it isn't infinite, then nobody has been able to find the end yet.[35] And if you include the Void, well . . .'

Samuel shuddered at the thought of how he had

💀 [35] Tricky business, infinity, and a lot harder to explain than one might think. One of the more interesting theoretical manifestations of infinity, and the problems and paradoxes associated with it, was proposed by David Hilbert, and takes the form of Hilbert's Hotel. Hilbert's Hotel is always full, but whenever a new guest arrives the hotel can always find room for him, because it's an infinite hotel with an infinite number of rooms. So, if a new guest arrives, he gets put in Room 1, the person in Room 1 moves to Room 2, and so on. Then an infinite coach, full of an infinite number of people, arrives, but the hotel can still fit them in. The manager moves all of the current guests into a room with a number twice as large as their current room – so Room 1 moves into Room 2, 2 to 4, 3 to 6, and so on. This means that an infinite number of odd-numbered rooms are now available for the infinite coach filled with an infinite number of guests. Unfortunately, Hilbert's Hotel can't exist in the real world because there are only ten to the power of eighty atoms in the universe, so there isn't enough matter to create an infinite-sized hotel. You wouldn't want to stay in it anyway: if you ordered room service, the food would take a long time to arrive, and it would always be cold; and if you forgot your key you'd have a terribly long walk back to reception.

almost lost himself in that emptiness. He could still feel a coldness deep inside him, and he wasn't sure if that element of himself touched by the Void would ever fully recover.

'Anyway,' continued Nurd, 'I sensed you as soon as you arrived. There's always been a part of me that's stayed connected to you. I don't know how, or why, but I'm grateful for it.'

'You used to turn up in my dreams sometimes,' said Samuel. 'We'd have conversations.'

'And you in mine,' said Nurd. 'I wonder if we were talking about the same things.'

But before they could continue an anxious-looking Wormwood approached, with Constable Peel close behind. Wormwood was about to say something, but Nurd stopped him with a raised hand.

'Samuel, I'd like to introduce you properly to someone. Samuel Johnson, this is my, well, this is my friend and colleague, Wormwood.'

And Wormwood, who had been called a lot of names by Nurd in his time, but never 'friend', stopped short as though he'd walked into an invisible wall. He blushed, then beamed.

'Hello, Wormwood,' said Samuel. 'It's good to meet you at last.'

'And you, Mr Samuel.'

'Just Samuel. I'm sorry if I was a bit quiet in the car. I wasn't quite myself then.'

'No apologies necessary,' said Wormwood.

Samuel extended his hand and Wormwood shook it, noticing that, when Samuel took his hand away, he didn't try to wipe it on his trousers, or on the ground, or on someone else. It really was a day of firsts for Wormwood.

A cough from Constable Peel, followed by a finger pointed at the sky, brought Wormwood back to reality with a vengeance.

'Oh yes. We need to get moving,' said Wormwood. 'Constable Peel has seen things circling below the clouds. We're being watched.'

They all looked up. The clouds had grown darker and heavier in the time that Samuel had been staring into nothingness, the thunder louder, and the lightning brighter.

'There's a storm coming anyway,' said Nurd. 'We have to get under cover.'

As they looked up, a winged figure broke through the clouds and hovered for a moment. To Samuel it looked at first like a bird with an elongated body, but then it dropped lower and he could pick out its forked tail, its bat wings, and the horns on its head. He thought that he could feel its interest in them before it twisted in the air and shot back into the clouds again.

'There,' said Constable Peel. 'Last time there were two of them.'

Nurd frowned. If Constable Peel was correct, it meant that one was keeping an eye on them while the other went off and informed of their presence. The question was: who was being informed?

Within sight of where they stood was a range of red-hued hills, the same hills that Samuel and Boswell had been making for when they encountered the Void. The hills were separated from them by what appeared to be marshland, over which hung a particularly noxious mist. Nurd knew that the hills were pitted with holes and caves. In any other part of Hell, they would probably have been turned into lairs for unspeakable creatures, but even the residents of Hell preferred to keep their distance from the Void, which was still visible from the higher points of the range.

'We can find a place to hide over there,' said Nurd. 'After that, we can try to plan our next move.'

They all piled into their respective vehicles, and Nurd led them in the direction of the hills, carefully steering a path through the stinking marshes. He was forced to roll down the windows so that he could peer out and check their progress, which made the car smell awful. At one point Samuel saw an eyeball protrude from the swamp, held up by a hand.

'What is it, Gertrude?' Samuel heard a voice say.

'Nigel, I do believe that there's an oik driving two other oiks and a small thingy through our garden.'

A second eyeball popped out of the water.

'I say, you chaps, bit of a cheek, what?'

'Sorry,' said Samuel. 'We didn't know it was your garden. We'll try not to make a mess of it.'

'It's a *swamp*,' hissed Nurd. 'If we did make a mess of it, it could only be an improvement.'

'Heard that!' said Nigel. Another hand emerged from the swamp and made itself into a fist, which it shook in the direction of Nurd's car. 'I'll give you what-for, and no mistake. Taking liberties with another chap's property, insulting his gardening skills. I mean, what's

Hell coming to, Gertrude? I'll get me sticks.' Both hands duly disappeared beneath the swamp.

'Quite right, Nigel,' said Gertrude, just as the ice-cream van emerged from the mist. 'Look! There's another one. I say, it's full of little fellows. How sweet!'

The dwarfs crowded to the serving hatch of the van, joined by Constable Peel.

'You don't see one of those every day,' said Jolly.

'No,' said Angry. 'You usually see two of them. Oi, darling, keeping an eye on us, are you? See what I did there, eh: keeping "an eye"?'

'Mind you don't drop it, love,' said Dozy. 'You won't have anything to look for it with.'

Gertrude, wisely, began to reconsider her opinion of the dwarfs. 'What dreadful little men,' she said, just as her husband's eyeball appeared beside her, and various hands brandishing sticks, clubs and, oddly, a stick of rhubarb.

'Come away from them, dear,' said Nigel. 'They're common, vulgar types. You never know what you might catch.'

'Common?' said Angry. 'We may be common, but we've earned the right to be unpleasant.'

'Sweat of our brows,' said Jolly. 'You've just inherited rudeness. We've had to work at it.'

'You're peasants!' shouted Nigel. 'Vandals! Get off my land!'

'Nyah!' shouted Angry, sticking his tongue out and wiggling his hands behind his ears in that timeless gesture of disrespect beloved in schoolyards every-where. 'Get a proper job!'

They emerged on to firmer ground, leaving the swamp behind. The dwarfs looked very pleased with themselves, and even Constable Peel and Sergeant Rowan seemed to have enjoyed the exchange.

'I love a good shout,' said Jolly.

'We should visit them on the way back,' said Dozy. 'I liked them. Eh, Jolly?'

But Jolly wasn't listening. Instead he was sniffing the air.

'Can you smell that?' he said.

'It's the swamp,' said Angry.

'No, it's different.'

'That was me,' said Dozy. 'It's all the ice cream. Sorry.'

'No, not that,' said Jolly. '*That.*'

They all sniffed.

'Nah,' said Angry, 'it can't be.'

'We're dreaming,' said Dozy.

'It's . . .' said Jolly, so overcome with emotion that he could barely speak. 'It's . . .'

'It's a brewery,' said Mumbles.

Everybody in the van looked at him, even Dan, who could barely see at the best of times.

'You spoke clearly,' said Jolly.

'I know,' said Mumbles. 'But this is important.'

And, to be fair, it was.

CHAPTER XXVI

In Which We Learn of the Difficulties in Recreating the Taste of Something Truly Horrible

We have already seen how exposure to life on Earth had changed Mrs Abernathy, and not necessarily for the better, depending upon how one might feel about net curtains and pot pourri. It had also changed Nurd, who had discovered that if he was any kind of demon at all, then he was a speed demon.

But the brief expedition to the world of men had also changed other denizens of Hell in a variety of ways. A shiver of burrowing sharks[36] had become quite fascinated by the game of rugby, even if they weren't very good at it because they kept eating the ball; a group

---

[36] And what a lovely collective noun that is, a *shiver* of sharks, because it's so apt. Similarly, you have to love a *smack* of jellyfish, which is exactly the sound a load of jellyfish make if you drop them; a *lounge* of lizards – hence the name 'lounge lizard' for a chap who hangs around in bars trying to look sophisticated; a *parliament* of owls, although this one is a little troublesome because owls actually look a lot smarter than most politicians, and therefore might find the use of 'parliament' a bit offensive as a description; an *unkindness* of ravens, who are clever but talk about other birds behind their backs; a *scold* of jays, who are always complaining to ravens for being unkind; and a *sleuth* of bears, as bears make very good detectives due to their foraging skills. Except for the Three Bears, obviously, because they took ages to work out who had burgled their house.

of ghouls, having locked themselves in a Biddlecombe sweet shop to escape from some rather aggressive young people, had become very adept at making chocolate, and were now distinctly tubbier than they had been, and therefore a lot less frightening; and a party of imps that had briefly glimpsed a Jane Austen costume drama on some televisions in a shop had taken to wearing bonnets and trying to find one another suitable husbands.

In the great clamour and disturbance that had followed the failure of the invasion, nobody noticed that two warthog demons, Shan and Gath, had disappeared, and there were now two fewer pairs of arms to shovel coals into the deep fires of Hell. Still, since it wasn't as if anyone was being paid a wage, and the fires of Hell showed no sign of going out any time soon, it was decided that Shan and Gath had merely found more suitable employment elsewhere, and they were quickly forgotten.

Prior to the opening of the portal, Shan and Gath had led uninteresting, fruitless lives. They had never really experienced hunger or thirst, so they didn't need to eat or drink. Occasionally they would gnaw on a particularly interesting rock, just to test its consistency, and they had been known to nibble on smaller demons, if only to see how quickly their limbs grew back. You had to make your own fun in Hell.

But their brief visit to Earth had opened their eyes, and their taste buds, to a new world of possibilities, for Shan and Gath's sole contribution to the invasion had been to spend the night in the Fig & Parrot pub in

Biddlecombe sampling free pints of what was then merely the experimental version of Spiggit's Old Peculiar. And while Spiggit's was, as we have established, a bit strong, and somewhat harsh on the palate, even for those who had previously dipped rocks in Hell's lava before sampling them, just to add a little taste, Shan and Gath still agreed that drinking it had been a life-altering experience, as well as briefly altering their sight and the proper working of their digestive systems. They had returned to Hell with only one purpose in mind: to find a way to replicate this wonderful brew and then do nothing else but drink it for eternity. They had therefore retired to a cave and set about their work, having absorbed a certain amount of brewing lore from some of the regulars at the Fig & Parrot, who had drunk so much beer in their time that their bodies were essentially kegs on legs.

Unfortunately, as Shan and Gath soon discovered, replicating the unique taste of Spiggit's Old Peculiar was considerably more difficult than they had hoped: successive tastings of their early efforts had played havoc with their insides, and it usually took a while for their tongues and sinuses to recover from more than three glasses. They had therefore decided to recruit a taster to test their various brews. The taster's name was Brock, a small, spherical, blue being with a good nature and two legs, two arms, one mouth, three eyes, and the useful ability to instantly reconstruct himself in the event of any unfortunate accidents.

As it happened, this latter quality had turned out to be particularly useful.

Inside Shan and Gath's cave were tubes, bottles, vats of water, and stocks of weeds that closely resembled wheat, oats, and barley. In an effort to imitate as closely as possible Spiggit's distinctive taste, Shan and Gath had also been forced to acquire a number of different acids; three types of mud; assorted dyes and corrosives; grit; oil; rancid fats; and various forms of wee.[37] Each variation was duly fed to Brock by Shan and Gath who, having encountered a couple of people dressed as mad scientists while drinking in the Fig & Parrot on that fateful Halloween night, had made themselves some white lab coats, and carried stone clipboards on which they carefully made notes of their experiments, as follows:

BREW 1: Subject hiccup, then vanish in puff of smoke.

BREW 2: Subject fall off chair. Appear to die.

BREW 3: One of subject's eyes fall out.

BREW 4: Two of subject's eyes fall out.

BREW 5: Subject claim that he can fly. Subject try. Subject wrong.

BREW 6: Subject claim that he can fly again. Subject try. Subject succeed. Gath remove subject from ceiling with broom.

☠ [37] And in case you think the idea of adding wee to beer is disgusting, there is actually a verb, *to lant*, which means to add wee to beer in order to flavour ale and improve its taste. And not just any old wee, but *aged* wee, which is known as 'lant'. Oddly, in olden days lant was also used in wool processing, for cleaning floors, as a glaze on pastry ('This bun tastes a bit funny.' 'Too much wee?' 'No, too little! Is there a shortage? If so, I can help . . .') and, oddest of all, as a means of keeping one's breath fresh, which raises the question: how bad must people's breath have smelled already if adding wee to it made it smell better? Frankly, you really don't want to know . . .

BREW 7: Subject beg for mercy. Threaten to sue. Fall
asleep.

BREW 8: Subject turn green. Become violently ill. Appear
to die again.

BREW 9: Subject say worst version yet. Subject say it wish
it really was dead. Subject plead for mercy.

BREW 10: Subject claim tongue on fire. Gath examine.
Subject's tongue actually on fire.

And so on. Beside each unsuccessful attempt to make
a drinkable version of Spiggit's Old Peculiar, Shan and
Gath had glumly added a big 'X'. But they now had
high hopes for Brew 19. This one looked like ale. It
had a nice frothy head, and its colour was a deep, rich
red. It even smelled like something that one might drink
without a gun being held to one's head.

They handed the stone cup to Brock, who examined
it carefully. He was becoming quite the expert. He
sniffed it, and nodded approvingly.

'That doesn't smell bad at all,' he said.

Shan and Gath nodded encouragingly. Brock took a
sip, held it in his mouth for a time, then swallowed.

'Well, I have to tell you, that's really very—'

Brock exploded, scattering pieces of himself over the
walls, the brewing equipment, and Shan and Gath. They
wiped Brock off themselves, and watched as the various
bits slimed and scuttled across the floor to reconstitute
themselves once again. When he was complete, and
apparently recovered, Brock looked warily at the liquid
that was now smoking on the stones by his feet.

'Needs a bit of work, that,' he said.

Shan sank to the floor and put his head in his hands. Gath groaned. All of that effort, and they still had not managed to create a drinkable beer, let alone a satisfactory imitation of the wonder that was Spiggit's Old Peculiar. They would never succeed, never. A second cup of Brew 19 stood beneath the stone tap. Gath was about to pour it down a hole in the floor when a dwarf entered the cave, followed by three more individuals of similarly diminished stature.

'All right, lads?' said Jolly, rubbing his hands together. 'I'll have a pint of your finest, and a packet of crisps.'

'That'll be two,' said Angry.

'Three,' said Dozy.

'Unk,' said Mumbles, who had reverted to type now that the beer had been found.

Shan and Gath looked confused. Not only were there unexpected dwarfs in their cave, but they were unexpected dwarfs with a death wish if they were actually prepared to sample the local brew.

'I wouldn't if I were you,' said Brock. 'It's got a bit of a kick.'

Jolly saw that Gath was poised to throw away the cup of Brew 19.

'Hey, hey! Don't waste that,' he said. 'Give it here.'

He ambled over to Gath and took the cup from his cloven hoof. Gath was too shocked to do anything more than gape. He had wondered if the dwarfs really existed at all, and had speculated that he had possibly been exposed to too many toxic brewing fumes. Nevertheless, this dwarf did seem to be speaking to him, and Gath no longer had a cup in his hand, so either the dwarfs were real or Gath needed to have a long lie-down.

'You'll never make any money that way,' said Jolly. 'You should pour it back in the barrel if it's bad. Nobody will notice.'

He sniffed at the cup.

'I'll tell you what,' he said to his comrades, 'it's Spiggit's, but not as we know it.'

He took a long draught, swirled it round his mouth, and swallowed. Shan and Gath immediately curled up and covered their heads, not terribly anxious to be covered in bits of dwarf, while Brock hid behind a rock.

Nothing happened. Jolly just burped softly, and said: 'Bit weak, and it's lacking a certain . . . unpleasantness.'

He handed the cup to the others, who each took a sip.

'I'm getting a hint of dead fish,' said Angry.

'Oh, definitely your dead fish,' said Jolly. 'No complaints on that front.'

'Is that petrol?' said Dozy.

'Diesel,' said Jolly. 'Subtle, but it's there.'

'Trusap,' said Mumbles.

The other three dwarfs stared at him.

'He's right, you know,' said Angry.

'Brilliant,' said Jolly. 'He has the tongue of a god, that boy.'

'I might be able to help,' said Dozy. He rummaged in his pockets and pulled out the core of an apple that was so old it practically qualified as an antique. He dropped it into the cup and swirled it around with his finger.

'Try it now,' he said, noticing that his finger was starting to burn, always a good sign when it came to Spiggit's.

Jolly did. For a moment he couldn't see anything at all, and his head felt as though a piano had been dropped on it from a great height. He teetered on his heels so that only the shelf of brewing equipment stopped him from falling over. Slowly his vision returned, and he found some stability.

'Wonderful,' he croaked. 'Just wonderful.'

Shan and Gath appeared at his shoulder.

'Just needed some rotten fruit,' explained Jolly. 'Apples are usually best, although I say that you can't beat a hint of strawberry. More rancid the better mind, but it's all a matter of personal taste.'

He handed the cup to Shan, who tried it and then passed it to Gath. They both winced, and reached out to support each other, then recovered.

'Hurh-hurh,' said Gath.

'Hurh-hurh,' said Shan.

And they held each other and laughed while the dwarfs looked on indulgently.

'It's that Spiggit's moment,' said Angry.

'That special moment,' said Dozy.

'That moment when you realize you're going to survive,' said Jolly. 'Probably. Magic, just magic.'

CHAPTER XXVII

In Which We Hear a Surprising Confession

Samuel, Nurd and Wormwood, with Boswell dozing beside them, sat at the mouth of the cave and watched the acid rain fall. It really was acid, too: it had corroded a coin that one of the dwarfs had dropped, and it left a faint smell of burning in the air after it splashed on the ground. They had managed to get the Aston Martin and the ice-cream van into shelter and Nurd had assured them all that they were safe for now. Nothing hunted or flew during the acid storms. Even demons didn't care much for unnecessary pain, or at least not self-inflicted unnecessary pain.

'What do we do when it stops?' asked Samuel. 'We can't hide for ever.'

'We know that there has to be a portal, and somehow Mrs Abernathy is in control of it,' said Nurd. 'If we find it then we can send you all back.'

A look of what might almost have been grief passed across Nurd's face, and was mirrored by Samuel. They were both thinking the same thing: after being separated and now, against all the odds, reunited, it just didn't seem right that they should be forced to part again so soon. Even though Samuel desperately wanted to return home, and Nurd wanted him to be in a place of safety, their fondness for each other meant that the ending for which they both wished was destined to cause them great unhappiness. All of this remained unspoken yet understood between them.

Strangely, Wormwood knew it too, for as his master and Samuel silently considered the fact that the best-case scenario would see them divided again by time and space and various dimensions, he coughed softly and said:

'I don't mean to be rude, but I'll be glad to see the backs of those dwarfs. They have the potential to be quite, um, troublesome.'

Samuel and Nurd recognized what Wormwood was trying to do, and were grateful to him.

'I don't think it's potential, Wormwood,' said Nurd. 'They are *actively* troublesome. They haven't been potential trouble since before they were born.'

At that moment the dwarfs were happily sharing Shan and Gath's new variation on Brew 19, helped by some frozen fruit salvaged from Dan's van. Dan, who was resigned to the fact that his ice-cream business was unlikely to recover in the current circumstances owing to the consumption of all his ice cream and most of his chocolate, had joined in the tasting, and was now a little tipsy. Even Constable Peel had consented to a 'small one', with Sergeant Rowan's permission, and the sergeant had found some unexpected common ground with Jolly, who had explained to him that the dwarfs' criminal behaviour was all society's fault. Sergeant

Rowan also believed this, mainly because society hadn't found a way to lock them up and throw away the key.

Angry, meanwhile, was demonstrating to Constable Peel the intricacies of pickpocketing, although this was less out of a desire to share hidden knowledge with the policeman than because Constable Peel had caught Angry trying to steal his handcuffs.

'I can't help it,' Angry was explaining in what might almost have been a sincere manner. 'I was just born this way. My mum says she brought me home from the hospital and found a stethoscope and two thermometers in my diaper. I can find a way to steal anything, me. It's a gift. Sort of.'

'I stole something once,' said Constable Peel suddenly.

Angry, along with Dozy and Mumbles, who had been listening to the conversation, looked taken aback.

'Really?' said Dozy.

Constable Peel nodded slowly. His cheeks burned with shame, and a little Brew 19 that had splashed on his skin and begun to irritate it.

'I was four,' he said. 'I was sitting next to Briony Andrews in kindergarten. We always got two biscuits at break, and I'd finished mine, but she had one left. So –'

Constable Peel covered his eyes with one hand and choked back a sob. Angry patted him on the back and tried not to laugh.

'Let it out,' he said. 'Confession is good for the soul.'

Somehow, Constable Peel found the strength to go on.

'So –'

'I can see where this is going,' said Dozy.

'Ungbit,' said Mumbles.

'Absolutely,' said Dozy. 'Briony Andrews is about to be one hundred per cent down in the biscuit department.'

'So –'

'Very tense this,' said Angry.

'I stole her biscuit!' concluded Constable Peel.

'No!' said Dozy, almost managing to sound surprised.

'Go on with you,' said Angry, not managing to sound surprised at all.

'Hardened criminal, you were,' said Jolly, joining in the fun. 'Stealing a little girl's biscuit? That's low, that is.'

'Devious,' said Dozy.

'Underhand,' said Angry.

'Sneaky,' said Jolly.

'I know, I know,' said Constable Peel. 'And it gets worse: I pretended she'd lost it. I even helped to organize the search party.'

'Oh, the hypocrisy!' said Angry, who actually thought that this did demonstrate a certain criminal cunning on the part of the juvenile Peel. It was almost admirable. He began to wonder if he might not have misjudged the policeman.

Constable Peel uncovered his face, revealing a fanatical gleam in his eye. 'But when I went home that day I vowed that never again would I engage in illegal activities, biscuit-based or otherwise. From that day on I was a policeman in spirit, and the law was my mistress.

I was Bob Peel, child lawman, and schoolyard wrong-doers trembled at my approach.'

There was silence as the dwarfs considered this before Jolly said sombrely:

'You must have been an absolute pain in the bum.'

Constable Peel stared at him. His chin trembled. His fists clenched. For a second, there was murder in the air.

'You know, I absolutely was,' said Constable Peel, and their laughter was so loud that dust from the cave roof fell in their beer, improving it slightly.

Back at the cave mouth, Wormwood nibbled on a wine gum as he, Nurd, and Samuel, joined by Sergeant Rowan, assessed their situation.

'The car has taken a beating,' said Wormwood. 'And the ice-cream van isn't going to last much longer. We're also nearly out of fuel, and it will take time to synthesize some more.'

'Is there any good news?' asked Nurd.

'We still have wine gums.'

'Will they power our car?'

'No.'

'Well, it's not really very good news then, is it?'

'No,' said Wormwood. 'Not really. Oh look, the rain's easing off.' He frowned. 'That's not good news either, is it?'

Nurd rubbed his eyes wearily. 'No, it's not.'

Soon the skies would once again be filled with eager, hostile eyes. Their enemies knew that they were in the area, and when the rain stopped they would begin to close in on them. They had no weapons, and little hope. There were days that just seemed to get harder and harder as they went on. Finding Samuel should have been a bright spot; after all, Nurd had spent so long wishing that he and his friend could be together again. Now that Samuel was here, Nurd just hoped to see him gone. Be careful what you wish for, he supposed; he hadn't wanted Samuel to be dragged to Hell just so that they could have another conversation. The dwarfs and Constable Peel appeared by his side, and together the little group gazed out as the rainfall grew gentler, and then ceased entirely.

'This is our chance,' Nurd told them all. 'It will stay dark and quiet for a while now that the rain has stopped. It's the way of things here. There'll be no lightning, and we can make some progress without being seen.'

'And the plan is that we find this woman, or demon, or whatever she is, and make her send us home?' said Angry.

'Or you find her, she tears you apart, and you don't have to worry about getting home any more,' said Nurd. 'It depends, really.'

'On what?'

'On how fast you can run once she spots you.'

'That doesn't sound like much of a plan,' said Jolly. 'And we've only got little legs. We're not really built for speed.'

'That's unfortunate,' said Nurd. 'Speed always helps on these occasions.'

'Doesn't look like you're much of a runner either,' said Angry. 'Big boots, bit of a belly. You're going to have trouble outrunning this Mrs Abernathy too, if she's chasing us.'

'But I don't have to outrun her,' said Nurd reasonably. 'I just have to outrun you . . .'

CHAPTER XXVIII

In Which Everything Goes Horribly Wrong

Preparations began for their departure while Samuel watched the clouds swirl. They moved less violently than before, as though worn out by their earlier efforts, the faces less visible now. There was a faint yellow glow to the sky and although the landscape before him was not beautiful, it was at a kind of peace. The rocky hillside descended to more muddy bogs, across which stretched a stone causeway. As before, a stinking, heavy mist hung over the bogs, and Samuel felt sure that it would hide them from any watchful eyes above as they drove.

He thought about his mother. She would be worried about him. He had lost all track of time since he had arrived in this place, but at least a day and a night had gone by, and perhaps more. Then again, time was different here. He wasn't even sure that there was time, not really. He supposed that, if eternity stretched before you, then minutes and hours and days would cease to have any meaning. But they had meaning for him: they represented moments spent separated from those whom he loved: from his mother, his friends, even his dad. Nurd was here, though, which was something.

Beside him, Boswell gave a little yip and got to his feet. He sniffed the air. His ears twitched, and he looked troubled.

'What is it, Boswell?' asked Samuel, as a shadow fell upon him, and the Watcher clasped a hand over Samuel's mouth so that he could not cry out, and pulled him into the air with a great flapping of his wings. By the time Nurd and the others grasped what was happening, Samuel was already disappearing into low clouds, clasped tightly in the Watcher's arms. Boswell ran down the hillside after them, barking and leaping up on his stubby back legs as though he might yet haul the massive red creature down.

But Samuel was gone, and it was left to Nurd to run to the little dog and hold him lest he get lost, or eaten, Boswell struggling all the time, desperate to follow Samuel, desperate to save him.

A craggy peak rose in the distance. Nurd thought that he saw a figure there, perched on the back of a basilisk. It was looking back at him, and he heard Mrs Abernathy's voice as clearly as if she were standing next to him:

'I will come for you, Nurd. I have not forgotten your meddling. For now, it is enough punishment for you to know that I have your friend, and I will sacrifice him to my Master. And then it will be your turn.'

But Nurd did not care about her threats, or about himself. He cared only for Samuel, and how he might be rescued.

* * *

The Watcher flew high. It held Samuel, and Samuel held it, for Samuel feared falling more than he feared the creature holding him. Its skin smelled of sulphur and ash, and was pitted with the scars of deep, long-healed wounds. Samuel felt the creature's consciousness probing at his own, trying to learn about him, exploring his strengths and his weaknesses. But as it tested him, so too it exposed something of itself, and Samuel was shocked by the strangeness of it, and he understood that even by the standards of Hell itself this was a peculiar, solitary being, one entirely unlike him but also unlike any other entity in that place.

No, not quite. It was allied to another, to—

For an instant, Samuel glimpsed the Great Malevolence, and had his first real inkling of the depths of the First Demon's evil, and wretchedness, and madness. It was so awful that Samuel's mind immediately put up a series of blockades to protect his sanity, which had the effect of closing out the Watcher. The rhythm of the creature's flight was momentarily interrupted, as though it were shocked at the strength of the boy's will. It gripped him tighter as a consequence, clasping him against its shoulder so that Samuel was looking back in the direction that they had come, back towards the hills still visible through wisps of cloud, and towards Boswell and Nurd, who were lost from sight.

A pale, emaciated figure broke through the clouds from above, its ribs clearly visible beneath its skin, its belly sunken. Its head was bald, its ears were long and pointed, and it had too many teeth for its mouth, so that they jutted forth from between its lips, snaggled and broken. It paused in mid-air, seemingly surprised to have come across them, then altered its position and began its pursuit. It was a wraith, a batlike demon little taller than Samuel himself. Its wings were attached to its arms, ending in sharp, hooked claws, and it had talons for feet. These talons it now stuck out, poised to strike like a falcon descending on its prey.

Samuel beat on the Watcher's back, and managed to cry out a warning. Instinctively the Watcher turned to its right, and the smaller creature's talons missed them by inches, one of its wings slapping against Samuel's face as it flew by. The Watcher shifted Samuel so that he was held only beneath its left arm, and Samuel felt sure that he would fall. He dug his nails into the Watcher's hard skin, and wrapped his legs tightly around its waist.

The wraith came at them again, this time from below, screaming over and over, summoning others like it to the chase. The Watcher struck out at it with a flick of its right arm, and its nails tore a hole in the attacker's belly. No blood came, but the wraith's wings stopped flapping and it spiralled through the clouds to the ground far below like a fighter plane crippled by gunfire, crying in agony as it fell.

Two more appeared, drawn by the shrieks of their brother. They dived together. One aimed blows at the Watcher's head, distracting it while the second tried to pull Samuel from his grasp, but the Watcher held on tightly. His free hand grabbed the wraith that was scratching at his eyes and broke its neck before discarding it. The second it almost decapitated with a swipe of its hand, leaving the head hanging from a fold of skin, and with that the attack was over, and they were alone in the skies once more. Samuel closed his eyes as they flew on, so that neither he nor the Watcher saw a final wraith that shadowed them for a time from above before it slipped away to report to Duke Abigor all that it had seen.

CHAPTER XXIX

In Which Various Dangerous Personages Put Their Plans In Motion

Mrs Abernathy's basilisk pounded across the warm stones, lost in the clouds of steam that had arisen in the aftermath of the recent showers. There was an acrid smell in the air, the stink of flesh and wood and vegetation corroded and burned by the falling acid, yet already what passed for life in that place was recovering. Clumps of brown seared weeds became slightly less brown; stunted bushes, blackened and smoking, reassumed their usual dull hue; and assorted small demons who had not been quick enough to escape the downpour began growing back arms, legs, toes, and heads. Some of them even grew an extra limb or two while they were about it, just in case an additional appendage proved useful in future. From holes in the ground and through gaps in the bushes they watched Mrs Abernathy pass, and they saw that her face was alive with triumph, and her eyes shone a deep, cold blue. Not all of them knew who she was, for there were parts of Hell where the Great Malevolence was little more than a rumoured presence hidden deep in his mountain fastness, and his dukes and generals and legions could have been figures from old fables for all the impact they had on the existence of these primitive entities. Yet they sensed that this curious figure was immensely powerful, and should probably be avoided if at all possible.

And then she was gone and they instantly forgot about her, for they had more immediate concerns such as when it might rain acid again, and what to do with that extra head they'd just grown.

Mrs Abernathy didn't even notice the movement around her. She sensed the conflict in which the Watcher was engaged far above her head, but she had never been less than certain of its capacity to annihilate any enemy that came within its reach. There had been a moment when she feared the Watcher might drop Samuel Johnson, an eventuality that might have put paid to her hopes of returning to the Great Malevolence's favour. After all, there wouldn't have been much to show of the boy if he'd been dropped from thousands of feet on to hard rock. True, his consciousness would have survived, but she wasn't certain that she could reconstitute a human as easily as a demon, and a mulch of messy blood, bits of bone, and fragments of tissue lacked a certain immediate identifiability. She could, she supposed, have scraped him into a jar, stuck a label on it reading 'Samuel Johnson (Most of Him)', and presented it to the Great Malevolence, but it wouldn't have had quite the same impact as delivering the boy, weeping yet intact, to her Master, and sharing in his revenge on the troublesome little human.

But even as Mrs Abernathy pictured in her mind the details of Samuel Johnson's impending humiliation, she remained troubled by the intervention of Duke Abigor. Abigor had always resented her position, but she was surprised by how quickly he had moved against her following the failure of the invasion. Some of those who had allied themselves to him, Dukes Guares and Borym among them, had once been her allies, and their betrayal stung her. For a moment she entertained herself by running through lists of the various agonies she would order to be visited upon them once she stood again at her Master's left hand, then pushed such pleasant images away, clearing her mind entirely so that she could concentrate on more important matters.

Abigor was risking a great deal by working against her: although she had been banished from the Great Malevolence's presence, no sentence had been passed upon her and she was still, theoretically at least, commander of his armies. Thus Abigor was technically guilty of treason, although she might have difficulty proving it should the necessity arise for as yet Abigor had done nothing directly to undermine her position.

Yet if he had laid hands on Samuel Johnson, what would he have done with him? He could have presented him as a gift to the Great Malevolence, just as Mrs Abernathy planned to do, but he would have experienced some difficulty in explaining how he had managed to drag his captive to Hell. No, Abigor was playing a different game here, the dimensions of which Mrs Abernathy was only beginning to grasp. The Chancellor, Ozymuth, was on Abigor's side, and Ozymuth, if the oozing Crudford was to be believed, was intent upon undermining the Great Malevolence by prolonging, and deepening, his grief. It hardly seemed possible, but Abigor was not interested merely in supplanting Mrs Abernathy. No, he wanted to take the place of the Great Malevolence himself, to become the ruler of Hell in place of its maddened king. And having already enlisted many of the dukes in his scheme, even if they were not yet aware of the full extent of it, he had no choice but to see it through to its end. If he were to abandon it now, and the Great Malevolence were to recover his wits and discover even some small element of the plot – as he most assuredly would, for if Mrs Abernathy did not tell him others involved would, if only in the hope of saving themselves from punishment – then Abigor and his co-conspirators could expect to end up frozen for eternity in the lake of Cocytus, if they were lucky and the Great Malevolence proved to be unexpectedly merciful. Abigor had gone too far to turn back now, and so he would have to gamble everything on the Great Malevolence's ongoing madness and the defeat of Mrs Abernathy. Both were linked to Samuel Johnson, for the sight of his enemy presented to him in chains might well bring the Great Malevolence back to his senses, and Abigor's plans would come to naught. But if Samuel Johnson were to be kept from him, then his mourning and lunacy would continue, and Mrs Abernathy would be doomed.

This was a delicate time. The boy was her captive, and she had to keep him safe from Abigor until she could bring him to the Mountain of Despair. The attack on the Watcher by Abigor's wraiths was just the beginning. Worse would follow.

As if to confirm her suspicions, the ground before her cracked and a wretched beast, yellow, eyeless and quivering, emerged from a hole. It was a Burrower, its lower half segmented like a worm's, its upper half that of a man, with a face resembling that of a rat or a vole. It had the legs of a millipede, except at its fore and rear parts where powerful webbed claws emerged from its body. It dwelt in the earth, only venturing entirely above ground when absolutely necessary, and formed a collective consciousness with its fellows, so that knowledge gleaned by one was shared by all. Although blind, Burrowers could identify the presence of other beings above ground by the vibrations of their footfalls, aided by their excellent sense of taste and smell. Such gifts made them useful spies, and they were loyal to Mrs Abernathy, for she would sometimes hand over her enemies to them, and they would drag the unfortunate creatures underground and feast on them.

'Mistress, we bring news,' the Burrower said. 'There are legions gathering. We hear whispers. They speak of a boy. They intend to besiege your lair, and take him from you. You are to be punished for plotting against the Great Malevolence.'

'Punished?' said Mrs Abernathy. She could barely believe the impudence of her enemies.

'Yes, Mistress. You were tried in your absence by a panel of judges appointed by Duke Abigor, and by unanimous decision found guilty of treason. It is said that you opened a portal between this world and the world of men in the hope of securing the Earth for yourself and creating a kingdom there in opposition to this Kingdom of Fire. You are to be apprehended, and taken to the farthest, deepest reaches of Lake Cocytus, where a place has been prepared for you in the ice.'

Mrs Abernathy was shaken. They had moved so fast against her.

'How much time do I have?' she asked.

'Little, Mistress. Although the forces that oppose you have not yet gathered in full at their place of rendezvous upon the Plains of Desolation, four legions have been sent ahead to secure your palace.'

'Whose legions?'

'Two legions each of Dukes Borym and Peros.'

'And what of my allies?'

'They await your command.'

'Instruct them to gather in the shadow of the Forlorn Hills. Send word to those of the dukes who remain uncommitted. Tell them that the boy is in my power, and the time has come for them to choose sides. Loyalty will be rewarded many times over. Betrayal will never be forgiven.'

'Yes, Mistress. And what of the legions that approach your lair?'

Mrs Abernathy thought for a moment.

'Drag them down, and consume them,' she said.

She spurred on her basilisk and it sprang away, leaving the Burrower licking its lips in anticipation of fresh meat.

CHAPTER XXX

In Which the Watcher Is Torn

Duke Abigor's wraith followed the Watcher's progress until it was almost within sight of Mrs Abernathy's palace, then banked away to report back to its master. But the Watcher had known of its presence all along, and as soon as it sensed that the spy had departed it changed course, using the clouds to hide itself as it made its way to a plateau on the Forlorn Hills. There it laid Samuel upon the ground, and placed a foot lightly on his chest so that the boy could not escape. From its perch, it stared down as Mrs Abernathy's army began to assemble itself below. Demons burst forth from the earth and emerged from caves. They descended from clouds and crawled from dank black pools. They formed themselves from ash, and sand, and snow, from molecules of water and the unseen atoms in the air. Horned beings, winged beings, finned beings; beings familiar, and beings shapeless; beings of fire and rock, and beings of water and ice; beings of tooth and claw, and beings of mind and energy: all had flocked to Mrs Abernathy's call.

Some had come out of loyalty, some out of fear, and

some simply because they were bored, and gambling on the outcome of a battle, even at the possible cost of future pain if they were defeated, at least broke the tedium of damnation. Lightning flashed, illuminating spearheads, and serrated knife edges, and thousands of bladed weapons. The Watcher moved its gaze to the right. In the distance, fiery hooves struck sparks from the ground, and booted feet marched in unison, metal clanking as the first legions of those dukes who had chosen to support Mrs Abernathy marched to her aid.

The Watcher allowed its consciousness to rove still further. It saw the four legions of Duscias and Peros moving purposefully across a cracked plain where once before, long ago even in its conception of time, a great lake of poisonous water had stood, fed by vile rivers that flowed from the surrounding peaks. The Great Malevolence had redirected the rivers to form the Lake of Cocytus, and in time the plain had dried up entirely. Now only dust flowed across it before falling into narrow crevasses that led deep into the ground below.

The four legions picked their way carefully across the treacherous landscape. They marched on foot, rank upon rank of demons, each heavily armoured and each carrying in his hand a pike topped by a thin, hard blade around which curled a second length of metal shaped like a corkscrew, the weapon designed to be thrust into the belly of an enemy, twisted, and then pulled out, dragging with it the internal organs and leaving the wretched victim in agony upon the ground, for even a demon will struggle to recover itself quickly after such a terrible injury. Short stabbing swords hung at their sides, and their gloves, their helmets, even the plates of their black armour were embedded with spikes, so that the armour itself was a weapon.

By the sides of the legions, mounted on skinless horses, their flesh raw and glistening, their muscles lean, rode the captains and lieutenants, their armour more ornate, their weapons bejewelled but no less capable of inflicting grave wounds. Banners waved in the cold wind, red and gold and green, the colours of the Houses of Peros and Borym, but above them all flew a single great standard, depicting a hand of fire against a sable background. This was the banner of the House of Abigor. There was no sign of Hell's own banner, the horned head of the Great Malevolence, the symbol of his armies. The dukes had made their loyalties public and were no longer primarily serving the Great Malevolence, but the demon who wished to succeed him.

It was the horses, their eyes and mouths lit red by the fires within, that first sensed the approach of an unknown threat. They whinnied and neighed, then rose up on their hind legs, almost unseating their riders. Confusion rippled through the ranks as Ronwe, a minor demon who had allied his nineteen legions with Borym and was now the second-in-command of all his forces, turned to shout an order, an order that was destined never to be heard as the ground opened up and swallowed both Ronwe and his steed. The crevasse before the front rank widened, forcing it to halt. Stinking green gases emerged from the revealed pit and the ground at the edges began to crumble, taking two dozen legionnaires with it into the depths. Those who had witnessed what had occurred, and who were thus aware of the danger, tried to retreat, but they were hemmed in by the ranks advancing from behind, and more tumbled down. Captains called out orders, attempting to halt the advance and permit the front ranks to fall back, but their horses were trying to throw them, and the troops were starting to panic, and the ground continued to crack and break, marooning whole cohorts of legionnaires on islands of dry earth that themselves began to crumble.

And then the creatures from below commenced their attack. Massive tentacles, ridged along their length with sticky, poisonous barbs, shot from the pits, dragging demon soldiers into the darkness. Giant red insects, their jaws capable of swallowing a man's head whole, poured forth, their palps twitching, their mouthpieces snapping. The arms of the troops were not strong enough to pierce their carapaces, nor was their armour capable of withstanding the force of the insects' bites. Worms long hidden beneath the earth opened their jaws, and what had once seemed solid ground became a trap filled with teeth, and feet were severed from legs, and heads from bodies.

But some of Duke Peros's finest soldiers had found solid ground at the edge of the lake bed, and were working their way carefully around the killing field, keeping their enemies at bay as best they could by discipline and force of will. They were halfway around the circumference, from which the surrounding hills rose precipitously like the sides of a volcano, when earth began to fall on their heads from above, revealing neat, round holes in the dusty soil, and webbed claws started to pull at their feet and arms and necks, and the Burrowers began to bite.

And the lake bed, long dry, ran red and black with the blood of demons.

The Watcher, distant yet aware, saw it all. This conflict threatened to tear Hell itself apart, but the Watcher remained uncertain of how to proceed, for the sound of the Great Malevolence's wailing still carried to it, and it seemed that the cries would never stop. If a king is mad, then what are his subjects to do?[38] Without the fear that the Great Malevolence inspired, it was inevitable that his subordinates would begin to fight among themselves, jockeying for power and position. But the threat posed by Abigor was greater than mere disorder, for Abigor was now in open rebellion against his lord.

The mass of demons below continued to swell as more and more of Hell's denizens flocked to Mrs

[38] For the most part, subjects just have to put up with them until someone kills the king in question. For example, the Roman emperor Caligula (12–41A.D.), who is said to have tried to make his horse, Incitatus, a consul of Rome, was stabbed thirty times. Eric XIV of Sweden (1533–77) was poisoned by pea soup laced with arsenic. Madness is something of a perennial problem when it comes to royalty, as a considerable number of kings have been distinctly suspect on the sanity front. Lesser known royal lunatics include Charles VI of France (1368–1422), also known as Charles the Mad – but not to his face – who believed himself to be made of glass and had iron rods placed in his clothing to prevent him from breaking, and once refused to bathe or change his clothes for five months. Meanwhile, Robert of Clermont (1256–1318), younger son of Louis IX of France, went mad after being hit on the head several times with a sledgehammer in the course of a joust, but then being hit on the head with a sledgehammer will do that to a person.

Abernathy's banner. Grand Duke Aym arrived with his twenty-six legions; Ayperos, Prince of Hell, with thirty-six; and Azazel, the standard-bearer of Hell's armies, took up a position on a great rock and unfurled the flag of the Great Malevolence.

Samuel twisted beneath the Watcher's feet, gazing out at the gathering forces with a mix of terror and amazement. The Watcher regarded him closely, its eight black eyes like dark planets set against the red sky of his skin. Even though the winged demon was more awful than any of the creatures assembled below, Samuel still found the courage to stare back at it in defiance.

'What are you waiting for?' said Samuel. 'Do whatever you're planning, and get it over with.'

He heard a voice speak in his head, and although the Watcher's insectlike jaws did not move, Samuel knew that he was hearing the demon's voice.

We wait.

'Wait for whom?' Even in this time of great peril, Samuel Johnson's grammar remained intact.

For Mrs Abernathy.

Samuel felt much of the courage he had mustered leach away. His body deflated, and all his strength threatened to leave him. He had been foolish to think he could escape her wrath, foolish to think Nurd could save him. He had been doomed ever since that first evening when he had watched as Mrs Abernathy and her loathsome companions had emerged from their world into his through a hole in an otherwise ordinary basement.

All of this, for you, said the Watcher, with what seemed like wonder in its voice. *All of this, because of a boy.*

'I didn't start it,' said Samuel. 'I didn't make Mrs Abernathy kill anyone. I didn't ask for her to invade the Earth. I just wanted to go trick-or-treating.'

But now look. Armies are mustering. Old loyalties have fallen apart, and new loyalties have been forged. Old enmities are forgotten, and new enmities are formed. And all the time, my master weeps. The bells must peal. There is no other choice.

'Your master?' said Samuel, picking up on something in the demon's tone that might almost have been love, but love so twisted and misguided that it was almost unrecognizable as itself. 'But don't you work for Mrs Abernathy? And what bells are you talking about?'

The Watcher did not reply, and Samuel, remembering his brief glimpse of the reality of the Great Malevolence, knew that the demon's loyalties were confused.

'So you work for the Devil, *and* for Mrs Abernathy?'

Yes. No. Maybe.

'You should probably make your mind up.'

Probably.

'I wondered what all that wailing was about,' said Samuel. 'You're telling me that it's the Great Malevolence, crying?'

Yes.

'Why?'

Because, after all this time, he came close to escaping his prison. After all this time, he had hope, and then the hope was gone, and he hates himself for giving in to hope. He, who exists only to kill the hopes of others, could not destroy the hope within himself. He is lost to his madness, and so he weeps.

'Can't say I'm sorry,' said Samuel, and thought to himself, the big crybaby. The Watcher's head tilted slightly, and Samuel was afraid the demon might have picked up on what he was thinking, but if it did, it gave no further sign.

'So why did those other demons attack us in the clouds?'

They are loyal to Duke Abigor. He does not want Mrs Abernathy to have you.

'Why not?'

Because she is going to hand you over to the Great Malevolence, and thus restore him to sanity, and herself to his favour, and he will forgive her for the failure of the invasion, and he will revenge himself upon you instead. But if Duke Abigor can prevent that, he will take Mrs Abernathy's place. He will take—

The Watcher broke off, unwilling to express its worst fear.

'Would Duke Abigor send me home, if he had me?' said Samuel hopefully.

No. Duke Abigor would keep you in utter darkness, and there you would stay for ever, for Death has no dominion here.

'Oh,' said Samuel.

Yes, 'Oh.'

'And what about you? What do you want?'

I want my Master to stop weeping. That is why I will let Mrs Abernathy hand you over to him.

And Samuel's hopes began to fade.

CHAPTER XXXI

In Which We Learn a Little of the Responsibilities of Command, and the Perils of Being Commanded

Duke Abigor slammed a mailed fist into the table of bones, which shattered under the impact, causing a number of the skulls to complain loudly about vandalism, and demons these days having no respect for antiques, and bones not growing on trees, and suchlike. Abigor lifted one of the dislodged skulls, which continued to chatter until it seemed to realize that its fortunes had suddenly taken a turn for the worse, something that, until recently, had seemed virtually impossible, given that it was a skull stuck in a table without much hope of advancement.

'My mistake,' said the skull. 'Don't worry about the damage.'

Abigor increased his grip, giving the skull just enough time to say, 'Gently, now –' before it was crushed to dust.

Abigor was dressed in his finest battle armour, its surface decorated with images of serpents that slithered over the metal and were, when required, capable of rising up and striking at an enemy. His blood-red cloak billowed angrily behind him, responding to the changes in its wearer's temperament.

'Four legions!' shouted Duke Abigor. 'We lost four legions!'

Before him, Dukes Peros and Borym blanched. They were soft, fat demons, conniving and ambitious, yet lacking the ruthlessness and drive that might have made them great. Peros looked like a vaguely ducal candle that had been placed too close to heat: his face appeared to have melted, so that his skin hung in hard folds over his skull, and any features that might once have resembled ears, a nose, cheekbones, and suchlike, had all been lost, leaving only a pair of green eyes sunk deep in the putty of his flesh. Borym's face, meanwhile, was almost entirely lost beneath a massive brown beard, bushy eyebrows, and hair so unruly that it fought back against any attempt to cut it, as a number of Hell's barbers had learned to their cost. Somewhere in Borym's mass of curls were four pairs of scissors, any number of combs, and a couple of very small imps who had been sent in to retrieve these items and become hopelessly lost.

The dukes' armour was even more ornate than Abigor's, but far less practical, for Peros and Borym were of the school of military command that believed ordinary soldiers, not dukes, should fight battles. Dukes claimed the victory, and divided the spoils; soldiers could relish the glory of war, and later raise a drink to their exploits on the field, assuming their hands were still sufficiently attached to their arms to enable them to raise anything more than a stump. So, whereas Abigor's armour, although beautiful, bore the marks of conflicts endured, the suits of Peros and Borym were decorated with feathers, ribbons, unearned medals, and carvings that depicted much slimmer versions of Peros and Borym vanquishing assorted enemies in unlikely ways, and therefore were barely on nodding terms with reality.

'My lord,' said Borym, who was smart enough to see trouble brewing, but not smart enough to avoid sipping from the resulting cup, 'we were only following your orders. It was you who advised us to cross the Lake of Dry Tears in an effort to take Mrs Abernathy by surprise.'

Abigor brushed his hands together, removing the last vestiges of the bone from his gloves. On the stones below, the dust and fragments began to move, flowing across the floor and gradually reassuming the shape of a skull.

'Ow,' said the skull.

'Are you suggesting that it was my fault?' asked Abigor softly.

'No, not at—' the skull began to say, before Abigor's metal boot stamped upon it, shattering it to pieces again.

'Of course not, my lord,' said Borym. 'I meant no such impertinence.'

'So whose fault was it, then?'

'Mine, my lord,' said Borym, in a vain attempt to rescue an already doomed situation.

'And mine,' said Peros, who was too stupid to keep his mouth shut.

'It is noble of you both to accept responsibility for your failure,' said Abigor.

He clicked his fingers and eight members of his personal guard, demons of smoke contained in suits of black steel trimmed with gold, their red eyes the only indication of the life within, surrounded the dukes.

'Cast them into the dungeons,' said Abigor. 'Then throw away the keys. With considerable force.'

Borym and Peros did not even try to protest as they were escorted from the room. Abigor clasped his hands behind his back and closed his eyes. Above him rose a vaulted ceiling like that of a cathedral. Waves of flame moved across it, blending with the fires that rose from slits in the floor and covered the walls in sheets of white and yellow, so that the whole room seemed to be afire. This was the heart of Abigor's residence, the innermost chamber of his great palace. Next to it Mrs Abernathy's lair was almost humble, but Abigor had always believed that nothing impresses quite like vulgar displays of wealth and power.

He should not have entrusted Borym and Peros with the task of surprising Mrs Abernathy and trying to secure the boy's capture. They were imbeciles who would have been hard pressed to catch a cold. Abigor's difficulty was that he had surrounded himself with traitorous dukes. Had he despatched one of his cleverer allies, such as Duke Guares, to attack Mrs Abernathy, then it was possible that Guares might either have forged a separate alliance with her, betraying Abigor, or tried to take the boy for himself. At least Abigor had no concerns about the loyalty of Borym and Peros, only their competence. Nevertheless, Abigor had enough self-knowledge to grasp that the loss of the four legions was, in part, his own fault, although he wasn't about to admit that to anyone else. When leaders started admitting their failings, their followers tended to seek alternative leaders with fewer failings, or less honesty.

A panel in the eastern wall of the chamber opened, and Chancellor Ozymuth stepped through the gap. Abigor did not turn around to acknowledge his presence, but merely said, 'Have you come to criticize me as well, Ozymuth?'

'No, my lord,' said Ozymuth. 'I was listening as you dealt with your fellow dukes, and have no desire to keep them company in their new quarters.'

'Your instincts for self-preservation are as finely honed as ever,' said Abigor. 'Still, Mrs Abernathy is cleverer than I thought and not all of her allies have deserted her.'

'She is a worthy adversary.'

'You sound almost as if you respect her.'

'It is as well to respect one's enemies, but I do not respect her as much as I respect you, my lord.'

Abigor laughed, but there was no mirth to it.

'You have a serpent's tongue, Ozymuth. I trust not one word that falls from it. What news of the boy?'

'He is with the Watcher. They await the return of Mrs Abernathy.'

'And where is she?'

'I was hoping that you might know, my lord.'

'She has avoided my spies, or it may be that my spies have been apprehended, for I have heard no word from any of them.'

Ozymuth shifted uneasily. He had to pose the question that was on his lips, but he risked angering Abigor by doing so.

'My lord, forgive me for asking, but you are still in control of the situation, are you not?'

Ozymuth tensed. Behind him the door in the wall remained open, and he was poised to flee through it and lose himself in the labyrinthine passageways connecting Abigor's palace to the Mountain of Despair should the duke turn on him, but instead Abigor gave the question some consideration.

'As long as the boy has not yet been handed over to the Great Malevolence, then victory remains within my grasp. Dukes Aym and Ayperos have remained loyal to Mrs Abernathy, as have some of the counts, but we outnumber their legions two to one. They have no hope against us on the field of battle, should it come to that.'

'An army is gathering at the foot of the Forlorn Hills,' said Ozymuth. 'Demons are heeding Mrs Abernathy's call to her banner.'

'They are of the lower orders,' said Abigor. 'They are untrained, and undisciplined.'

'Yet they are many.'

For a moment, Abigor looked troubled. 'What will she do, Ozymuth?'

'She will assemble her army to protect the boy, then march on the Mountain of Despair with her prize.'

'So we must ensure that she does not reach it. Go, Ozymuth: continue to whisper your poison into the ear of the old lord. Keep him mad. When I rule Hell, I will make sure he is well looked after.'

Ozymuth bowed low and left the room, the chamber door closing silently behind him. When he was gone,

Abigor clicked his fingers once again, and the captain of his guard entered.

'Inform the dukes that they are to gather their forces before the entrance to the Mountain of Despair,' said Abigor. 'Tell them to prepare for battle!'

CHAPTER XXXII

In Which Samuel and Mrs Abernathy Meet Again, Which Only Delights Fifty Per Cent of Those Involved

Mrs Abernathy's basilisk was chained to a post, its scaly skin covered in saliva, its eyes glazed with exhaustion. Mrs Abernathy had ridden it hard and they had encountered a number of obstacles along the way, although Mrs Abernathy had dealt with them admirably. Those obstacles had included five of Duke Abigor's spies, whose heads now hung from the basilisk's saddle, the heads still arguing among themselves about which of them was most to blame for their misfortune. Mrs Abernathy paid them no heed. Her attention was focused on the boy who sat at the base of a large gilded cage not far from the door to Mrs Abernathy's small but perfectly formed palace.

Samuel watched her carefully through his glasses, one lens of which had cracked as he struggled vainly to escape the Watcher's grip when it became clear that Mrs Abernathy's arrival was imminent. Now, face to face with the woman who hated him more than any other creature in the Multiverse, he found himself examining her closely in the hope that some weakness might reveal itself. To be honest, Mrs Abernathy didn't look at all well. Some of the stitches keeping her face together had come loose, exposing a little of the reality of the monstrous form beneath, and her skin was discoloured, marked with patches of green like mould on bread. Her clothing was filthy and torn, her hair matted and dishevelled. As she circled Samuel she nibbled at one of her fingernails, and seemed surprised when it fell off.

'How are you, Samuel?' said Mrs Abernathy at last.

'I could be better,' said Samuel. 'After all, I'm in Hell. With you.'

'It's your own fault. I warned you against meddling in my affairs back on Earth.'

'I didn't have any choice but to meddle in them. You sent demons to kill me.'

'And very unsatisfactory they were too, given that they failed. It's so hard to get good staff these days. That's why I took it upon myself to drag you to Hell and, lo and behold, here you are. If I'd taken the time to kill you myself back in Biddlecombe, think of all the trouble I'd have avoided. Your home would be a place of ash and fire by now.'

'Well, sorry it didn't work out for you,' said Samuel.

'Don't be sarcastic, Samuel. It's a very low form of wit.[39] You know, now that I have you, you seem so much less worthy of the pursuit. I've spent all this time raging against you, planning the horrors I would inflict upon you, and it made me forget that you're really only

[39] The people who say that sarcasm is low wit are usually the ones who keep getting caught out by other people being sarcastic at their expense. Sarcasm is the lowest form of wit? Oh, you don't say . . .

a little boy, a little boy who got lucky for a while, and whose luck has now run out. Yet such trouble you've caused me, and so much distress and humiliation.'

'Is that why you're falling apart?'

Mrs Abernathy examined the index finger that had just lost its nail.

'Yes, in a way,' she said. 'Cut off from my master, I am like a tree without sunlight, a flower without water, a kitten without milk, a—'

She stopped talking when she sensed that the examples she was using were hardly appropriate for an arch-demon of Hell. Flowers? Kittens? She was sicker than she thought . . .

She stretched out a hand in the direction of the vast army of demons that had assembled, awaiting her command.

'You're the cause of all this,' she said. 'Armies are marching because of you. Demon stands against demon, duke against duke. I have ordered the annihilation of four legions in order to keep you safe. Hell has never seen such conflict, such turmoil. And all because of a little boy who couldn't keep his nose out of the business of others, and a demon who believed that he could escape my wrath in a fast car.'

At this, Samuel could not hide his shock.

'Oh, that's got your attention, hasn't it?' said Mrs Abernathy gloatingly. 'You thought I didn't know about your friend Nurd, the so-called Scourge of Five Deities?'

'He doesn't call himself that any longer,' said Samuel. 'It's just Nurd. Unlike you, he doesn't have any delusions of grandeur.' Samuel had heard his mother use that phrase about Mrs Browburthy, who was the chairperson of practically every committee in Biddlecombe and ruled them all like a dictator. He was rather pleased that he'd found an opportunity to use it now.

'Delusions?' said Mrs Abernathy. 'No, I have no delusions. I was great once, and then I was humbled, but I will be great again, mark me, and you will be the gift that restores me to my rightful place. As for Nurd, I will hunt him down when I have handed you over to my master. He will be tortured, just as you will be, but the greatest torment that I can devise will be to ensure that you and he never set eyes on each other again. You will have eternity to miss him, and he you, assuming you can find time for such fine feelings amid your own sufferings.'

She leaned in close to the bars and whispered to Samuel: 'And you can't even begin to imagine what I'm going to do to your rotten little dog, but I'll make sure that you can hear his howls of misery from wherever you are.'

Mrs Abernathy turned her back on Samuel and walked to the edge of the cliff that overlooked her army. She raised her right hand, and opened her mouth.

'Heed me!' she cried. The demons assembled below grew silent and gave her their attention. 'We are close to the moment of our triumph. The boy, Samuel, who foiled our invasion of Earth, who ensured that we would continue to suffer in this place, is in my grasp. We will take him to our master, the Great Malevolence, and we will offer the boy to him like a juicy fly to a spider. Our Dark Lord will arise from his grief, and all who were loyal to me will be rewarded, and all those who took arms against me and, in doing so, betrayed our master, will be punished for ever.'

A great cheer rose from the demons, and blades and claws and teeth flashed.

'But first our foes must be vanquished,' Mrs Abernathy continued. 'Already they gather before the entrance to the Mountain of Despair, intent upon instituting a new order in Hell, as if their ambitions can ever compare to the purity of our master's evil. They are led by the traitor Abigor, and great will be his suffering when victory is achieved. Now, look upon our prize!'

The Watcher ascended, and its claws grasped the ring at the top of the cage. The gilded prison rose into the air before suddenly Samuel was falling fast as the Watcher descended over the lines of demons, tens of thousands strong, all screaming their hatred at him as the cage flew barely inches above their heads, their spears and knives and sharp claws aimed at him as though hoping that they might save the Great Malevolence the trouble of ripping him apart. Samuel saw demons mounted on dragons and serpents, on toads and spiders and living fossils. He saw battle machines: catapults, and cannon, and great spiked wagons. He saw, amid the chaos of the lesser demons, the massed, ordered ranks of the legions, their loyalties distinguished by the banners of each duke, although those banners always flew lower than the standards depicting a horned figure set against a black background.

At last Samuel was lowered on to a flat wagon, where

Mrs Abernathy was already waiting for him. She ordered a black cloth to be placed over the cage, 'a taste of the greater blackness to come', and Samuel's last sight as the cloth fell was of Mrs Abernathy's triumphant, grinning visage.

The Watcher resumed its perch above the gathering. It saw the legions take the head of a column that began to snake toward the Mountain of Despair, the untrained masses falling loosely into place behind the troops. A fresh mount had been found for Mrs Abernathy, a massive hybrid of horse and serpent, its snake head snapping at its bridle, upon which she sat sidesaddle at the head of her army. She had even donned a new dress for the occasion, a little blue number with a lace collar. The wagon bearing the covered cage was surrounded by a phalanx of legionnaires who had been gifted to Mrs Abernathy by the allied dukes, and now bore a new coat of arms: a lady's handbag, decorated with a yellow daisy.

Curious, thought the Watcher. Appropriate, but . . . curious.

CHAPTER XXXIII

In Which a Third Force Intervenes
in the Conflict

The wagon rumbled beneath Samuel, tossing him from side to side as its rough-hewn wheels passed over the uneven ground. The repeated impacts against the cage were bruising his body, so he tried to hold on tight to the bars to prevent himself from being injured further. The cloth that covered the cage was quite thick, although Samuel's silhouette was still visible to those outside when lightning flashed, and he could just make out a tiny sliver of landscape visible through a hole in the material. When the wagon at last found itself on even ground, Samuel crawled over to the hole, knelt down, and peered out.

Elevated as he was above the surrounding horde, Samuel could see some distance across the Plains of Desolation. The Mountain of Despair rose before him, so big that it dominated the entire horizon, the extent of its base impossible to measure, its peak lost amid the battling clouds. There was an opening visible at the foot of the mountain, tiny by comparison with the great mass of black rock, but still huge enough to accommodate a hundred men standing on one another's shoulders, with room to spare so that the topmost man would not bang his head. Samuel had seen that opening before: through it, the Great Malevolence had briefly emerged just as it seemed his invasion of the world of men was destined to succeed. The memory reminded Samuel of what he was about to face: the vengeance of the most fearful being the Multiverse had ever known, an entity of pure evil, a creature without love, or pity, or mercy.

Terrified though he was, Samuel did not weaken. It is one thing to be brave in front of others, perhaps for fear of being branded a coward and becoming diminished in their eyes, but another entirely to be brave when there is nobody to witness your courage. The latter is an elemental bravery, a strength of spirit and character. It is a revelation of the essence of the self, and as Samuel crouched in his cage, slowly approaching the place in which his doom would be fixed, his face was calm and his soul was at peace. He had done nothing wrong. He had stood up for what he believed was right in order to protect his friends, his mother, his town, and the Earth itself. He did not rail at the unfairness of what was to come, for he understood in his heart that it would serve no purpose and would only make his torment harder to endure.

Had there been a soul inside Mrs Abernathy for her to examine, or had her vanity and lust for power and revenge not clouded her insight, she might have come to understand that she did not so much hate Samuel Johnson as fear him. There was an essential goodness to him that she could not touch, a decency that remained untainted by all that he had experienced so far in his short life. Samuel Johnson was human, with all of the flaws and foibles that came with his species. He could be jealous and sad, angry and selfish, but in him a little part of the best of humanity glowed brightly, just as it illuminates so many of us if we choose to let it. What Mrs Abernathy did not grasp was that, despite all that she or her master might visit upon him, she would never, ever defeat Samuel Johnson, and no matter how deep or dark the place in which he was interred, his soul would continue to shine.

The wagon ascended an incline, and as it reached the top Samuel gasped, for arrayed on the plain before him was another mighty army: row upon row of demon legionnaires, their long shields catching the reflection of the bolts of lightning that broke through the clouds above with greater and greater frequency and ferocity, as though the angry spirits in the skies were urging on the opposing forces, seeking on the battlefield below a reflection of their own wrath. Mounted cavalry were moving into position, the eyes of their skinless steeds like hot coals set in ash, their hooves striking sparks from the stony ground.

Behind the main ranks strode the monsters of the underworld: cyclopses, and minotaurs, and snake-headed hydrae; gigantic gorgons, their faces masked with plates of gold until the order came to reveal themselves, but their serpentine locks already writhing in anticipation of the fighting to come; and lurching, predatory creatures with the bodies of men and the heads of vicious animals. Many of the beasts seemed familiar to Samuel, and not merely because they had formed part of the huge force originally destined to conquer the earth. These were the monsters that shadowed all of the Earth's mythologies and religions, the beings that had appeared to the ancients in nightmares and had found their way into legends and fairy tales, books of myths and books of faith.

Allied with them were jumbled entities that had never been imagined before, for only madness could have conjured up such visions: heads on legs, scuttling sideways like crabs, sharp teeth snapping; creatures that were hybrids of shark and spider, of toad and bat, of earwig and dog, as though segments of every animal that ever existed on Earth had been tossed in a great vat and allowed to fuse with one another.

And then there were beings that bore no resemblance to anything from Samuel's world, even in the most passing of ways: shifting masses of matter that reached out with wisps of darkness, probing for prey; fleshy globes with a thousand mouths; and entities that existed only as painful sounds, or poisonous smells. It seemed that no force could stand up to such horrors and triumph, yet similar creatures, and worse, had gathered to serve Mrs Abernathy. Her army might have been more ragged and less disciplined, with fewer of the trained legions to array themselves meticulously for battle, but Samuel believed that Mrs Abernathy's strength was greater overall. The conflict would be a test of strategy against might, of military training against sheer weight of numbers.

But regardless of who won, Samuel would ultimately lose, for all here wished him harm.

The Watcher flew high over the battlefield, higher even than the winged scout demons of Mrs Abernathy and Duke Abigor, so high that the gathering combatants were lost to it and there was only cloud below and the peaks of the Moutain of Despair rising before it. The Watcher had made its decision. It could not stand by and watch Hell torn apart. Its loyalty was to one, and one only: the Great Malevolence.

It was time for the bells to ring.

At the entrance to the Mountain of Despair Edgefast and Brompton were regarding the awesome armies, the greatest ever gathered in conflict in Hell's long history, with the slightly bored air of men who are watching a repeat of a football game to which they already know the score, and which hadn't been very interesting first time around.

'Busy out there today,' said Brompton. Despite the fact that he could quite easily have had himself reassembled after Mrs Abernathy tore him apart, he was still a severed head resting beside a pile of assorted limbs and bits of torso, although he now had a cushion, thanks to an uncharacteristic moment of weakness on the part of Edgefast. Brompton had elected to remain a talking head because a) he claimed that his experience had altered his view of Hell, and he now saw the world, quite literally, from a different angle; b) he no longer had to worry about laundry, or tying his shoelaces; and c) he could spot anyone really small who might try to sneak in. This had seemed perfectly acceptable to Edgefast, who didn't want to have to bother getting to know another new guard.

'Suppose so,' said Edgefast, picking at his teeth. 'If you like that kind of thing.'

'Makes a change, though, doesn't it, all them demons milling around? Very exciting, I'd say.'

'I don't approve of change,' said Edgefast. 'Or excitement.' He shifted from one foot to another, and looked uncomfortable. 'Mind you, I shouldn't have had that last cup of tea. Gone right through me, that has. I'm about to have an accident. Look, mind the shop for five minutes while I go and, you know, make myself lighter in a liquid way.'

'Right you are,' said Brompton. 'I'll look after things.'

Desperate though he was to relieve himself, Edgefast took a moment's pause.

'Now, you know this is a big responsibility.'

'Yes, absolutely.'

'You can't let anyone in who isn't supposed to be allowed in, and since nobody is supposed to be allowed in – Chancellor Ozymuth's orders – then you mustn't let anybody in, full stop.'

'Understood.'

'Not anybody.'

'They shall not pass,' said Brompton sternly.

'No passing. Not a one.'

Edgefast moved away, then came back again.

'Nobody, right?'

'No. Body. Nobody.'

'Good.'

Edgefast shuffled off. Brompton whistled a happy tune. It was his first time alone at the entrance, and he liked being in charge. He was a good guard, was Brompton. He didn't nip off for naps, he took his job seriously, and he was happy to serve. He had the right spirit for a guard.

Unfortunately he had the wrong body, namely none at all.

He heard the beating of wings and two large red feet landed in front of him. Since he couldn't move his head, Brompton did his best to look up by raising his eyebrows and squinting. The Watcher's eight black eyes stared down at him in bemusement.

'Nobody's allowed in, mate,' said Brompton. 'You'll have to leave a message.'

The Watcher considered this possibility for a moment, then simply stepped around Brompton and marched into the heart of the mountain.

'Oi!' shouted Brompton. 'Come back. You can't do that. I'm the guard. I'm guarding. You can't just step around me. It's not fair. Seriously! You're undermining my authority. Back you come and we'll say no more about it, all right?'

The sound of the Watcher's footsteps grew distant.

'All right?' repeated Brompton.

There was silence, then more footsteps, this time lighter, and approaching with the reluctant shamble of someone who is returning to work but really would prefer not to be.

'Yeah, all right,' said Edgefast. 'Feel much better, thanks. Forgot to wash me hands, but never mind. Anything I should know about?'

Brompton thought carefully before answering.

'No,' he said. 'Nothing at all.'

CHAPTER XXXIV

In Which We Encounter Some Cunning Disguises

There were many curious and alarming vehicles dotted among the opposing sides on the battlefield: war wagons, their steel-rimmed wheels accessorized with bladed spikes, their beds protected by layers of metal to shield the driver and the archers beneath; primitive tanks with long turrets through which oil could be pumped and then ignited by a standing flame at the mouth of the turret; siege weapons shaped like serpents, and dragons, and sea monsters; and field catapults crewed and ready for action, their cradles filled with rocks.

A word about the rocks, or, indeed, a word *from* the rocks, which might be equally appropriate: as we have already seen, there were numerous entities in Hell – trees, clouds, and so on – that were sentient when, under ordinary circumstances, they should not have been. Among them were certain types of rock that had developed little mouths, some rudimentary eyes, and an overestimation of their own value in what passed for Hell's ecosystem.[40] Thus it was that a number of

💀 [40] Like a great many organisms straining for sophistication, they had also created their own basic form of music. Please insert your own joke here.

the rocks residing in the cradles of the catapults were complaining loudly about their situation, pointing out that they would, upon impact, be reduced to the status of pebbles or, even worse, rubble, which is the equivalent of a king or queen being forced to live in a tent and claim unemployment benefit. Nobody was listening, of course, since they were rocks, and there's a limit to the amount of harm a rock can do unless someone gives it a bit of help by flinging it at someone or something with considerable force. As these rocks would very soon be headed in the direction of the enemy, it was felt that they could address their complaints to interested parties on the other side, assuming the individuals in question a) survived having a rock flung at them; and b) were in the mood to consider the rock's complaints about its treatment in the aftermath, which seemed unlikely.

So when a large rock with four eyes began pressing through the ranks of Mrs Abernathy's demons, it barely merited a second glance, even if it did appear to be growling more than most rocks tended to. Neither did the vehicle following in its wake attract much attention, even if its effectiveness as a machine of war was debatable given that its weaponry consisted solely of four wooden posts stuck to its front and rear parts, the remainder of its body being covered by a white dust-proof cloth with slits at eye level. What was beyond question, however, was the ferocity of the four small demons riding upon its back. Horns protruded from their foreheads, and their faces dripped with disgusting green and red fluids of indeterminate origin. Somehow they contrived to be even more terrible than the two warthog demons escorting the larger vehicle, and who discouraged those unwise creatures who tried to peer under the dustcloth from investigating further by hitting them very hard with big clubs.

'Coming through,' shouted Jolly. 'Mind your backs.' He nudged Dozy. 'And stop licking that raspberry and lime from your face. You're ruining the effect.'

'One of my horns is coming loose,' said Angry.

'Then use more chewing gum,' said Jolly. 'Here, take mine.'

He removed a lump of pink material from his mouth and handed it to Angry, who accepted it with some reluctance and used it to stick his ice-cream cone horn more securely to his forehead.

'Grrrrrr!' said Mumbles, waving one of D. Bodkin's staplers in a threatening manner.

'Let us at them!' said Dozy. 'We'll tear their heads off and use them for bowling balls.'

'Sissies, the lot of 'em,' cried Angry, getting into the spirit of the thing and making a variety of rude gestures at Duke Abigor's forces in the hope that at least one of them would be understood as an insult by the opposing side.

'Easy, lads,' said the voice of Constable Peel from somewhere under the dustcloth. 'We don't want to attract the wrong kind of attention.'

'What kind of attention would that be?' asked Angry, and received his answer as a black arrow whistled past his ear and embedded itself in the body of the ice-cream van. 'Oh, right. Fair enough.'

The little convoy made its way slowly alongside the wagon on which rested Samuel's hooded cage. Dozy and Mumbles produced some paper cups and began pouring drinks for the demons surrounding the wagon.

'Drink up, boys,' said Dozy, handing down the cups. 'And girls. And, er, whatever you are. Haven't you ever heard of having a drink before the war?'

And while the demons drank, temporarily sacrificing their eyesight, their balance, and their desire to live to cups of not-quite-right-but-still-not-too-bad-all-things-considered imitation Spiggit's, Angry and Jolly dropped from the roof on to the bed of the wagon. Mumbles threw them a sack, and the two dwarfs, with their burden, slipped silently under the cloth.

Mrs Abernathy raised a hand to halt her troops. Three horses, on which were mounted members of Abigor's personal guard, advanced from the opposing lines. A white banner fluttered from a pike held by the leader of the three, the captain of the guard. They rode to within hailing distance of Mrs Abernathy, and halted.

'By order of Duke Abigor, we demand the surrender of the traitor, Mrs Abernathy,' said the captain.

In the distance Mrs Abernathy could see Abigor mounted on his great steed, his red cloak bleeding into the air behind him. Surrender? Could he be serious? She thought not. He was covering himself in case questions later arose about his conduct. Yes, he could say, I gave her the opportunity to surrender and avoid conflict, but she refused, and so I had no choice but to proceed against her.'

'I know of no traitor by such a name,' said Mrs Abernathy. 'I know only of the traitor Abigor, who has taken arms against the commander of Hell's forces. If *he* surrenders to *me*, and orders his demons to lay down their weapons and disperse, then I can promise him . . . nothing at all, actually. Regardless, he is doomed. It is merely a matter of how deep in the great lake of Cocytus I choose to inter him.'

'He also demands that you hand over the boy, Samuel Johnson,' said the captain, as if Mrs Abernathy had not spoken. 'He is an interloper, a pollutant, and an enemy of the state. Duke Abigor will ensure that he is imprisoned securely, that he may do no further harm.'

'That, too, I refuse,' said Mrs Abernathy. 'Is there anything else?'

'Indeed there is,' said the captain. 'Duke Abigor orders you to reveal the whereabouts of the portal between worlds, a portal that was opened without the knowledge or approval of our master, the Great Malevolence, and threatens the stability of this realm.'

Mrs Abernathy said nothing for a time, as though composing a suitable response. Eventually the captain of the guard grew tired of waiting.

'What answer should I bring to Duke Abigor?' he said. 'Speak now, lest he unleash his wrath upon you.'

'Well,' said Mrs Abernathy, 'you can say – oh, never mind, I'll let you work it out yourself.'

From her back emerged her lethal tentacles. Before the three riders could react, they were enveloped, and within seconds they and their horses had been ripped apart. Mrs Abernathy gathered up the remains, crushed them into a ball of flesh and bone, leather and metal, then hurled it in the direction of Abigor's lines. The mess rolled as far as Abigor's mount, where it bounced off the horse's front legs and came to rest.

'I think that was a "no",' said Abigor. 'I was rather hoping it would be. Jolly good. Carnage it is, then.'

The Watcher moved swiftly through the Mountain of Despair. The arches and alcoves that had echoed with laughter and mockery during Mrs Abernathy's last visit were now silent. The creatures that dwelt within them retreated to the shadows, fearful of drawing the attention of the Watcher to themselves, and only when it had passed did they peer out at it. It was a long time since the Watcher had walked through those great halls, but the memory of it had remained. Its presence in the mountain was a reminder of an older order, and as it walked it seemed to grow larger and more powerful, as though feeding upon an energy meant for it alone.

Chancellor Ozymuth waited for it at the end of the causeway. He raised his staff and the Watcher halted.

'Go back, old one,' said Ozymuth. 'There is no place for you here. Your time is over. A new force rises.'

The Watcher's black eyes stared at him implacably. In them, Ozymuth was reflected eight times, a pale figure against the darkness, as though he were already lost.

'The Great Malevolence is mad,' continued Ozymuth.

'Another will rule in his stead until his wits are restored. Mrs Abernathy must bow to the inevitable, and you must find some dusty, forgotten corner of this kingdom where you may fade from remembrance, lest you share the fate of your doomed mistress. Cocytus is wide and deep, and there is a place in it for you, should you continue to resist the inevitable. Your time of service to your mistress has come to an end.'

The voice of the Watcher spoke in Ozymuth's head.

Mrs Abernathy is not my mistress.

Ozymuth's desiccated features formed themselves into the semblance of a grin. 'You see sense, then?'

I serve another.

'You speak of Duke Abigor? It may be that he can find some use for you.'

No. I serve another.

Ozymuth frowned. 'You answer in riddles. Perhaps age has addled your brain after all. Go! I am done with you. We are all done with you. Your fall will be great.'

Ozymuth was about to turn away when one of the Watcher's hands grasped him by the throat and lifted him from the ground. Ozymuth tried to speak but the Watcher's grip was too tight, and Ozymuth could only gurgle as he was held over the edge of the causeway, his eyes widening in understanding. Beneath him opened a swirling vortex of red like the interior of a volcano, but its very centre was dark, the blackness within stretching for ever.

You have poisoned my master. You have brought us to the brink of war.

Ozymuth managed to shake his head, his feet kicking,

his hands clawing at the Watcher's arms as he heard the last words he would ever hear.

It is your fall that will be great.

The Watcher released him, and Ozymuth began his eternal descent.

CHAPTER XXXV

In Which Battle Commences, and a Rescue Mission is Mounted

Samuel turned at the sound of his cage bars rattling. A match flared, and he experienced a moment of pure terror at the sight of the demonic figures revealed until one of the ice-cream cone horns fell from Angry's forehead once again, and Jolly rubbed some of the 'blood' from his face, licked his fingertips, and said, 'It's just raspberry ripple! Oh, and sweat.'

'All right, son?' said Angry. 'We'll have you out of there in no time, as long as the lightning holds off for a minute or two.'

From somewhere on his person he produced a set of picks, and began working on the lock.

'What's happening?' asked Samuel. 'I can't see much from in here.'

'Well,' said Jolly, striking another match as the first one died, 'that Mrs Abernathy woman was asked to surrender and hand you over, but she didn't think much of that idea so she tore the messengers apart, rolled them in a ball, and sent them back where they came from. Strong female, she is. Model of her kind, assuming anyone could tell what kind she is exactly. My guess is that, any time now, there's going to be a lot of shouting, and stabbing, and general warmongering going on all around us.'

'What about Nurd, and Boswell, and the others?'

'All fine, and all nearby.'

There was a loud *click*, and the cage door opened.

'Barely worth the name "lock", that was,' said Angry. 'I've had cans of beer that were harder to open.'

'So what's the plan?' asked Samuel, as he clambered out of the cage.

'It's Mr Nurd's,' said Jolly. 'And it's genius.'

He opened the sack and revealed what lay within.

'You can't be serious,' said Samuel.

But they were.

Duke Abigor raised a hand, and a horn rang out. From behind him came the sound of a thousand arrows being nocked, and a thousand bowstrings being drawn tight.

'On my command!' cried Abigor, then let his hand fall. Instantly the arrows were released, darkening the sky as they hurtled towards the enemy lines.

'Oh, crumbs,' said Constable Peel, peering through the slit in the cloth that covered Dan's ice-cream van. 'That's a lot of arrows.'

But just as the arrows reached the top of their arc and began to fall, they burst into flames, and a cheer rose up the ranks of Mrs Abernathy's army. The lady in question was visible upon her mount, her arms raised and smoke and flames pouring from her fingers.

'I'm glad she's on our side,' said Constable Peel.

'Only until she finds out that we are on *her* side,'

said Sergeant Rowan. 'Then she'll take a very different view.'

Another flight of arrows was unleashed against them, but this time in greater number, and some of them broke through Mrs Abernathy's fiery defences and embedded themselves in the flesh of demons. The demons didn't seem terribly perturbed about their injuries, though, and for the most part just stared at the arrows in mild annoyance.

'Well, they don't seem to be doing much harm,' said Constable Peel, just as a nearby entity, a hunched being of black fur and bad teeth, tugged at the arrow in its chest and promptly exploded in a shower of flesh and white light.

'On the other hand . . .'

Abigor ordered his first wave of cavalry to attack, and the skinless horses carried their riders towards Mrs Abernathy's army. The cavalry wielded heavy lances with vicious, multi-bladed tips, and although half of them fell beneath the onslaught of spears, arrows, and complaining rocks that ripped through their ranks, the remainder hit the first line with incredible force, tearing a hole in the shield wall and impaling the soldiers behind before casting the long lances aside and swinging maces and swords to brutal effect.

A second wave of cavalry attacked, followed by the demonic rank and file, led by Duke Abigor and his personal guard. Meanwhile two legions had commenced a flanking movement, hoping to encircle Mrs Abernathy's army entirely. In response, Mrs Abernathy's forces unleashed torrents of flame and clouds of arrows, while

Mrs Abernathy herself waded into her opponents, the tentacles on her back whipping and writhing, pulling riders from their horses and ripping them apart like bugs. The gorgons at last revealed their hideous visages, turning to stone those who did not look away in time, while those who did hide their faces found themselves vulnerable to attack. The cyclopean giants swung their clubs, tossing aside ten soldiers at a time. Dragons on both sides set hair and skin and flesh burning, while sirens attacked from above like birds of prey, their outstretched claws impaling themselves in flesh and armour, inflicting awful wounds that turned instantly black as the poison in their talons infected the tissue. The fighting drew closer and closer to where the disguised car and the ice-cream van stood, hemmed in by the thronging mass of demons anxious to join in the fight.

'Guard the cage!' screamed Mrs Abernathy, for the discipline of Abigor's legions was beginning to tell, and she felt the battle turning against her. A second line of demons surrounded the wagon, their blades unsheathed, forming a wall of sharp metal and sharper teeth through which none could penetrate. Only a few noticed that the original guards were more than a little unsteady on their feet, and seemed to be having trouble focusing, but then more arrows began to descend and avoiding impalement took precedence over all else.

There was blood, and screaming, all lit by bolts of lightning from above as Hell tore itself apart.

CHAPTER XXXVI

In Which a Certain Someone Wakes Up
With a Sore Head

It was Dozy, now back in the relative safety of the ice-cream van, who noticed it first, just as he finished helping Jolly and Angry back inside after the successful completion of their rescue mission.

'Did you hear that?' he said.

'All I can hear is the noise of battle,' said Constable Peel.

'No, it was something else. Like an echo, but before a sound has been made to cause it.'

Slowly, bells began to toll deep in the heart of the mountain, growing louder and louder. The sound of them was so loud and so resonant that all who heard them covered their ears in pain. The vibrations caused the ground to tremble. Cracks appeared on the plain. In the Hollow Hills caves collapsed, and from the icy mountains to the north great avalanches flowed down and smothered the faces of those unfortunates who broke the surface of Cocytus. The Sea of Unpleasantness was riven by earthquakes beneath its surface, and tsunamis of black water rose up and broke upon the barren shores. On the battlefield weapons fell from hands, and horses threw their riders. Ears bled, teeth were loosened in their gums. Demons cowered, wailing in agony. Over and over the bells sounded, shaking stones from the Mountain of Despair, until the very notion of Hell itself was reduced to a single essence: the awful pealing of the bells that had been silent for so long, heard only at the times of greatest crisis in that place.

And then suddenly they stopped, and demons of all shapes and forms turned their heads in the direction of the Mountain of Despair. Flames flickered deep in its heart as a shape appeared in the doorway. It was the Watcher, now many times taller and broader than before, its red skin glowing as though the creature had recently been forged in the fires within, a being of metal or stone that would slowly cool to grey and black.

'How did it get in?' hissed Brompton to Edgefast, as the shadow of the Watcher advanced before them.

'It must have sneaked by,' said Edgefast, trying not to catch Brompton's eye.

'It's forty feet tall! What did it do, wear a hat and dark glasses? Some guard you are.'

But all questions about the Watcher, and any amazement that the guards, and the two armies, and Mrs Abernathy and Duke Abigor, might have felt at its altered appearance faded away as it became clear that another presence was emerging from the mountain, a figure that dwarfed the Watcher just as the Watcher towered above most of the demons arrayed on the field. A fierce stench of sulphur swept across the plain and the light from within the mountain was lost, the flames hidden by the mass of the approaching creature. All was utter stillness and silence among the assembled armies. Even the dwarfs were quiet, seemingly frozen into muteness and immobility by what they were seeing. In Nurd's Aston Martin, Boswell buried his muzzle in Samuel's armpit, and closed his eyes in terror, just as his nose twitched at the stink of what was coming, forming a picture of it in his dog brain that he was unable to erase.

So enormous was the Great Malevolence that he had to crouch in order to pass beneath the lintel of the mountain's door. When he stood erect at last there was a grandeur to the sight; a sense of awe infected all who witnessed it, for here was not merely the most ancient and ferocious of evils, but the element of Evil itself given form. From this being flowed all that was wrong, all that was foul, all that blighted hope in world upon world, universe upon universe. His crown was formed from spurs of bone that grew from his own skull, jagged and yellow. His great frame was still sheathed in the armour that he had donned in expectation of his crusade upon Earth, etched with the names of every man and woman born and yet to be born, for he hated them all and wanted to remember his fury at each one, the great litany of names constantly being added to as more humans entered the world. Some of those names burned, for there were those who had damned themselves by their actions, and so were destined to join him.

Most of the flesh on the Great Malevolence's face had long since decayed, leaving a thin layer of brown, leathery skin draped over his bones, broken at his cheeks so that the muscles and bone beneath were clearly visible. His teeth were jagged and double-rowed, set in blackened, diseased gums, and a pale pink serpent's tongue licked at his rotted lips.

But terrible though his face was, it was his eyes that truly chilled, for they were almost human in the depth of their feeling, filled with unbounded rage and a dreadful, poisonous sadness. From where he watched inside Nurd's car, Samuel understood at last why this being hated men and women so much: he hated them because they were so like himself, because the worst of them was mirrored in him. He was the source of all that was bad in men and women, but he had none of the greatness, and none of the grace, of which human beings were capable, so that only by corrupting them was his own pain and regret diminished, and thus his existence made more tolerable.

Now he stared out over the battlefield, the Watcher poised before him, and as he spoke all trembled in fear.

'WHO HAS DARED TO RAISE OPPOSING ARMIES IN MY REALM? WHO SETS DEMON AGAINST DEMON?'

As if by a prearranged signal the armies separated, putting as much space as possible between themselves and their commanders, so that Mrs Abernathy and Duke Abigor stood isolated.

'My lord and master,' said Abigor, bowing his head. 'It is good to see you restored to us. Without your hand to guide us we have been lost, and we have been betrayed by our own. I have been forced to act to protect this great kingdom against the treason of one who was once beloved of you, this –' he gestured at Mrs Abernathy with disgust – 'polluted personage, this patchwork woman.' He seemed about to say more, but the Great Malevolence raised a clawed finger and Duke Abigor was silent as his master turned his attention to Mrs Abernathy.

'DOES ABIGOR LIE?'

'No, my master,' said Mrs Abernathy. 'For we have been lost, and we have been betrayed, but the treason was not mine. Look to the standards: I fight under your banner, but Abigor fights only under his own.'

'Permit me to explain—' began Abigor, but his words turned to fat black flies that buzzed against his cheeks and tongue, and Mrs Abernathy allowed herself a sly grin as her opponent tried to spit out the insects, but with each one that he ejected two more came into being until Abigor's mouth was filled with them.

'I set out to make amends to you for my failings, and I have done so,' continued Mrs Abernathy, now that she had silenced Abigor for a time.

'YOUR FAILINGS WERE GREAT. SO TOO MUST BE THE RECOMPENSE.'

'And it is,' said Mrs Abernathy. 'For I have brought you the child who sabotaged all that we had worked for. I have brought you Samuel Johnson!'

She waved to the wagon driver, who urged on his horses, bringing the covered cage to the clearing on the battlefield. Beside her Abigor had found enough power to disperse the flies, and interrupted her.

'She lies, my master! I fight beneath my own banner only because she uses your standard to hide her treason.

293

She has compounded betrayal with more betrayal. She stole the child from me. It was I who found a way to open the portal, but she took the boy from my castle that she might claim credit for his capture.'

The wagon drew nearer, its prize waiting to be revealed, lightning flashing to reveal the shape inside the cage.

'And where is the portal that you opened, Duke Abigor?' asked Mrs Abernathy. 'Show it to us, that we may marvel at it. Display it for our master, that we may harness its potential for another invasion.'

'It vanished,' spluttered Abigor. 'I could not keep it open for long. I could only find time to snatch the boy before it closed again.'

Mrs Abernathy raised her arms.

'Let me give you proof of his treason, my master,' she said. 'For I know the location of the portal. I know, for it lies . . . within me!'

Her eyes shone a cold blue, and a blue glow filled her mouth. The air around her seemed to swirl, forming a column of dust and ash that caught the light coming from within her, so that she became the centre of her own blue world. As she grew taller and taller she was both Mrs Abernathy and her old, ancient self, the demon Ba'al, its tentacles writhing, its massive head visible beneath Mrs Abernathy's stretched skin, like one transparent image overlaid upon another. Her segmented jaws opened wider and wider – ten, twenty, thirty feet in width – revealing a tunnel of dark light with a blue heart.

'Behold, my master!' she cried. 'Behold the portal! And behold – Samuel Johnson!'

The wagon master whipped away the black cloth, and the crowd gasped at the figure of Mr Happy Whip, grinning his plastic grin at the assembled forces of Hell.

And at that moment a rock with four eyes shot from the ranks, followed closely by a cloth-covered wagon adorned with unimpressive horns. The disguises fell away, revealing Dan, Dan the Ice-Cream Man, hunched over the wheel of his beloved van, urged on by Sergeant Rowan, and Constable Peel, and four determined dwarfs; revealing Samuel Johnson in the Aston Martin once owned by his dad, Boswell held tightly in the crook of one arm, the other hand resting on the shoulder of a goggle-eyed Wormwood.

And revealing Nurd: Nurd, no longer Nurd the inept, Nurd the coward; no longer Nurd, the Scourge of Five Deities. No, this was a Nurd transformed. This was Nurd, the Vanquisher of Demons. This was Nurd, the Triumphant.

This was Nurd, the Frankly Terrified.

Before Mrs Abernathy could react, Nurd had driven the car straight into her mouth, the ice-cream van barely inches behind him. As they disappeared through the portal, the faint strains of 'How Much Is That Doggie in the Window?' floated from Mrs Abernathy's jaws over the great plain.

Even on a battlefield where two massive armies faced each other, and the Devil himself towered over them both seeking an explanation for what was going on, a pair of motorized vehicles driving straight down a demon's throat, a throat recently transformed into a gateway between universes, still counted as something quite out of the ordinary. Nothing happened for a number of seconds, apart from the occupants of the two vehicles falling through a wormhole of sorts, with all that entailed, including being stretched to the point of agony and then compressed in a similarly painful manner, but all this was hidden from the denizens of Hell, who continued to stare at Mrs Abernathy to see how she might respond to this recent turn of events.

Mrs Abernathy might have hidden the seeds of the portal within herself, but she had not intended it to be used in the manner to which Samuel, Nurd and company had just put it. She had planned on manifesting it at a point outside herself and then, with her master's help, drawing all the power that she could from the Collider in one fell swoop and reversing the portal's direction of travel, so that instead of moving objects from Earth to Hell, it would move them from Hell to Earth. It would not be enough to pass an army through, but it would be enough to transport the Great Malevolence and herself to the world of men, and there they would create a new Hell, just the two of them. Unfortunately that plan now looked like it would have to be put on the back burner, for Mrs Abernathy had more pressing concerns.

Her body shuddered. She gagged and choked, like someone who has swallowed a piece of food that has gone down the wrong way, which in a vehicular sense was more or less what had happened. The blue light grew stronger and brighter, so bright that the assembled demons, even the Great Malevolence himself, were forced to look away from it, so bright that it turned from blue to white, and burned so strongly that Mrs Abernathy screamed.

The portal collapsed, and Mrs Abernathy imploded, her being turning in upon itself, the substance of her spiralling inward as every atom in her body was separated from the next. Her disguise of human skin was sucked from her, revealing the old monster within. Her segmented jaws were pulled into her throat, her tentacles folded themselves over the front of her body as though to protect her, and there was a soft popping sound as the portal closed and the fragments of her being were scattered throughout the Multiverse.

CHAPTER XXXVII

In Which We Get to the 'Happy Ever After' Part

There was a blue flash on Ambrose Bierce Drive and two vehicles appeared: an Aston Martin, its windows so cracked that it was impossible to see through them, its four wheels splayed outward like the legs of a collapsing animal so that the car rested on its underside; and a very battered ice-cream van, containing four similarly battered dwarfs covered from head to toe in raspberry ripple; two policemen whose hats had melted; and one bewildered ice-cream salesman with smoking hair.

'Next time we take the train,' said Jolly, staggering from the back of the van. 'I feel like I've been dragged through a washing machine backwards.'

His fellow dwarfs joined him, Dozy utilizing one of his horns to scrape up the last of the ripple. Acrid smoke began to emerge from beneath the van, quickly followed by flickering flames. Dan, Dan the Ice-Cream Man looked on mournfully as the remains of his business went up in smoke.

'Perhaps I wasn't really cut out to be an ice-cream

salesman,' he said. 'At least the insurance will cover it, I suppose.'

Jolly tapped him on the arm. 'Think you'll buy a new van, then?'

'Probably. Don't know what I'll do with it, though.'

'Funny you should mention that,' said Jolly, adopting his most trustworthy of expressions. 'How would you feel about transporting four hard-working, self-motivated individuals to a variety of business engagements?'

'Sounds all right,' said Dan.

'It does, doesn't it?' said Jolly. 'I wish we actually *knew* four hard-working, self-motivated individuals, but in their absence, how about driving the four of us around instead?'

Sergeant Rowan and Constable Peel helped Nurd, Wormwood, Samuel and Boswell to free themselves from the Aston Martin, as the doors had buckled badly when they travelled through the portal.

Nurd patted the roof of the car sadly. 'I think she may have taken her last trip,' he said, as Wormwood wiped a tear from his eye. Wormwood had grown to love the Aston Martin almost as much as he loved Nurd; more so, even, as the car had never hit him with a sceptre, used unpleasant language towards him, or threatened to bury him upside down in sand for eternity.

'At least you have a car, or what's left of one,' said Constable Peel. 'How are we going to explain the loss of our patrol car, Sarge? And where did it go?'

'We'll never know, son,' said Sergeant Rowan.[41]

Suddenly there was movement in the flaming ice-cream van, and seconds later Shan and Gath emerged from the conflagration, patting out small patches of fire on their fur.

'Forgot about them,' said Angry, with the casual air of someone who has left a shoelace undone rather than abandoned two creatures to an inferno of metal, plastic and assorted ripples.

'Where did they come from?' asked Constable Peel.

'We hid them in the fridges while you were up front with the sarge and Dan,' said Jolly. 'Sorry. I mean, it wasn't like we could leave them in Hell, not after that winged bloke found Samuel at their cave. It wouldn't have been fair.'

💀 [41] Somewhere in the depths of Hell, a massive invisible floating demon named Fred had just arrived home to his invisible wife, Felicity, and invisible child, Little Fred. 'Where have you been, then?' asked his invisible wife. 'I don't know what you think you are, sauntering about like you haven't a care in Hell, leaving me all alone to keep Little Fred amused. Most of the time, it's like you're never here at all.' Fred, being invisible, was tempted to point out that, even when he was there, it was like he was never there at all, but he didn't think this was the time, as, although he was invisible, and therefore should have presented a hard target for his beloved missus, she seemed to have an uncanny ability to score direct hits upon him with various household objects. Instead he put a police car and a van beside Little Fred, or where he thought Little Fred might roughly be. In the manner of kids everywhere, Little Fred immediately picked up the vehicles and banged them together, before running their wheels across the dirt while making 'brrrmmmm-brrrmmmm' noises.

'They're supposed to come with little men', said Fred, 'but I know he'd just lose them.'

'What about me?' asked Felicity.

'Just a kiss for you, my love,' said Fred.

He pecked lovingly at the air.

'I'm over here, you idiot . . .'

'We've brought four demons to Earth,' said Sergeant Rowan. He had gone rather pale. 'They'll have my stripes.'

Constable Peel grinned. 'I don't have any stripes.'

'I know. They'll have your guts for garters instead.'

'Oh.'

'Yes, "Oh." Not grinning now, are you?'

'But we'll get into terrible trouble, Sarge, and I've had enough trouble to last a lifetime. The chief constable isn't going to approve of us bringing demons back from Hell. He doesn't even like going abroad for his holidays because it's full of foreigners. If we tell him what we've done, we'll be directing traffic for the rest of our lives.'

Sergeant Rowan looked at Shan and Gath. Having put out the flames on their fur, they were now fortifying themselves with the last of their home brew.

'Then we won't tell him,' said Sergeant Rowan.

'But we can't just leave them and Nurd and Wormwood to wander around. It wouldn't be right.'

'We're not going to leave them to wander around either,' said Sergeant Rowan. 'Constable Peel, I have a plan ...'

Nurd looked at the blue sky above his head, clouds scudding across it, lit by the amber glow of a beautiful setting sun. He smelled flowers, and grass, and burning ice-cream cones. He saw a cat scratching its back against a pillar, and a bird pecking seeds from a feeder. He felt exhilarated, and free.

And very afraid. He was an alien creature here, a demon. They might hate him, or fear him, and lock him away. What about Wormwood? Wormwood had barely been able to look after himself in Hell. Without Nurd he'd be lost, but even Nurd wasn't sure how they were going to survive in the world of men.

A hand grasped his, squeezing it tightly. Nurd looked down and saw Samuel. Beside him, Boswell wagged his tail.

'It's going to be OK,' said Samuel. 'Look, it's a brave new world.'

The whole trip to Hell, with all of its traumas and triumphs, had lasted a mere three hours on Earth, and his mother, although worried, had not yet begun to actively fret, although she did as soon as Samuel explained to her what had occurred. A cup of tea was definitely in order, but this time Mrs Johnson went out to get the milk herself while Samuel had a bath. When Mrs Johnson returned Wormwood was in the bath, and Nurd was wearing one of Mr Johnson's old bathrobes and blowing bubbles from a small plastic pipe.

'What are we going to do about those two?' asked Mrs Johnson as she arranged tea and cake on a tray. 'They can't stay here for ever. We don't have enough room.'

'There's a plan,' said Samuel.

And there was.

Samuel went to school as usual the following morning. To those who were perceptive enough to spot the changes, like Tom and Maria, he seemed older somehow, but also stronger and more determined, even before he told his two closest friends all that had happened the previous day. Then, his spare glasses fixed firmly upon his nose, he strode up to the canteen, where he found Lucy Highmore and two of her friends finishing some homework at one of the tables.

'Hello,' said Samuel to Lucy. 'Can I talk to you for a moment?'

Lucy nodded, and her friends packed up their books and departed, giggling. Lucy looked hard at Samuel Johnson for the first time. She had never been very unkind to him, but neither had she exchanged more than a couple of words with him before. They were in different classes, and only mixed at assembly. Now, face to face and with no distractions, she thought that he was quite handsome in a funny way, and although they were the same age there was a sadness, and a wisdom, in his eyes that made him appear older than she.

'My name's Samuel.'

'I know.'

'Yesterday I asked out a letter box, thinking it was you.'

'Do I look like a letter box?'

'No, not really. Not at all, actually.'

'So it wasn't an easy mistake to make, then?'

'No.'

'That's good to know.'

'Yes, I would expect so.'

There was a silence between them for a time.

'Well?' said Lucy.

'Well,' said Samuel, 'I was rather hoping that you might like to join me at Pete's for a pie after school on Friday, if you weren't busy.'

Lucy considered the offer, then smiled regretfully.

'I'm sorry. I'm busy on Friday.'

'Oh,' said Samuel. He bit his lip, and turned away. At least I tried, he thought.

'I'm not busy on Saturday, though.'

'How did it go?' asked Maria, when she encountered Samuel in the corridor later that day.

'She said "yes",' said Samuel.

'Oh, good,' said Maria, and walked away, and Samuel thought that she seemed to be troubled by something in her eye.

Life can be difficult. In fact life is often difficult. It's especially difficult when you're young and trying to find your place in the great scheme of things, but, if it's any consolation, most people do find that place in the end.

In a basement deep in the headquarters of Spiggit's Brewery, Chemical Weapons & Industrial Cleaning Products Ltd, Shan and Gath, dressed in pristine white coats, moved intently around a laboratory equipped with the latest in brewing technology. Beside the laboratory were their living quarters, with comfortable beds, seats, a television, and a pinball machine, a game at which Shan in particular was surprisingly adept, when he had the time and inclination to play it, which wasn't very often. After all, Shan and Gath had discovered one of the secrets of happiness: find something that you would have done anyway as a hobby, and convince someone to pay you good money to do it instead.[42] Their days were now spent developing Spiggit's new boutique range of beers: Spiggit's Summer Rain Ale, Spiggit's Gentle Sunbeam Amber, Spiggit's Strawberry Sunrise Lager, that kind of thing, beers of gentle fragrance and delicate taste designed for the gentler, more discerning drinker.

Or big girly men, as Shan and Gath liked to think of them.

They were also responsible for a separate line of beers for those with a more 'robust' constitution. These included Spiggit's Very Peculiar, Spiggit's Distinctly Unpleasant, and the notorious Spiggit's Old Detestable, which now came in extra-thick glass bottles with a lock on the cap after the yeast in one batch tried to make a break for freedom. But there was always a place in their fridge, and in their hearts, for Spiggit's Old Peculiar.

After all, there was no improving on perfect imperfection.

Some days later, in another, much larger, basement area, within sniffing distance of the chimneys of the Spiggit works, a sleek red sports car careened out of control and struck a brick wall with so much force that its rear wheels lifted from the ground as the hood crumpled

---

☠ [42] Most people will spend their lives doing jobs that they don't particularly enjoy, and will eventually save up enough money to stop doing those jobs just in time to start dying instead. Don't be one of those people. There's a difference between living and just surviving. Do something that you love, and find someone to love who loves that you love what you do.

It really is that simple.

And that hard.

and pieces of engine, car body, and possibly passenger body as well flew into the air. The back of the car seemed to hang suspended in its death throes, then fell back to the concrete with a bang.

For a time, there was only silence.

A creaking noise came from somewhere in the mass of twisted metal. The driver's door opened or, more correctly, the driver's door fell off, and a dazed-looking Nurd staggered from the wreckage. Wormwood ran to him and helped him remove his crash helmet and gloves. Nurd gazed up uncertainly at a long window, behind which various engineers, designers, and safety experts sat, their heads craned to catch Nurd's words. Samuel Johnson stood close to the glass, clearly relieved. No matter how often he watched this happen, he was always glad, and surprised, when his friend survived relatively unscathed.

'Well,' said Nurd at last, 'the seat belt works, but you might need to take a look at the brakes . . .'

As I said, most people, and some demons, find their place in life in the end.

CHAPTER XXXVIII

In Which We Discover the Limitations of the Term 'Happily Ever After'

Professor Hilbert, Professor Stefan, Ed, Victor, and the senior Collider scientists were gathered in a meeting room at CERN, as the Collider rumbled about its business around them.

'And the boy says that he was dragged to Hell?' said Professor Stefan.

Professor Hilbert nodded. 'The return of the Aston Martin, or what's left of it, seems to support his story.'

'And he was there along with four dwarfs, two policemen, their patrol car, an ice-cream salesman, and an ice-cream van?'

Professor Hilbert nodded again.

'An ice-cream van? You're sure it was an ice-cream van?'

'A Mr Happy Whip ice-cream van,' confirmed Professor Hilbert.

'Mr Happy Whip,' repeated Professor Stefan solemnly, as if this fact were particularly important.

'They didn't bring any, er . . .'

'Demons?'

'Yes, demons, they didn't bring any *back*, did they?'

'The policemen, Samuel Johnson, and Mr Dan, Dan the Ice-Cream Man, who is now apparently managing the dwarfs, all confirm the general absence of demons from this world.'

'And the dwarfs?'

'The dwarfs are very unpleasant. In fact, for a time we thought that *they* were demons,' said Professor Hilbert. 'One of them threw a beer bottle at Ed.'

Ed pointed to a large bump on his forehead. 'He was nice enough to empty it first, though.'

'Have you examined the boy?' said Professor Stefan.

'His mother wouldn't let us,' said Professor Hilbert. 'She seems to think that we're partly to blame for his disappearance, since we were the ones who turned on the Collider again. She was quite adamant about that, and used some very strong language to that effect.'

'And the policemen?'

'The policemen wouldn't let us examine them. They also presented us with the bill for a patrol car, with thirty days to pay.'

'And the dwarfs?'

'We tried to examine them, but it didn't go well. Suffice it to say that those dwarfs are *very* unhygienic.'

'But despite all that they say, you claim they weren't really in Hell?'

'Wherever they were, it wasn't Hell,' said Professor Hilbert. 'Hell doesn't exist. Where they were was simply another world, another universe. I believe it to be a dark matter universe. We're close, Professor, very close. We can't shut down the Collider, not now. Our understanding of our place in the Multiverse is about to change utterly. The answer to whether or not we are alone in the Multiverse has been answered. Now we are duty bound to explore the nature of the life forms with which we share it.'

'What do you suggest that we do?'

'Nothing. We say nothing. We do nothing. We ignore the boy and his story. We continue with the experiment.'

'What if they go to the newspapers?'

'They won't.'

'You seem very certain of that.'

'I am. The mother is frightened enough for her child as things stand. She won't want the media camped on her doorstep, assuming they believe the boy's story, and we can make sure they do not. The policemen have been warned by their superiors not to say anything to anyone about what they experienced, and the ice-cream salesman just wants his insurance money. As for the dwarfs, they're not the most reliable of witnesses.'

Professor Stefan still looked uneasy.

'What are the risks?'

'Five per cent. At most.'

'And that five per cent contains the threat of invasion, possible consumption by unknown entities, and the potential destruction of the entire planet?'

'Possibly.'

Professor Stefan shrugged. 'I can live with that. Anyone for a biscuit?'

Deep in the heart of the Mountain of Despair, the Great Malevolence brooded. The time of his madness had passed. Now his mind was clear again.

'A BOY. A BOY, AND A DEMON.'

The Lord of all Evil spoke as though he could not quite believe his own words. The Watcher stood silently at his feet, awaiting its master's command. Above it the great bells, the bells that had pulled its master from his madness, were silent once again. The portal was gone. Mrs Abernathy was gone. Duke Abigor and his allies were frozen in the lake of Cocytus, where they would remain for ever. Only the Great Malevolence prevailed.

'DOES THE COLLIDER STILL RUN?'

The Watcher nodded.

'GOOD.'

The Watcher frowned. The link between Hell and the world of men was no more. Whatever power Mrs Abernathy had harnessed to create the gateway had vanished with her. It would take time to find a way to access the Collider's power again, and surely the men and women responsible for it would be more careful this time. As far as the Watcher was concerned, the kingdom was once more isolated.

The Great Malevolence, seeming to read his servant's thoughts, spoke again.

'THERE IS ANOTHER KINGDOM.'

And the Watcher, almost as ancient as the one it served, understood. There was a kingdom that existed alongside the world through which men walked, a kingdom filled with dark entities, a kingdom of beings who hated men almost as much as the Great Malevolence himself.

The Kingdom of Shadows.

'PREPARE THE WAY.'

The Watcher departed, and the Great Malevolence closed his eyes, allowing his consciousness to roam across universes, touching those who were most like himself, evil creatures intent upon doing harm to others, and in each mind he left a single order.

SEEK THE ATOMS. SEEK THE ATOMS WITH THE BLUE GLOW. FIND HER . . .

Acknowledgements

Thanks to my editors and publishers at Hodder & Stoughton and Simon & Schuster, my agent Darley Anderson and his staff, and to Dr Colm Stephens, administrator of the School of Physics at Trinity College, Dublin, who was kind enough to read the manuscript and correct my errors. Any that remain are entirely my own fault.